Mrs. Claus and the Santaiana Slayings

"An exceptional series launch . . . This fun, well-plotted
mystery is the perfect holiday entertainment."
—*Publishers Weekly* (starred review)

Mrs. Claus and the Halloween Homicide

"Brings the Christmas cozy to dizzying new heights of cuteness."
—*Kirkus Reviews*

Entertaining . . . Ireland makes suspending disbelief surprisingly
easy. Fans of offbeat, humorous cozies will clamor for more."
—*Publishers Weekly*

"This is a wacky story with a bit of *Elf* meets *Nightmare Before
Christmas* meets *Murder She Wrote*. It will definitely entertain
readers during the HalloThankMas holiday season."
—*The Parkersburg News & Sentinel*

Mrs. Claus and the Evil Elves

"A fresh take on a Christmas cozy. It's a delightful mix of humor,
technology, and murder in an unconventional mystery."
—*Library Journal*

"*Mrs. Claus and the Evil Elves* is the coziest of cozy mystery series,
and well-worth a read for anyone wanting an extra touch of
whimsy, seasonal or otherwise, with their whodunits."
—*Criminal Element*

Mrs. Claus and the Trouble with Turkeys

"An absurd cozy for those who enjoy Tamara Berry's
books or holiday mysteries." —*Library Journal*

"Readers of cozy mysteries will gobble up this seasonal
novel with a fun plot and featuring naughty and nice
humans, elves and reindeer." —*Toronto.com*

Books by Liz Ireland

Mrs. Claus Mysteries

MRS. CLAUS AND THE SANTALAND SLAYINGS

MRS. CLAUS AND THE HALLOWEEN HOMICIDE

MRS. CLAUS AND THE EVIL ELVES

MRS. CLAUS AND THE TROUBLE WITH TURKEYS

MRS. CLAUS AND THE NIGHTMARE BEFORE
NEW YEAR'S

Anthologies featuring Mrs. Claus

HALLOWEEN CUPCAKE MURDER
(with Carlene O'Connor and Carol J. Perry)

IRISH MILKSHAKE MURDER
(with Carlene O'Connor and Peggy Ehrhart)

Published by Kensington Publishing Corp.

Mrs. Claus

and the

Nightmare Before

New Year's

Liz Ireland

Kensington Publishing Corp.
www.kensingtonbooks.com

KENSINGTON BOOKS are published by
Kensington Publishing Corp.
900 Third Avenue
New York, NY 10022

ISBN: 978-1-4967-4894-2 (ebook)

ISBN: 978-1-4967-4893-5

First Kensington Trade Paperback Printing: October 2024

10 9 8 7 6 5 4 3 2 1

Mrs. Claus and the Nightmare Before New Year's

Chapter 1

You don't know the meaning of "mixed emotions" till you've waved your beloved spouse off on a round-the-world trip in an overloaded antique sleigh powered by flying reindeer. I mean, who doesn't love that iconic sight of Santa aloft, silhouetted against the night sky, giving a cheery wave and bringing joy to children around the world? The vision made even me half-woozy with nostalgia and happiness. Yet I also watched the takeoff with my heart lodged in my throat. That was my husband, Nick, ho-ho-hoing up there, and that sleigh didn't even have seat belts.

Worse still, the weather this December had been completely unpredictable. Santaland had already dug itself out of two blizzards, and snow squalls had been whipping up periodically. What if one of those storms materialized while Nick was up in the sleigh?

As I stood on the steps of Municipal Hall in Christmastown in the minutes after watching Nick depart on his annual errand, all around me the elves were celebrating the big send-off with a jubilant frenzy of cheers, singing, and dancing. For them, the night marked the joyful culmination of a year of almost nonstop preparation. The fact that the holiday had brought a break in the unpredictable weather gave them even more reason to cut loose.

A series of zip lines had been set up in downtown Christmastown, including one strung from the roof of Municipal Hall to the old, sturdy cedar that marked the entrance to Peppermint Park. Now the street resounded with gleeful whoops of elves zipping overhead. Reindeer weren't known for their sense of humor, but even they were kicking up their heels and laughing at some of the zip-lining elves wearing felt antler beanies.

The Santaland Symphony Orchestra played a full-throttle rendition of "Sleigh Ride" that had other elves dancing a crack-the-whip down the middle of Festival Boulevard where just moments before Nick had been making last-minute checks on his sleigh. Someone had passed out sparklers in the crowd, which, along with the twinkle lights everywhere, set our snow-and-tinsel world aglow.

Sparklers weren't all that was lit, either. Vendors selling spiced cider, grog, and eggnog—spiked and plain—fueled the exuberant mayhem.

And there I stood, feeling like an astronaut wife seconds after liftoff. Nick, the elves accompanying him, and the nine reindeer drawing the sleigh were just a speck in the sky now; I could barely make out the dim flash of the lead Rudolph's nose against the ribbon of vibrant northern lights.

The astronaut wife analogy ramped up my anxiety another notch. Would this trip be Santaland's Apollo 13?

Stop it, I scolded myself. Nick would be back safe and sound in a day and a half, what with travel time and all the crossing of time zones. One of the first things you know when you marry Santa Claus is that you'll spend part of every Christmas wearing out the carpet with anxiety on his behalf.

My friend Juniper tugged on the sleeve of my puffy winter coat, pulling my focus away from the sky. "Come on, April."

Her curly hair was covered by an elf cap decorated with big gold jingle bells. "Come join the fun."

"I'm not sure I feel like dancing."

She glanced up, tracking my gaze. "Your eye strain isn't going to help Nick navigate. Worrying won't help anything."

It was the kind of thing Nick would say—in fact that he *had* said just this morning when I woke up shivering with fear for him and babbling again about seat belts.

"It's too late now to retrofit the sleigh with seat belts," he'd told me in his maddeningly sensible voice.

Frantic laughter had bleated out of me. "No, five decades ago was too late. Seat belts have been required in most places at least that long."

"Santaland isn't most places."

As if I needed a reminder of that. After several years at the North Pole, I was still adjusting. During the first years after my marriage, the sleigh thing had seemed so novel. I put my trust in Santaland magic, like a child. Now I knew bad things could happen. Nick's sister, Lucia, had been in a sleigh accident earlier this month when she'd been caught in a snow squall. She came out fine—Lucia was as tough as a boot—but just hearing about it had rattled me. I found it much harder to remain calm about my husband circumnavigating the globe in a contraption that had been built before the Wright brothers were even born . . . and hadn't been altered since.

Nick had shaken his head at me when I worried something terrible could happen. "Haven't you heard the saying we have here at the North Pole? 'Santa always comes back.'"

"I don't give a hoot about local sayings," I'd shot back. "I'm worried about *you*."

Having our last discussion be an argument, even one about my fears for his safety, made me feel even more upset now.

I gave myself a mental shake. *I'm Mrs. Claus.* That title

came with many official duties—and being an elf joy buzz-killer wasn't one of them.

I still wasn't sure about dancing, though. "I'll have some grog," I told Juniper.

Her hat jangled in approval as Juniper bounced on her heels. "Oooh—good idea!"

She grabbed my double-mittened hand and we threaded our way through the throng of elves, reindeer, and snowmen. I was surprised at how few people mingled among elves in the crowd. Usually the humans in Santaland hung around after ceremonial occasions to make a point of being seen—Nick was keen to make the extended Claus family, who mostly lived in the old chateaus on Sugarplum Mountain, less aloof from the population at large. Where was everyone?

My mother-in-law, Pamela, was in bed with a head cold. But that left quite a few people unaccounted for. Other than Nick's young nephew, Christopher, darting off with some of his friends, the only other person I spied was Nick's cousin Amory Claus standing next to the Gert's Pretzels cart, looking jolly and almost Santalike himself. We exchanged a wave.

Juniper and I finally made it to the front of the line at Sniffles's Grog Wagon.

"Hello, Mrs. Claus." The twinkle in Sniffles's dark eyes told me he'd been sampling his own wares. "Small tankard or large?"

I almost said small, but then I remembered that endless sky Nick was traveling across. "Very large," I said.

"That's the spirit." Juniper ordered the same for herself.

When Sniffles handed the large cups to us, Juniper and I raised them together. "To absent friends," I said, not just thinking of Nick. Claire, my friend from my hometown in Oregon who'd moved to Santaland after I did, was spending Christmas in the north with her boyfriend, Jake Frost (distantly related to Jack). They wouldn't return till after New Year's.

The grog, which was bitter with a touch of sweetness, had a kick that took a little of the edge off my anxiety. As Juniper and I wove through the crowd, I thought about the good bottle of champagne I'd put by for this New Year's. Maybe I would go ahead and pop it open when Nick got home. And then I'd apologize profusely for having been such a worrywart before he left.

My New Year's resolution: Next year I would be a less naggy, more confident Mrs. Claus.

My arm hit something pointy and someone barked at me. "You there—watch your step!"

The voice belonged not to one of Santaland's two police constables, but to a snowman named Pumblechook. The stick I'd bumped into was his arm. Last year Constable Crinkles gave Pumblechook one of his uniform hats, and ever since the snowman had acted as if law and order in Santaland rested solely on his frozen shoulders. Arguing with him was pointless. He was convinced he was Santaland's answer to Joe Friday.

"Sorry, Mr. Pumblechook." I saluted him. "Won't happen again."

"Really?" At such easy compliance, surprise registered in his charcoal eyes. His public reprimands rarely met with anything other than exasperation or laughter. "Well! See that it doesn't."

"Yes sir."

When we were out of earshot, Juniper tsked at me. "You shouldn't encourage him."

"Why not? He's about as good at police work as the actual policemen in this town."

As if to prove my point, our local lawman, Constable

Crinkles, skimmed overhead on the zip line, squealing like a toddler and waving lit sparklers in each hand. Our chief constable's perfectly round body was squeezed inside the zip line body harness. His blue uniform with shiny brass buttons and tall hat made him resemble a miniature, manic Keystone Cop. Tonight he'd decorated the top of his hat with a gold pom-pom with tinsel streaming from it.

Juniper laughed at the spectacle. "He looks like a flying Christmas ball."

"Or an over-decorated wrecking ball."

We had to dive out of the way of oncoming line dancers. Were they doing the conga or the bunny hop? It didn't seem to matter. The dance line absorbed anyone in its path like a joyous amoeba.

It wasn't until the whooping dancers had passed that a strangled cry of distress overhead registered. Juniper and I looked up. Constable Crinkles dangled helplessly from the zip line, his arms and legs flapping uselessly.

"Help!" He waved his sparklers to get attention. The chin strap of his cap seemed to have his head trapped at an awkward tilt. "I'm stuck!"

The tinsel streaming from the pom-pom ball at the top of the constable's uniform hat had managed to get jammed up in the pulley mechanism that was guiding him across the wire. As a result, the lawman was stalled out midway over Festival Boulevard.

His nephew, Deputy Ollie, appeared at my side, a younger, thinner shadow of his employer-relation. He gaped up at his uncle. "What should I do?"

"Get me unstuck!"

"Oh! Okay, I'll be right there. Don't move!"

"I *can't* move."

That last grumbling retort was lost on Ollie, who was already charging into Municipal Hall to rush to the rooftop

and render emergency aid. Meanwhile, a crowd gathered below Crinkles. Everyone was calling advice up to the flailing
constable.

"Try twisting, Constable!" one elf called out.

"No," another said, "you need to swing your legs."

"That won't help," someone behind me opined. "They'll
have to cut him out of the harness."

Butterbean, the elf who had come up with the idea for the
zip lines, waved his hands to nix that, his boyish blond cow-
lick quivering at the idea. "Those harnesses were expensive."

"But we can't just leave our chief constable dangling from
a wire," Juniper pointed out.

"Ollie'll get him down," Butterbean said, expressing more
confidence in the abilities of the deputy constable than anyone ever had before.

The crowd's collective gaze pivoted toward the top of the
Municipal Hall, where a hurriedly harnessed Ollie slid onto
the zip wire to make his way toward the constable. Immediately it became clear that he'd taken off too fast. The wire was
designed to rush people along on a downward trajectory, and
now Ollie whooshed headlong toward his uncle.

Cries of alarm and warning went up from the crowd. Too
late. The deputy hit his uncle like one ball bearing crashing
into another.

"Ouch!" the constable cried out. "You rammed right into
my shoulder."

"Sorry, Unc, I couldn't figure out a way to make this
crazy doojabber slow down."

"Never mind—just get me out of this."

"Okay." The deputy reached up—but his hand came just
short of the pulley holding the constable hostage. "Um, how?"

Butterbean cupped his hands like a megaphone and called
up to Ollie. "Hoist yourself up to the wire, shimmy over, and
twist his hat from the pulley."

Following those instructions would have been difficult even if Ollie had possessed the build of a capuchin monkey. But lacking both long arms and a prehensile tail, and encased in his own harness, it was nigh on impossible. Now both our constables were dangling over the street.

"What next?" Juniper wondered aloud.

"We could call the Fire Brigade," I said. "But they'd be coming from Tinkertown, so . . ."

Tinkertown was Christmastown's sister city, a good twenty-minute sleigh drive away.

Juniper stood directly underneath the constables' dangling booties, her mittened fists on her hips. Her brow crinkled in thought until an idea struck her and she whirled toward the gathered elves. "I know! Let's make a pyramid."

This idea was taken up immediately by the elves nearest us. It was a practical suggestion, since we didn't have a ladder at hand. And elves love to make elf pyramids, the higher the better. Maybe it's because their lower center of gravity makes them sturdier, or the fact that they're usually performing these feats on snow-covered ground that softens any potential falls. But they really are quite adept at stacking themselves up in impossibly high elf piles.

At least, they're *usually* adept. When they're sober.

"I'll join in," I said, moving forward.

Smudge, a friend of Juniper's and my fellow percussionist in the Santaland Concert Band, put an authoritative hand out to stop me. "Sorry, April. You'd throw off the symmetry."

I tried not to take offense. I was taller and longer limbed than an elf, so my involvement would create a lopsided pyramid. It was hard to stand back and do nothing, though, as inebriated elves clambered on top of one another. Twice they collapsed and had to reorder themselves. And Juniper was going to be at the apex of the tottering mess. I decided that I could at least spot her, and stood at the bottom, arms stretched out ready to catch her if she tumbled off the precarious tower of elves.

When her time came, Juniper scrambled to the top without much problem and reached to unhook the constable's pom-pom from the pulley. She was to the right of Constable Crinkles, on the downward wire side. As Juniper was wrenching the pom-pom from the mechanism, something in the distance caught her eye. "Look! There's a big sleigh coming from the north!"

The moment she said the words, the pom-pom finally pulled free. Several things then happened in quick succession. First, half the elves in the pyramid twisted to see if they could spot the aforementioned sleigh. Then Crinkles and Ollie, set free, slipped down the zip line, acting like a giant bowling ball against the elf-sized pins that were Juniper and the two elves beneath her. The top several rungs of elves tilted off balance, causing the structure to sway, which rippled down to the elves at the base. Before I knew what was happening, an elf avalanche was cascading toward me.

If you've never been buried beneath a pile of twenty-plus elves, let me tell you, it's a shock. Elves might be small, but twenty of them together flattened me into the snowy ground. For a moment I was stunned, suffocating beneath all those small but solid woolen-clad bodies. Finally those at the top started to squirm free, allowing a little air to penetrate to those of us at the bottom. When a hand finally reached down to help me to my feet, it was Juniper's.

"Are you okay, April?" Her tumble to the ground hadn't fazed her.

I tested my legs. "Everything seems to be functioning." A Christmas miracle.

Her brow scrunched as her gaze aimed north again. "Whose sleigh do you think that was?"

The sleigh! I'd forgotten about it. What if Nick had crashed and was making his way back?

"Do you think it's Nick?" I asked. What if he was hurt?

She blinked in surprise. "No—golly gumdrops, I'd recognize Santa's sleigh. There were only two reindeer pulling this one. It was traveling fast from the north."

North of Santaland was a vast snowy plain that stretched to our border with the Farthest Frozen Reaches, an icy mountainous wilderness populated with wild elves, snow monsters, Santaland's criminal exiles, and other unsavory characters. It was also where Claire was vacationing with Jake's family.

I brightened. "Maybe it's Claire and Jake."

She shook her head. "I don't think so."

Smudge said, "Could be someone coming to Christmastown to join the celebration."

"Why would anyone show up *now*, when Santa's already taken off and the fun's almost over?" Juniper asked.

It didn't seem like the celebration was winding down to me. In fact, the stuck constables and the toppled pyramid had just been a hiccup in the proceedings, judging from the way the assembled crowd had resumed their revelry. The orchestra was playing "Here Comes Santa Claus" and elves were once again jigging down the street, singing along. Having made it to the end of the zip line, the constables were out of harness and queued up at Sniffles's Grog Wagon.

The celebration had already grown so loud again that it took a moment to hear the arriving sleigh's brassy blast, which was like a cross between a hunting horn and an emergency klaxon. The orchestra ceased playing and the crowd parted to allow the vehicle through.

The reindeer pulling the sleigh were rough, shaggy creatures, unlike the more manicured animals from the herds around Christmastown. I recognized the boxy, weathered wood sleigh behind them, although I hadn't seen it in a while. The vehicle belonged to an elf named Boots Bayleaf, who rarely ventured far from his shack full of unfortunate taxidermy animals in the northern snowdrift, just south of the Farthest Frozen Reaches. The grizzled old elf's eyes were frantic as he careened down the street thick with revelers. He was forced to stop where Gert's pretzel cart blocked the road.

"I need to see Doc Honeytree right away," he shouted.

Constable Crinkles and his deputy stepped out of the grog line to peer into the back of Boots's sleigh. "What you got there, Boots?"

Ollie, who was taller than his uncle, rose on the pointed toes of his booties to see. His eyes bugged. "Those are people!"

Not elves, he meant. Since I knew all the people in Santaland, I was curious, too, and concerned.

But these people were strangers to me. Two men and a woman lay sprawled unconscious on the flatbed in back of Boots's sleigh, covered with old woolen blankets. Yes, they were definitely humans—their size was a giveaway. Judging from their faces, which was all I could see of them, all three were adults. Maybe in their thirties? It was a bit hard to be sure of ages; the men had shaggy beards dotted with ice, and all three had a pallor that was mottled red over pale marble. A sure sign of prolonged exposure to extreme cold.

"You know them?" Boots asked me.

I shook my head. It was hard for elves who'd lived all their lives in the close-knit world of Santaland to grasp that I might not know every member of my species. "Their faces aren't familiar to me."

"Strangers!" Juniper said, aghast.

While friends or relations who were known to the residents of Santaland were welcome to visit—as long as they pledged to keep Santaland's secrets—random outsiders were forbidden. Our country was a secluded, magical place. No one wanted to see Christmastown and the surrounding area exploited as a tourist destination.

The constable stood with his arms akimbo and glared at the backwoods elf. "Have you lost your hooting senses, Boots? We can't have random visitors here."

"I didn't invite them, I found them just this side of our border—three lumps of nearly frozen humans in the snow. I need to get them to the Santaland Infirmary. One looks real bad."

Boots yanked the striped blanket off one of the men. A collective gasp went up from the crowd.

A large antler was lodged in the man's back.

"Go," I told Boots. I was already dialing the doctor's number. "I'll alert Doc Honeytree that you're on the way."

But elves remained crowded around the sleigh, making it impossible for Boots to maneuver around them.

"Was he gored by a reindeer?" Ollie asked.

Constable Crinkles puffed out a breath. "Well, there *is* a big pointy antler sticking out of his back."

One well-toned reindeer obviously from the Comet herd nosed his way forward. "Reindeer are not murderers." The vehement pronouncement was accompanied by a loud sneeze that made elves dart out of his snout's pathway.

"Hmph." Crinkles's lips pressed together. Next to him, Ollie shifted uncomfortably.

Was it my imagination, or were the elves gathered around avoiding looking at each other?

"It's outrageous!" the reindeer snapped.

Was it? Even Constable Crinkles had a hard time ignoring the gruesome evidence before his eyes. His pallor made me worry that he might faint. I wasn't feeling too good myself.

Boots bit his lower lip. "I, uh, asked the man who attacked him. He was almost unconscious at that point, and I had to lean close to hear his reply. He said, 'An animal.' And that was it."

Everyone shifted, and pointedly did not look at the reindeer.

"We're not the only animals in Santaland," another reindeer called out, to murmured agreement among his fellow ruminants.

He wasn't wrong. Technically, humans and elves were animals.

The other man lying in the wagon of the sleigh let out a groan.

"All right, everyone—break this up!"

It wasn't Crinkles trying to scatter the crowd. Pumblechook the snowman had shuffled forward and was now trying to direct traffic and herd elves out of the sleigh's path.

"Everyone make way for Boots's sleigh!" he barked.

The elves dutifully followed instructions, moving back and pushing the Gert's Pretzels cart out of the way. I was slower to react, still distracted by the people in the sleigh. Why were they here—and what were we going to do with them? The future of Santaland might hinge on the answer. What if one of these people was a travel writer or journalist who'd been blown off course?

Way off. Santaland was nestled in an unmapped arctic valley nearly impossible to find.

Yet these three had found it. Had they meant to, or were they lost?

It didn't matter. What mattered now was helping them to the extent we could, and then getting them out and back to where they came from with Santaland's secrets preserved.

"Egress!" Pumblechook shouted at the stragglers— including me. "Let the sleigh through."

As the sleigh nosed forward, one of the men's eyes opened. He blinked groggily at Pumblechook. "A talking snowman?"

He fell back again, delirious, but that question made my heart sink. Preserving Santaland's secrets might prove an even trickier business than I'd feared.

Chapter 2

Christmastown leaders gathered at the Midnight Clear diner for an emergency meeting. A retro eatery with a strong Christmas vibe was an unlikely venue to discuss weighty civic matters, but Municipal Hall was closed up for the holidays, while the diner was open late and toasty, and practically empty since the street celebration was still underway.

Besides myself, Constable Crinkles and Mayor Firlog of Christmastown were also present. And of course, where the mayor appeared, Mrs. Firlog was never far away. I'd asked Amory Claus to join us, too. Given that Pamela, Nick's mother, was in bed with a cold, and Nick's nephew, Christopher, the future Santa, was only thirteen, it seemed logical to include Amory as another representative of the Claus family.

At the celebration I'd also managed to collar Plummy Greenbuckle, who earlier in the year had taken my place as Santaland Events Coordinator. She sat pencil at the ready to take notes for this impromptu meeting on an overturned order pad that she'd borrowed from our waitress.

Rounding out the table were Boots, Juniper, and Butterbean. Boots, we hoped, would fill in more about how he'd found the strangers, and I wanted Juniper there to be a friendly face. Butterbean's presence was puzzling, except that Butterbean was always percolating with ideas. He was an employee at the Santaland Scoop, my friend Claire's ice cream parlor. Since the Scoop was closed during her absence, Butterbean was at loose ends and apparently eager to insert himself into this difficulty.

We waited to hear word from the infirmary. It was hard to decide what our course of action should be until Doc Honeytree rendered his verdict on the state of the health of the three strangers. In the meantime, Constable Crinkles had ordered a Holiday Popper Platter—a large serving dish piled with fried balls of dough and cheese. He and Boots had already put a serious dent in it.

"Maybe they'll just stay unconscious until Nick comes back," I said, just thinking aloud.

Mayor Firlog nodded. "And if one of them wakes up, Doc can always just knock them out again."

Juniper almost choked on a popper. "That would be unethical."

The major drew back. "I didn't mean that Doc should clunk anyone over the head. But surely he could administer . . . well, a pill or something." He drummed his hands anxiously on his potbelly, which was covered by a blue velveteen vest embroidered with snowflakes. "What would be the harm in that?"

Having the doctor slipping a mickey to these unfortunate travelers seemed only marginally less unethical to me than clunking them on the head.

"No harm," agreed Mrs. Firlog. Her high column of teased hair worthy of a 1960s Nashville chanteuse ensured that she towered over her husband. "The challenge is knocking them out before they see anything they could blab about to the outside world."

"We still don't know who these people are," Amory Claus said. "They could be desperadoes."

"Desperadoes!" Crinkles's eyes widened in panic. "Should I tell Ollie to get the prisoner cell ready at the constabulary?"

The jail at the Christmastown Constabulary was as punishing as a kindergarten time-out corner—and about as secure as one, too. The cell was really just the spare room of the cozy cottage the constabulary was housed in, complete with tidy twin beds with double wedding ring quilts, an unbarred window, and en suite bath. A true desperado could break out of that place in less time than it took the average child to tear the wrapping off a Christmas present.

"Why assume the worst about people?" Juniper asked. "Maybe they're just tourists who got lost."

The mayor's wife gaped at her incredulously. "What would tourists be doing in Santaland, especially wandering around the wilderness near our border with the Farthest Frozen Reaches?"

Her husband nodded, adding, "Even elves don't venture thataway if they can help it."

Boots cleared his throat. "I think the strangers are shipwreck survivors. And possibly professional spies."

Amory laughed. "Oh sure."

It was hard to know which sounded more absurd—North Pole espionage or the business about the shipwreck. Santaland was nestled as far inland as was possible at the North Pole.

Boots said, "See, they weren't together when I found them, or even close. First I spotted the woman—that red parka of hers was hard to miss in the snow."

I hadn't seen the parka—just Boots's stained blanket covering the woman.

"She was unconscious when I loaded her into the back of my sleigh and started driving south toward Christmastown. But further on I saw the poor man facedown in the snow with the antler in his back. I loaded him next to her and got a little farther this time when I ran across the second man. He was in better shape than the other two and mumbling before he passed out partway here."

"Did he tell you who they were, or where they came from?" I asked.

Boots shook his head. "He just said, 'Wreck,' over and over. And then he mumbled, 'Find the ship.' Didn't make sense to me. I asked him if there were any other survivors of this wreck, and he shook his head."

"What makes you think that they might be spies, though?" I asked.

"Isn't obvious?" Amory asked. "They were spreading themselves out to infiltrate Christmastown by stealth."

Boots cast his gaze toward the floor, hesitating. "The thing is, after the last one passed out, I went through his pockets." He dug into his own tunic pockets now and produced two items, extracting them carefully.

"Forty-two American dollars," he said, showing us a wad of bills. "I found that in the pocket of the man who was gored."

"Why were you going through their pockets?" I asked.

"To find out who they were, where they lived." Deep creases appeared at the sides of his mouth. "I live alone, isolated. I thought maybe these three might belong to someone around here. But then I found this." He placed a business card down on the table. The card had a photo of a waterfall as the background.

Sam Bradford—Photography and Videography

Underneath, there was contact information and an address in Los Angeles.

The possibility that we were dealing with a professional photographer worried me. What if this really was a trio of journalists who'd come looking for Santaland?

Anxious glances ricocheted around the table, and hands reached for poppers. Nervous chewing ensued.

"A professional photographer," Mrs. Firlog said. "And what about the others?"

"They might be travel writers, or journalists," Amory said, with rising panic. "If these people get out and spread the word about Santaland, next thing you know there'll be planeloads of tourists being unleashed on us, and all the messy development that brings. Santaland will become a Las Vegas version of itself."

"Suffering cranberries!" Mayor Firlog exclaimed. "This could be the end of our entire way of life."

Constable Crinkles's face slackened with dread. "The end of Santaland as we know it." Two more poppers disappeared.

The end of Santaland as we know it. Not on my watch. I wasn't going to have Nick return to a Santaland on its way to becoming a theme park.

"We need to get these people out of Santaland ASAP." I turned to Amory. After all, he was in the line of succession to take over the role of Santa Claus, after Nick and Christopher. "You must have experience in flying big sleighs. Nick's everyday sleigh is parked in the sleigh shed by the castle." The everyday sled was almost as big as the ceremonial sleigh—not as large as a sleigh bus, but sturdy enough to stand up to a long journey. It was as big as a sleigh could be and still be flown. "Do you think you could manage the trip?"

Amory froze. "You mean *tonight*? It's almost Christmas . . ."

Juniper turned to me. "It'll be hard to find elves to help him run an errand like this on Christmas."

"I'll go!" Butterbean said excitedly.

"We don't want elves going." This needed to be handled quietly—and Butterbean rarely did anything quietly. "Lucia can go with Amory." Nick's sister was good at long trips; unlike me she never got sleigh-sick, even after her crash.

Amory bleated in protest. "You want me to make a treacherous flight to Alaska with *Lucia*?"

I couldn't deny that Lucia wouldn't be the greatest company. She was naturally antisocial and could be witheringly caustic. "You just need to drop the three people off at the nearest hospital before they're fully conscious. It'll take two days of traveling, tops."

Could anything be more reasonable? But Amory was still loath to leave the cozy hearth of his mountaintop chalet just when he was expecting—like everyone else in Santaland—a week of uninterrupted R & R.

"Even if I agreed to go on this errand," he said, "where on this of all nights could I round up a big team of reliable reindeer on such short notice? Nick's taken the cream of the crop, and now the herds have been out celebrating with the rest of Santaland."

"It's true." Constable Crinkles gave a regretful shake of his head. "Ollie came across a bunch of juveniles behind Municipal Hall, dipping their muzzles into a bucket of grog."

"And one of those reindeer who spoke tonight seemed sickly," Amory added. "Did you notice him sneezing?"

Honestly. "If there's one thing Santaland is never short of," I said, "it's eager reindeer. I'm sure my two would be ready to step up to the plate."

Amory laughed. "How far do you think could I get with Cannonball and Wobbler? They're like the Laurel and Hardy of reindeer."

I bristled. Just this year, Lucia had recruited two misfit reindeer to pull my hybrid sleigh when needed. Granted, knobby-kneed Wobbler didn't have the strongest nerves, and Cannonball was a little—to put it kindly—big boned. Aside from that, they were both solid gold.

"Cannonball's been on Lichen-Fast for two months," I

informed Amory. "He's so fit now, he could pass for one of the Comet herd."

"Oh sure." Amory snorted. "He's reduced from cannonball to bowling ball."

"There's no reason to be offensive," I snapped.

"You're asking me to take a treacherous journey with defective reindeer."

"Defective!" I repeated, my voice looping up in outrage.

At that moment, the Midnight Clear's door banged opened, and cold air rushed through the cafe. Doc Honeytree's nephew-assistant, Algid, hurried to the cashier counter. The elf behind the register was ready with a big to-go bag for him. As I looked around, I noticed that sometime during the argument at our table, Boots had disappeared. He'd left the business card, though. And the forty-two dollars.

Before Algid could also dash out, I flagged him down. He came over to our table. Algid was wraith thin and always a little bloodless looking, like an elf who'd spent the majority of his life in a basement lab. Which he had.

"I'm just getting takeout sandwiches for my uncle, Nurse Cinnamon, and me," he explained.

"How are the patients?" Amory asked.

"Can they be flown out of Santaland soon?" I added.

A frown creased his sallow cheeks. "My uncle extracted the antler—fortunately it hadn't pierced any vital organs—but now we have to worry about infection. That man, like all three of them, is weak from cold exposure. Right now, though, it's the woman we're most concerned about. My uncle's about to operate."

I hadn't seen anything wrong with her, but of course she'd been mostly covered up by Boots's blanket. "Operate on what?"

"Her left big toe," Algid said. "We're going to have to

amputate it. Frostbite. If we don't operate quickly, the woman could lose a whole foot." Algid shook his head. "Mind you, in the state they're in, I would advise against moving any of them." He bit his lower lip in thought. "Except the man who *wasn't* gored by an antler. He could probably stand the trip."

The one named Sam, he meant. Five minutes ago, getting the photographer out of Santaland seemed a priority. But what was the point of moving him while the other two were still here?

"How long will they have to stay in Christmastown?" the mayor asked.

Algid hiked his to-go bag on his hip. "A week?"

After Algid hurried back to the infirmary, our table descended into thoughtful silence accompanied by Brenda Lee singing "Rockin' around the Christmas Tree" on the corner jukebox.

"A week?" I repeated. What would we do?

From the glum expressions around me, I wasn't the only one asking that question.

This was the week when elves were able to enjoy a little leisure. Eggnog flowed, gifts were exchanged, and carols and games were constant. There was a figure skating show planned, and the iceball opening game would be played at Peppermint Pond. The reindeer were holding their annual Hop-n-Snort. And on New Year's Eve there was Grog Night, a huge gathering at the top of Sugarplum Mountain that would welcome in the New Year with drink, elf clogging, and musical acts.

"What do you think, Mayor?" Juniper asked Mayor Firlog.

Christmastown's foremost elected official drew a blank.

Mrs. Firlog pushed aside her mug of eggnog. "We'll have to be careful that these strangers don't realize where they are."

"Exactly!" Her husband echoed his agreement. "Very careful."

"Why?" Juniper asked. "Won't they just think they're in a normal hospital?"

I nearly choked on my coffee. True, the Santaland Infirmary's rooms were sterile and neat as a pin—Nurse Cinnamon was scrupulous about hygiene—but its furnishings suggested an old inn more than a typical hospital. And even if the visitors accepted the building's antique appearance, they'd eventually notice that the place was staffed by elves.

The elves didn't grasp this at first, but Amory did. He seemed thoughtful—an unusual look for him. After a moment, he snapped his fingers. "We just need to get rid of all the elves. Relocate them all to Tinkertown."

"Not happening!" Juniper said.

Amory frowned. "It's just for a week."

"*Christmas* week," Juniper reminded him.

Plummy Greenbuckle gasped, drawing all eyes toward her. "What are we going to do about Santa's return?" she asked.

A worried silence fell over the table. Santa's return wasn't met with the same raucous jubilation that marked the send-off, but a huge crowd turned out for it after a lantern high atop the tower of Castle Kringle's old keep was lit to let Santaland know that the sleigh had been spotted. It would be hard to hide a swarm of elves and reindeer greeting a giant sleigh landing on Christmastown's main thoroughfare. Especially when the rooms of the Santaland Infirmary provided a view in that direction.

"We'll need to reroute Nick out of town," Amory said. "And the elves will just have to stay home this year."

Faces gaped at him with a mix of shock and outrage.

"You mean—the sleigh will *just land*?" Plummy asked.

"No welcoming?" Mayor Firlog said.

"No spiked eggnog and cake?" Crinkles drooped, crestfallen at the prospect.

Elves always brought eggnog and Christmas cake to welcome Santa home.

"No reindeer gathering, either?" Juniper asked. "The herds aren't going to like that."

She was right. The pulling of Santa's sleigh was the focus of reindeer activity. Being told to stay away wouldn't go down well. I already suspected there would be rising tension coming from the reindeer because of that antler in the stranger's back. Whether the man survived his wound or not, reindeer would have to be interrogated to find out who the culprit was.

Plummy piped up, "*No one's* going to be happy if you're telling us that every big celebration planned for the next week will need to be canceled. What about tomorrow's ice show?"

"And the iceball season opener," Crinkles chimed. Our constable moonlighted as the coach of the Christmastown Twinklers.

"And Grog Night!" the mayor and Amory exclaimed in unison.

My stomach began to churn. This could turn into a nightmare.

"It's not fair," Plummy pouted. "This is my first time as Holiday Week Events Coordinator, and now you're telling me that all my efforts should be put on hold?"

"If the Twinklers can't have the iceball opener at Peppermint Pond," Crinkles said, "we'll just have to move our iceball opener from Peppermint Pond to Tinkertown Arena."

"The Reindeer Hop-n-Snort is going to be held in Tinkertown Arena that night," Plummy reminded him in an exasperated voice.

The Hop-n-Snort was an all-herd social held every year during Christmas week. The reindeer thought of it as the equivalent of high school prom. It was one of the few reindeer-centric events of the year that wasn't a competition. Telling the reindeer that they couldn't have the arena for their

Hop-and-Snort would curdle elf-ruminant relations faster than vinegar curdled eggnog.

Crinkles pursed his lips. "Maybe the reindeer could switch to another night."

"You can't just go changing things!" Plummy burst out in distress. "This week has all been carefully planned." She added almost tearfully, "I made charts."

"You're all missing the point," Amory broke in. "If the visitors in the hospital can see out their window, it won't matter *what* activity is going on at the pond. They'll see *elves*. They'll see Christmastown. How long will it take for them to realize they're in Santaland?"

Plummy tossed her pencil down on the Formica tabletop in frustration. "We should just keep those people locked up somewhere until they're well enough to get rid of. Or better yet, let's get rid of them right now."

Her bluntness shocked me, yet as the others around the table nodded along with her, I started to see the sense in what she was saying. Was an entire country supposed to cancel its entire holiday just so three lost strangers could be kept in the dark about being here? Even if the three of them survived to return to the United States, with wild tales of being in Santaland, what were the chances that their reported tales of elves and talking snowmen would gain any traction? If I'd heard anyone blabbing about a magical country at the North Pole anytime before I moved here, I would have recommended that they find a good therapist.

"Exactly." The mayor thumped his hand on the table. "Just get rid of them."

Mrs. Firlog agreed. "As soon as Doc Honeytree gets them patched up, Amory or Lucia or anyone else who wants to volunteer can fly them out of here. Preferably while they're still delirious."

The murmurs and nods around the table indicated that

everyone concurred. I was about to add my own assent, when Juniper stood up. "Listen to yourselves!" With all eyes on her, she said forcefully, "We can't send the three strangers away. You heard what Algid said—they're all unwell, and one of them is dangerously hurt. Maybe he was even hurt by one of Santaland's own. Besides, it's *Christmas*."

Heat of shame crept into my cheeks, and the sheepish expressions of the others told me that her words had the same effect on them. We were Santaland, for pity's sake. We couldn't turn away strangers. I was embarrassed that I had even entertained the un-Clausian idea of "getting rid of" these three people who needed our help.

"Juniper's right," I said. "Doc told us it would be dangerous to move them. Until their health is stable and we learn a little more about their situation, we need to accommodate them. It's the right thing to do. I'm sure Nick would think so, too."

Mentioning Nick had the effect of tossing a blanket on a fire. Santa Claus might be flesh and blood here in Santaland, but his name still carried the weight of conscience. *He knows when you are sleeping, he knows when you're awake . . . He knows when you're booting perilously injured people out of the country so that your entertainment schedule won't be interrupted . . .*

"We'll have to think of a plan," I finished.

Plummy Greenbuckle flipped to a blank page on the pad on her clipboard and poised her pencil over it to write. All eyes turned to me expectantly.

I gulped. I hadn't meant that *I* should come up with a plan, but evidently that's what they expected me to do. "Well, first . . . um . . . we should scale back the Christmas week activities."

Mrs. Firlog bristled. "*Scale down* Christmas in Santaland? I never thought I'd live to see the day that a Claus would suggest that. How could it even be done?"

My mind a blank, I pivoted toward Amory. He froze like a reindeer in the headlights. Then he turned to Butterbean.

Butterbean might resemble an elf-eared embodiment of the Big Boy restaurant logo, but idea-wise, he's part Thomas Edison, part P. T. Barnum. Not all of his schemes are good ones, and a few have been borderline disastrous. But when you're desperate, you're desperate, and as always, Butterbean had a plan. He hopped to standing on his chair and took charge.

"Friends, everyone can get what they want here," he declared in that optimistic tone that for years had been luring Santalanders to skip after him like children following the Pied Piper. "We just need to make it look like this *isn't* Santaland."

"How?" I raised my hand, indicating the low-ceilinged room, the Christmas twinkle lights everywhere, the *three*—count 'em—fully decorated Christmas trees, and holiday-themed everything around the place right down to the little nutcracker salt-and-pepper shakers on all the chrome dinette tables. And the Midnight Clear wasn't an anomaly in Santaland, where there was no such thing as going overboard with Christmas decor.

"*Lots* of places go berserk with decorations at Christmas," Amory said. "Aren't there towns in the United States that become de facto Christmas villages in December?"

"Sure," I said, "but there's no way that we're going to convince those three people that they've just landed into a holiday-centric town in the US. For one thing, unless they're all suffering from amnesia, they'll remember that they got lost somewhere around the Arctic Circle."

The elves chewed on that for a moment. Literally. The holiday popper platter was rapidly disappearing.

Butterbean snapped his fingers. "What about Canada? It's cold, and they celebrate Christmas."

"So the elves of Santaland are going to pretend to be Canadians?" Juniper asked skeptically.

Butterbean nodded. "Very short Canadians."

I was skeptical, but I held my tongue. I didn't have any better ideas.

"It might work," Mrs. Firlog said, turning toward me. "Do you think you can recruit Clauses to be around the strangers as much as possible and minimize their contact with elves?"

"Probably . . ." I said.

"Splendid!" Butterbean hopped on the balls of his feet. "And even if the strangers do happen to see an elf or two from the infirmary windows, they won't be able to judge perspective very well."

Amory rubbed one of his extravagant side whiskers thoughtfully. "There's a whole warehouse in Christmastown loaded with shoes and other items of human clothing that were overproduced back in the day. We can distribute these surplus, unwished-for items to the elves in central Christmastown, where the strangers might be most likely to see them."

"I'll make an announcement that no elves should wear curly-toed booties," Butterbean said.

Mrs. Firlog gasped. "Not even a slight curl?"

Her husband shook his head. "We'll all have to make sacrifices, dear."

"Also," Butterbean continued, "we'll need full ear coverage, either by earmuffs or hats with earflaps. Maybe the Order of Elven Seamstresses could help modify available hats."

"You'll have to ask the reindeer to stay on the ground as long as there are strangers around," Juniper said. "And the snowmen will need to stay quiet for a few days." She frowned. "Snowmen don't talk where these strangers are from, right?"

I sputtered into my coffee. "No."

Plummy dutifully wrote everything down. "Hide ears, ground the reindeer, mute the snowmen."

"I'm still not sure we'll be able to convince the strangers that they're in Canada," I said.

"Why not? If we tell them they are, why would they doubt us?" Amory said. "We need to think of another name for Christmastown, to change the signs and such. Something sort of similar."

"Centertown?" Mrs. Firlog suggested.

Plummy took that down.

"Better make it Centretown with *r-e*," I said. "It's more Canadian."

Mayor Firlog stood and stretched. "That's it, then. Meeting adjourned." He gaveled us out with his butter knife.

"Wait," I said. "Shouldn't we discuss the antler?"

"Oh." The mayor glanced over at Crinkles. "What do you think, Constable?"

Crinkles had just stuffed the last popper into his mouth, which had already been full. His cheeks bulged like those of a chipmunk fully loaded with acorns. He swallowed with the aid of a long drink of eggnog. "Maybe that antler attack didn't even take place in Santaland. It might have happened in the Farthest Frozen Reaches."

Out of his jurisdiction, in other words.

"Besides, does the antler matter?" he continued, looking a little worried that he might be asked to actually investigate something. "Doc says the wound probably won't prove fatal. And you know how reindeer are. They close ranks."

"A man was stabbed in the back. Maybe it wasn't even a reindeer who did it. Reindeer are high-strung and competitive, I know, but capable of murder?"

Silence fell around the table, as though all the elves had something in mind they weren't telling me.

"What?" I asked.

Crinkles shook his head.

Even Butterbean seemed hesitant to speak.

Mrs. Firlog finally said, "I suppose Mrs. Claus is right. We can't appear to do nothing."

The constable sagged in his chair. "The reindeer won't like being questioned. It's Christmas week."

It's Christmas week was like a mantra with the elves. They were ready to kick back and have fun. But even Constable Crinkles finally had to admit that they couldn't overlook a violent attack on a stranger in our land.

"What we need is someone who can ask questions without getting the herds riled up," he said. "Someone like Lucia."

All gazes swung back in my direction. Dread clawed at me. Nick's sister, Lucia, was a friend to all reindeer and probably wouldn't welcome an interrogation much more than the herds themselves.

"Getting Lucia to convince the herds to comply with Crinkles's investigation can be *your* job, April," Amory told me with a smile.

Great. When I'd said there needed to be an investigation, I didn't think that *I* would get dragged into it, even in a minor way.

Then again, there was never anything minor about dealing with Nick's formidable sister.

Chapter 3

On the sleigh ride up Sugarplum Mountain to Castle Kringle I checked my phone for any messages from Nick. Nothing. Of course, it was early hours yet—no doubt Nick and his team were still over the Pacific. Hard to find Wi-Fi hotspots mid-ocean. Besides, he probably had more pressing matters to consider than texting me, like keeping that overloaded sleigh aloft.

It was a glorious night. Even though I was dragging with fatigue, I couldn't help marveling at the frozen beauty of the world around me. Castle Kringle stood halfway up Sugarplum Mountain, jutting out of the snow like something from a fairy tale. Below it smaller but still impressive stone chateaus decorated with lights dotted the nighttime landscape like glistening jewels. These houses belonged to "lesser" Clauses and other humans who had, mostly through marriage, been absorbed into the closed world of the North Pole.

From its vantage midway up the mountain, Castle Kringle shone like a beacon that was probably visible all the way to Mount Myrrh, Sugarplum Mountain's slightly sinister sister peak in the Farthest Frozen Reaches. Our castle was a beloved landmark to all of Santaland. Anywhere else, it would have been made into a picture postcard and become an iconic image of the country. But postcards and the tourists who would buy them were exactly what Santaland *didn't* need.

The reindeer pulling my sleigh, Cannonball, slowed down on the last approach to the castle.

I leaned forward. "Would you like some motorized assistance?" I should have thought to ask sooner. My sleigh was a hybrid, and the battery was charged up.

"No . . ." Clouds puffed out of Cannonball's snout as he exhaled. Reindeer were proud creatures. "I'm good."

He didn't sound good. I remembered the sneezing Comet from earlier this evening. I didn't want Cannonball to get sick. I happened to know that he was eagerly anticipating the Hop-n-Snort later this week.

"It's late," I said, pushing the button to engage the battery. "I'll give you a little boost."

With just a tap on the accelerator, the pressure taken off the exhausted reindeer was immediate. He shook his head, then held it higher and trotted with a lighter gait as the sleigh glided up the approach to the castle.

He looked abashed as I stepped off my little sleigh, though. "Sorry, Mrs. Claus. I might have overindulged in oat cookies at the celebration."

The groundskeeper elf, Salty, met us to help Cannonball back to the castle stable and unburden him of harnesses and sleigh. "I told you to watch out for those cookies," he said.

I laughed. "Everybody falls off the wagon every once in a while, Cannonball. You've made great progress."

"Thank you. Back to lichen shakes tomorrow, I guess. I want to look smart for the Hop-n-Snort."

What a dismal prospect. Was any dance worth chugging down diet beverages made from tree algae?

After they jangled away toward the reindeer barn, I took a last deep breath of night air and went inside. Something about my return seemed odd. It took a moment for the reason to dawn on me: no Jingles.

It was rare that I arrived home without the castle's steward, Jingles, greeting me at the door. Of course, it was late—perhaps Jingles was asleep. All the castle seemed quiet, and I hadn't expected to stay so long in Christmastown.

I was tired but still too keyed up to go to bed. Thoughts of Nick in that antique sleigh, probably still over an ocean, caused my heart to thump a little faster. I headed toward the kitchen to make myself a hot toddy.

When I pushed on the swinging door, I almost smacked into a young female elf in a white coat and cap. "Excuse me!" She scrambled back. "Oh—you're Mrs. Claus, aren't you?" Her whole body seemed to tremble. Even the hot water bottle in her hand jiggled nervously. "One of them, I mean."

Three Mrs. Clauses resided at Castle Kringle. I was the wife of Nick, the acting Santa Claus; Pamela, his mother, was the dowager Mrs. Claus; and my sister-in-law Tiffany was both the widow of Nick's late brother and mother to Christopher, the future Santa Claus.

"I am," I said. "Who are you?"

"Coco."

"Cocoa—like hot chocolate?"

"No *a*." She dropped another curtsy. "Excuse me."

She streaked out the door, leaving it swinging behind her.

Puzzled, I crossed the kitchen to make myself some tea. The kettle on the stove contained hot water left over from Coco filling up her hot water bottle. While tea steeped in the biggest mug I could find, I located a bottle of bourbon to splash into my brew.

Who was Coco? Jingles hadn't mentioned anyone new here at the castle. He usually came into my room first thing in the morning with coffee to update me on Santaland gossip, staffing issues, and anything else he thought I needed to know.

Back in the hallway I heard faint instrumental Christmas music coming from the corridor leading to Nick's office. A slit of light showed beneath the door.

Not sure why I felt the need to be silent in my own home, I tiptoed over and peeked in.

Nick's long, wood-paneled office, usually a soothingly calm place with a fire lit at one end, a modest Christmas tree in another corner, and a map of the world on one wall, had been transformed into a bright command central. The map had been replaced by a sixty-inch screen showing blue ocean crisscrossed with lines of longitude and latitude. Before it was Lucia, Nick's sister, stalking back and forth across the carpeted floor. Her long blond hair hung in its usual braid down her back. She wore a Fair Isle sweater topped with a quilted vest, and corduroy pants tucked into shearling-lined suede boots that reached her knees.

Wherever Lucia was, her reindeer friend, Quasar, was usually never far away. Tonight he knelt close to the fire, snoozing peacefully. Quasar was a misfit reindeer of the Rudolph herd, which you could tell at once from his nose. Even as he snored lightly, his muzzle fizzled like a light with a short in its socket.

Jingles was in the room, too, which explained why he wasn't on door duty. Though an elfman—his mother had been a human—he could have passed for a full-blooded elf while standing next to Lucia, who towered over everyone at Castle Kringle except Nick. Jingles wore his red-and-green tunic and cap of the castle elves. His striped stockings ended in curly-toed elf booties, and he was bobbing on them now to get a better look at the screen.

"There!" he said excitedly. "I saw something on the map. It was a wink of light."

Lucia's eyes narrowed in the direction he indicated. "That was just a reflection from some goofball opening the door from the hallway."

I—the goofball in question—stepped in and closed the door. "What's going on?" I didn't like the anxious way Lucia was pacing. "Is this something to do with Nick?"

Jingles turned to me to explain. "Lucia put a tracking device on Santa's sleigh."

"Butterbean found it for me." Her lips tightened in a frown. "It doesn't seem to be working. We haven't gotten a ping from the sleigh since the Andreanof Islands."

"The what?"

"That long tail of islands trailing off of Alaska."

I should have paid more attention to geography in school. Of course, back then I never dreamed that I'd end up married to someone circumnavigating the globe in a glorified sled.

I backed up and sank into a leather chair opposite Nick's massive oaken desk to check my phone. Still nothing from Nick. "I haven't received a message from him, either."

"Well, it's early hours yet." Lucia scowled at me. "You look terrible. What's wrong?"

My husband is being flown by reindeer in an overloaded sleigh across the world's largest ocean.

"Just a little tired," I said.

"You should have let me know when you were arriving," Jingles said. "I intended to have a tray prepared for you."

I waved a hand. "I had some food at the send-off."

"Junk, probably." Lucia jerked her thumb in the direction of a table in the corner. "There's some walrus jerky over there. Have some. It's pure protein."

The leathery brown strips on a tray did nothing to settle my stomach. Jingles, who knew my tastes better, fluttered over to the table in question and piled a few shortbread cookies on a dainty plate and brought them to me. I took one gratefully. Give me comforting carbs over pure walrus protein any day.

"Some of the town leaders met at the Midnight Clear diner at the end of the celebration," I told her. "I didn't expect to be there so long."

Lucia dragged attention away from her map. "What was the meeting about?"

I told them about Boots bringing the three strangers in, and how Doc said they couldn't be moved because one of them was getting a toe amputated from frostbite and the other had been seriously wounded. And then I explained the plan to make Christmastown seem like a normal—if very holiday-centric—place in northern Canada.

Lucia crossed her arms. "How are the elves taking this decision?"

I shrugged. "I guess we'll find out tomorrow."

Jingles looked excited by the idea. "It's like a whole week of pretending we're at a costume party." He puffed up a little. "Of course, *my* ears aren't as pronounced as most elves are, so *I* don't have to walk around in earmuffs all week."

"I doubt you'll have to worry about it. We're going to try to confine the strangers to the infirmary."

"Oh." Jingles deflated a little. He liked dressing up—his Halloween costumes were always the best at the castle.

"You mentioned that one of the men was wounded," Lucia said. "Is he expected to live?"

"I think so . . ." I slugged down the last of my bourbon-laced tea. Here's where things got tricky. I'd promised to ask Lucia to liaise with the herds and encourage them to cooperate with the investigation. You had to tread carefully with Lucia, though. "The thing is, it appears that he was wounded by a reindeer."

Her expression darkened. "Where did you get that idea?"

"From the antler that was sticking out of his back?" I

hated the way my voice rose up doubtfully, but Lucia's flinty dark blue eyes could make me doubt whether snow was cold.

"I'm guessing that no reindeer was attached to this antler when the man was found."

"Well, no." I frowned. "That would have made Constable Crinkles's job a lot easier."

Her eyes widened. "What does the constable have to do with this?"

Wasn't it obvious? "He's got to investigate, Lucia. The man could have been killed. For all we know, he might still die. Then we're looking at murder."

"Maybe a murder done in self-defense. People from outside Santaland can be barbaric when it comes to reindeer."

"Boots didn't mention the man having a weapon on him. And that seems like something Boots would have noticed." I hitched my throat. "Boots asked the man who stabbed him, and the man said an animal had done it."

"But he didn't specify *which* animal."

"No, but . . ." I forced myself to play devil's advocate. "Come on. Reindeer are the first suspects to come to mind when there's been an antler attack, right?"

Lucia wasn't ready to concede that much yet. "And so Constable Crinkles is going to—what? Interrogate every reindeer in Santaland?"

"Well, he's probably going to start with the leaders of the herds and go from there."

"They're not going to like this," she declared. "I don't, either."

Great. I'd been told to enlist Lucia's help in smoothing over the herds' ruffled fur over the inevitable investigation. Instead, all I'd managed to do was get her back up. Not a good start.

She strode over to Nick's desk and leaned against it, crossing her long legs in front of her. "For one thing, it's December. Most reindeer have already shed their antlers, except the females. Does are the least aggressive creatures in the world unless one of their young is threatened. And most of the fawns aren't trailing after their moms anymore at this time of year. So that's the first reason that suspecting reindeer makes no sense."

Everything she said was true.

She continued, "Another thing: With all these antlers being shed in Santaland, anybody could have picked one up and attacked these strangers. It could have been a Santalander, or a wild elf from the Farthest Frozen Reaches."

It was like facing a clever lawyer in the courtroom. Lucia was the Perry Mason for reindeer, and I was the unlucky Hamilton Burger, pop-eyed and dumb in the face of arguments I hadn't stopped to consider.

"Or it might have been Boots himself." Jingles sniffed. "I never liked that elf. So uncouth."

"Boots *saved* those people," I reminded him.

"So he says," Lucia said. "When the victim wakes up—*if* he wakes up—we might hear a different story."

"No one would stab a total stranger for no reason and then try to save them."

"Who said there was no reason?" Lucia argued. "We don't yet know what those strangers were doing out in our wilderness. Boots might have had a good reason for attacking the man."

"Then why wouldn't he have said so?" I asked.

She shrugged.

I wanted to laugh it off as Lucia simply bending over backwards to divert attention away from the most likely suspects, the reindeer. But then I remembered that Boots had gone through the men's pockets. And that he had found very little.

Suspiciously little. Except the card, which identified one of the men. And money. Handing over money indicated that

Boots hadn't wanted to steal from the people he'd found. Except American money wasn't much use in Santaland . . .

Also, I'd seen something in the grizzled old elf's eyes when he was telling us his story that made me suspect that he wasn't divulging everything he knew.

"Anybody can grab an antler and sharpen it to a deadly point," Lucia said. "But you know who can't hold an antler and do that?"

"Who?"

"Reindeer."

From the corner, the sound of Quasar rising to his hooves distracted our attention. I hadn't noticed that he'd awakened. "S-sorry, Lucia," he said in his Eeyore-like voice. "That's not true. The Dashers are well known for vanity and often w-wear antler racks with sharpened points."

It was true. During the winter months, the leaders of that herd often sported what the other reindeer called "antler toupees."

If it were anyone besides Quasar contradicting her, Lucia might have been resistant to the argument, but after she listened to him, she nodded. "Okay, I guess it's true that the constable will need to start somewhere, and the herd leaders are as good a place as any." She leveled a warning look on me. "But I won't have them bullied."

The idea of Crinkles bullying anyone almost made me laugh. "We were hoping that you'd talk to the herd leaders first. You could just emphasize the importance of cooperating with the constable."

I expected an argument, but she bit back a sigh. "Okay, I'll go talk to them in the morning."

"Thank you!"

"You should try to get some sleep," she told me. "Nothing you can do about anything right now."

I was staring at the map, which still hadn't shown any sign of a ping from Nick's tracking device.

"What about you?" I asked.

"I'll keep watch for a while longer," she said.

"As will I," Jingles said.

"You'll let me know if you hear anything from Nick, right?" I asked.

"Sure," she said, practically hustling me out of the situation room.

I went up to my bedchamber. It was one of the most luxurious rooms in all of Santaland, but it was decorated for maximum coziness. The large four-poster bed was a cloud of fluffy pillows and warm comforters. Almost as inviting was the opposite corner, a lounging area Nick and I had fashioned near the room's big fireplace. There we had a couch, a television for private movie nights, and a little bar area for refreshments. I opened the walnut cabinet that camouflaged the mini fridge I'd had installed. The bottle of bubbly I'd bought for our New Year's celebration was still tucked in there.

I took a quick shower, donned the downy-soft flannel nightdress stitched for me by the Order of Elven Seamstresses, and crawled under the covers of the sprawling bed that seemed all the bigger in Nick's absence. Before plugging my phone into its charger, I checked it once again.

No messages. It would probably still be a while before he was within texting range.

Didn't mean I couldn't send him one, though. I thought about relaying the news of what had been going on in Santaland in the hours since he'd taken off, but I decided to simply text him a heart. Nick already had enough on his plate to worry about in the coming day.

Turns out, I didn't know the half of it.

Chapter 4

The moment my eyes opened the next morning, I reached for my phone. Sometime while I was off in dreamland, Nick had replied to my heart text with a picture of the Sydney Opera House lit up for Christmas, plus a heart of his own. My spirits lifted, and I bounded out of bed.

I needed to let Lucia and everyone know that I'd heard from him. I showered and was in the last stages of getting dressed for the day—Christmas Eve!—when Jingles knocked and came in with my morning coffee tray. I was accustomed to a disdainful glance if he didn't approve of whatever outfit I'd chosen for the day, but today his bloodshot tired eyes widened in horror when he looked at my red-and-green wool dress.

"You're going into Christmastown wearing *that*?" he asked, like a disapproving 1960s dad seeing his daughter about to traipse out the door in a miniskirt.

There was nothing at all risqué about my dress. It was somewhat fitted but high-necked, and the colors were blocked out in a Mondrian-style pattern. "What's the matter with my outfit? It's Mrs. Clausy yet modern. I've worn it dozens of times and you've never disapproved of it before."

"But isn't it . . . well, *too* Mrs. Clausy?"

I glanced at myself in the mirror. In addition to the dress, I was wearing soft leather boots, shearling lined for warmth, and red wool stockings. The ensemble gave off a definite holiday vibe, but to me that was a good thing. "It's Christmas Eve. What's the problem?"

"The visitors," he said in an urgent growl, as if someone might be eavesdropping on our conversation.

Nick's message and thoughts of Christmas Eve had nudged the strangers at the hospital from my mind. Now I gave myself a more critical once-over. I still didn't see the harm in showing a little holiday color.

Jingles informed me what had been going on while I'd been sleeping. "The elves brought out a warehouse full of clothes and shoes and they've been distributing them this morning, trying to hide their elfiness in case one of the foreigners should glimpse them through the infirmary windows."

"They wasted no time getting to work on that," I said, impressed.

"Of course not. They're elves." He continued, "Shouldn't you be trying to set an example and tone it down, too?"

I could see where he was coming from, but still. "People dress for Christmas. The visitors won't think there's anything notable about me."

"Whatever you say."

Jingles had a talent for making me as uneasy when he deferred to my opinion as when we were in full-throttle disagreement.

I shook off my doubts and took a sip of the coffee he'd set on the edge of my dressing table. "I need to talk to Lucia. I got a text from Sydney from Nick."

"She heard from him, too," Jingles said. "He's sent her another message since—he's already on his way further west."

I swatted back the little pinprick of jealousy that news gave me. Nick knew that Lucia was keeping track of the sleigh's route. She would be answering any inquiries from elves who had a family member on the sleigh as a Santa's helper, and of course she'd be conveying information to the herds, as well.

Jingles continued, "Anyway, Lucia's not in the castle right now. She's gone down to talk to the herds, just as you asked her to do."

"In that case I'll let Pamela know everything that's been happening." My mother-in-law would be glad for news of Nick, too.

Jingles took a step forward as if to block my passage to the door. "You'll need an appointment."

A laugh hovered on my lips, but then I took in Jingles's dead-serious expression. This wasn't a joke. "But she's sick. Shouldn't I visit her?"

"She has a nurse. Coco."

I remembered the elf with the water bottle. "That little elf I saw last night in the kitchen?"

Jingles nodded. "Mrs. Claus—the dowager Mrs. Claus— sent word that all visiting requests should go through Coco."

"That's the weirdest thing I've ever heard. Is Pamela worried about contagion?"

"I'm not supposed to question orders."

My mother-in-law and I didn't always have the most simpatico relationship, but it felt strange just leaving her alone when she was sick. Especially during the holidays.

Then a terrible, unworthy thought occurred to me: If Pamela was *that* sick, she probably wasn't up for doing crafts. No matching holiday sweaters!

I know that any gift offered with love is a marvelous gesture, but I'd only been Nick's wife for three years and already the sweaters of Christmas past were taking up a lot of space in my cedar chest. And part of me wished that some year we'd have holiday photos where we didn't all look like a *Far Side* cartoon family with deplorable fashion sense. Last year, for instance, we'd all received fuzzy sweaters done in metallic yarn that made us look like a clan of sparkling yetis.

"I was hoping to sound her out to see if there was anything special she wanted for Christmas," I said.

"You still don't have a gift for her?" Jingles gulped. "Not anything?"

"That's just it. I don't want to buy her just anything." Relations between my mother-in-law and me had been improving this past year. I wanted to get her something she'd really like. Even if she had to tell me what that would be.

"There's always a subscription," Jingles said. "You enjoyed that Fudge-of-the-Month subscription Juniper bought you from Dash's Candy and Nut Shoppe."

It was hard to beat the gift of fudge. "Maybe I'll find something in town today. I have to be there for Tiffany's ice show tonight."

"Goodness—I almost forgot." He pulled out a pad of paper and held it slightly away from him. He needed glasses but was reluctant to get a pair. *Vanity, thy name is Jingles.* "Plummy Greenbuckle called and left a message for you. She'd like to know if this evening's ice show at Peppermint Pond should be canceled."

"Absolutely not." For months my sister-in-law, Tiffany, a former competitive ice skater who now gave lessons, had been rehearsing her Tiny Gliders class in routines choreographed to excerpts from *The Nutcracker.* Canceling would break her heart—not to mention the tiny hearts of all those Tiny Gliders. "Why would it be canceled?"

"Too Christmassy?"

I sighed. "Christmas is *not* the problem. As long as the elves don't look conspicuously elfy."

The Tiny Gliders were elfy . . . but they were also adorable. And I doubted little skaters on Peppermint Pond could be seen in too much detail from any of the patients' windows.

The infirmary stood on the rise of a hilly block and afforded a good view of much of Christmastown, but it was several blocks away from the pond.

I made a note to meet up with Plummy Greenbuckle and get this straightened out.

"Okay," I said. "I'll go into town after breakfast and meet with her."

"You can skip the breakfast here at the castle." He flipped a page on his notepad. "Juniper called this morning and asked me to have you text her when you're up and about. She wants you to meet her this morning at the We Three Beans coffee-house. It seems she's dug up some information on Santaland's unexpected guests."

Salty had my sleigh ready to go at the castle entrance. Harnessed to it was Wobbler, a rangy reindeer with knobby knees, shaky nerves, and boundless enthusiasm. "Happy Christmas Eve, Mrs. Claus!" A merry jangle of harness bells accompanied his greeting.

I returned the sentiment, then turned and asked Salty in a low voice, "Is Cannonball okay?"

He kept his tone sotto voce. "He's got a touch of indigestion this morning. Too many reindeer cookies last night. He worried that he might be"—he lowered his voice another notch—"gassy."

I nodded, thankful for Cannonball's consideration. I really wasn't up to riding behind a flatulent reindeer this morning. "It's good of you to step in for him, Wobbler."

"It's one of my New Year's resolutions—to be more pro-active in putting myself forward. I'm calling it my 'On, Wobbler!' plan for building greater self-confidence."

"Very apt." Wobbler was a reindeer who insisted on the formalities, like my calling out, "On Wobbler!" whenever he was guiding my sleigh.

Now didn't seem like a good moment to tell Wobbler that henceforth he would need to be silent—at least until the three strangers left Christmastown. We were still miles from the Santaland Infirmary, so I figured that stricture could wait a little while.

I climbed onto the sleigh and shouted out a robust, "On, Wobbler!"

The sleigh leapt forward and soon we were skimming across the frozen path.

That text from Nick had been a tonic for my spirits. As we threaded through beautiful Kringle Heights, each chateau surrounded by evergreens dripping with lights and decorations, I couldn't help smiling. The sun was shining, and it was Christmas Eve—*our* Christmas Eve. In some parts of the world, it was already Christmas Day, and children were already waking up to find what Nick had brought them.

Wobbler had to maneuver around several snowmen making their way up the snow path. I waved at them as we passed. They were probably heading up the mountain for Grog Night at Kringle Lodge, which was located up at Sugarplum Mountain's timberline. Grog Night was seven days away, but snowmen moved slowly. Some would probably be stopping for a rest at the castle.

At the end of one of the snowy driveways, Carlotta and Clement Claus were checking their cheery red mailbox. I asked Wobbler to stop.

Wobbler, who hated to have errands interrupted, resisted slowing down at first.

"We're not on a strict timeline," I assured him. I still had plenty of time to make it into town and meet Juniper at We Three Beans.

Wobbler drew up, but the sleigh overshot the mouth of the lane. I hopped off and walked back to talk to Clement and Carlotta.

Clement was laughing. "I see Secretariat's driving the sleigh today."

I decided to ignore the barb. "We missed you at the send-off last night. Is everything okay?"

Carlotta and Clement, twins, exchanged glances in that conspiratorial, understanding way close siblings often have. "Audrey wanted to go gather mistletoe. But then she texted while she was out to tell us that she was lost. Took us forever to find her."

Carlotta shook her head in amused exasperation. "She'd gone the wrong way and ended up picking her way across some lake north of town."

"And one of her snowshoes broke," Clement said. "By the time we got back here, we didn't feel like braving the crush of the sleigh send-off."

Audrey, their younger sister, had been "living away" for several years, ostensibly attending college in Florida. Claus family members sometimes went away when they became adults. Like the Amish, they were encouraged to go test the outside world before deciding if they wanted to spend their entire lives at the North Pole. If they stayed longer than one or two years, it would be assumed that they preferred the outside world and the benefits of being a Claus in Santaland could no longer be taken for granted. Audrey had stayed away five years.

Maybe those five years had made her forget that mistletoe was available everywhere in Christmastown—in stores, at the florist, and of course, hanging from trees. You certainly didn't have to wander out into the countryside looking for it.

"Flock and Ivy's has mistletoe up to the rafters," I said.

The siblings exchanged an eye roll. "Since coming back to us, Audrey's determined to do things just so," Carlotta explained. "She thought picking her own mistletoe would be more authentically Santaland than going to the florist."

Clement said, "Turns out, authenticity is rather exhausting."

"But we're happy to go along with her ideas," Carlotta assured me. "On her deathbed, Mother made us promise that we'd look after her."

Clement tried to look solemn, but then laughed. "Caught us in a weak moment."

Carlotta gave him a playful swat and then leaned toward me. "Audrey's just trying to show everyone that she's a true Santalander. I keep assuring her that she's not going to get voted off the island just because she stayed away so long." She raised her brows at me. "Right?"

As if my opinion counted. In truth, Audrey was more of a true Santalander than I was. I'd only lived here for three years. Audrey had been away five years, but she'd grown up here. She had Santaland in her blood.

"I sometimes wonder if the person that's she really trying to convince that she belongs here is herself," Clement said. "Part of her has to be homesick for the south."

To Santalanders, anything south of the North Pole was "the south."

It struck me that Audrey and I were probably similarly conflicted. I dearly loved Santaland, Nick, and all the friends I'd made here, but sometimes I missed Cloudberry Bay. I still owned my inn in that little Oregon oceanside town, and spent every summer running it. Summer was Santaland's slow season, so Nick usually accompanied me during this annual working vacation. The crazy thing was that while I was in Cloudberry Bay, even when I was there with Nick, I felt nostalgic for my life here in Santaland. Torn between two places, just like Audrey probably felt.

I looked down their laneway toward the chateau. "Where is Audrey now?"

Clement blinked at me. "At the infirmary."

"When she heard that they were looking for Clauses to volunteer at the Santaland Infirmary this morning, she leapt at the chance to help out."

"*Leapt,*" Clement echoed.

"She's intent on being a contributing member of Santaland society."

"Does she know anything about nursing?" I asked.

"No, but Nurse Cinnamon said that it didn't matter. She said that all Audrey has to do is wander around and look human."

I nodded, understanding. Audrey would be a prop nurse to deflect the patients' attention from Nurse Cinnamon, an elf.

Clement let out a dramatic sigh. "Those poor people."

"They're lucky that Boots found them when he did," I pointed out.

"*Lucky?* I heard that poor woman lost a toe." Carlotta bit her lip. "Although I suppose it could have been worse. She could have lost her nose."

"Or her life," Clement said.

Carlotta looked doubtful. "Would life be worth living without my nose?"

Her brother leveled a serious look on her. "Who nose?"

When his lame pun sank in, the two of them dissolved into whoops of laughter.

They were a world unto themselves, these two. The C & C show. I wondered how Audrey felt being back in the old family house, with her tight-knit siblings. She was younger than they were by a decade.

"Well, I'm glad you all made it back from last night's misadventure in one piece," I said.

Clement saluted. "Bent, but not broken."

"And not gored by a reindeer, fortunately," Carlotta added.

"Those antlers can be ghastly. Grandfather once showed me a collection of Antlers of the Greats from the Old Keep. Dasher the Third's antlers were like Ginsu knives."

I frowned. The Old Keep was the original building of Castle Kringle. The ceiling had partially collapsed long ago and that part of the castle was unused now—although still accessible. I'd been through there a few times, but I'd never seen the Antlers of the Greats. They must have been locked up somewhere.

Behind me, Wobbler stamped and let out a long snort— the reindeer equivalent of someone clearing their throat.

"I'm late for a meeting," I explained, as if I were off to the General Assembly of the UN instead of coffee with Juniper.

"Don't let us keep you," Clement said.

"We'll see you soon," Carlotta added, waving me off.

She didn't say when, but she didn't have to. There was no shortage of activities in Christmastown during the next week. We were all going to see each other plenty of times.

I hopped back on the sleigh and with a quick "On, Wobbler!" we were on our way again, fast-trotting the well-worn path down Sugarplum Mountain into the picturesque village. Christmastown reminded me of a porcelain set my grandmother used to keep in her breakfront cabinet of a snowy Bavarian village decorated for the holidays. The sloping rooftops below me were all covered in a blanket of fresh snow, with brick and stone chimneys peeking through. From above, it even looked as if the whole town were perched on a bed of cotton wool.

But of course, off in the distance far beyond Christmastown loomed the high craggy peak of Mount Myrrh, where wild elves lived alongside snow monsters, as well as creatures rumored to be even worse. Cheery Santaland was safe from such things—usually—but Mount Myrrh always reminded me that the outside world wasn't too far away.

"WE THREE BEANS COFFEEHOUSE!" Wobbler announced as he stopped in front of the half-timbered edifice. His voice was loud enough to turn heads up and down the entire block. It was time to have *the talk*.

I climbed down and spoke to him face-to-face. "Because of the strangers in town, we're having to change our behavior in Christmastown somewhat. Even reindeer."

He nodded, jangling his harness bells. "I'm here to help. What can I do?"

It broke my heart to pop the bubble of so much well-intentioned eagerness. "I'm afraid you'll have to be silent."

His big eyes blinked. "You mean not talking at all, *ever*?

"It's just until the strangers leave," I explained. "I'm sorry."

He drooped his head, looking dejected.

"Wobbler?"

He didn't respond.

"Wobbler, is something wrong?"

"You told me not to talk!"

"Right." I gave him a hearty pat. "Good job."

I headed off to meet Juniper. The street surrounding We Three Beans bustled with elves doing their last-minute holiday shopping, but these elves looked . . . different. I frowned.

And then it struck me. Their clothes. There wasn't an elf cap in sight. Instead, the elves were wearing strange headgear for these parts: fedoras and knit watch caps like the ones humans wore. Beneath the hats they were sporting some kind of knitted flaps that covered their ears. It was a bizarre look. And gone also were colorful elf tunics, breeches, and hose. These elves wore jeans and khakis rolled up to fit them, and dated-looking sweaters and sweatshirts under puffy human coats.

One elf walked by in a baseball hat with a Vancouver Grizzlies patch on the front. As I caught his eye, the elf's feet shot out from under him and he went flying, landing on his backside.

I reached down to help him up. "Are you okay?"

He took my hand but scrambled up quickly. I'd never seen an elf lose his balance before, or slip on the snow. That was something *I* did.

"It's these darn slippy-doody shoes." He looked up at me, his face reddening. "Excuse my language, Mrs. Claus, but it's the truth."

I glanced down at his feet, which were encased in old-fashioned tennis shoes that looked as if they had no grips at all on their rubber soles, like pre-Air Jordan sneakers from the early 1980s. "No wonder you slipped," I said.

"Beg pardon?" he said, tilting his head.

He couldn't hear me, I realized, because of the knit flaps over his ears.

Something told me this was going to be a long week.

Chapter 5

If any spot in Santaland could be called my happy place, it would be the We Three Beans coffeehouse. The cafe's motto, "A caffeinated elf is a happy elf," went double for this human, and finding a moment in a busy day to visit there always helped smooth out life's little stresses. The atmosphere was warm, almost like a European pub. The long room boasted timbered ceilings, and the owner, Trumpet, kept a blaze going in the stone fireplace. Of course, the room was designed with elf comfort in mind—all the comfy furniture was slightly smaller than what I was used to, and holiday tunes piped through ceiling speakers all year long. Elves enjoyed singing along.

Today, however, when I pushed through the heavy old cedar door and entered the coffee shop, there were no Christmas tunes playing, and the only voice raised in song was Anne Murray's, and she wasn't singing a Christmas carol, but "You Needed Me," a syrupy ballad from the 1970s.

Disoriented, I made my way to the counter where Trumpet stood waiting to take orders. Instead of his usual cheerful, slightly jaunty elf cap, he sported an orange and blue hat with *DYN-O-MITE* knit into it. He also had little knit muffs over his ears. He didn't look happy.

Neither did the other elves scattered among the tables in their unfamiliar clothes and earmuffs.

"GOOD MORNING, MRS. CLAUS," he said. I wasn't sure if he was talking loudly because he couldn't hear, or because the volume on Anne Murray was cranked up.

"You don't have to do this," I told him. "The three strangers are at the infirmary. Even if they were all conscious and looking out their windows—which I doubt they are—they don't have laser vision. They can't see inside We Three Beans."

"We were told to act Canadian," he said determinedly. "Butterbean's scaring up some more Canadian flags for me and another mix tape." The prospect didn't appear to cheer him. "He mentioned something about Celine Dion's greatest hits."

There was already a garland of maple leaf flags draped like swag over the menu board. I studied the offerings and felt my eyes narrowing. "What is hot maple eggnog?"

"Eggnog with maple syrup, heated up to warm you so that you'll swear you're sitting by a potbellied stove in a cozy Toronto cabin."

"I'm pretty sure Toronto is the place where there aren't cabins." And just thinking of that gluey eggnog with even more sticky sweetness added made me shudder. "I'll have a straight latte, no eggnog."

"Maple syrup?" he asked.

"No syrup."

He shook his head as if I were being unpatriotic. "Whatever you say . . ."

I waited for my latte and then, as "Snowbird" started to play, I claimed a table near the fireplace. I was cold-natured, so I rarely passed up an opportunity to cozy up to a heat source. The Anne Murray playlist must have been on repeat, because some of the elves were starting to sing along to "Snowbird." Of course. Any lyric having to do with snow was bound to catch on with them sooner or later.

Juniper hurried into the coffee shop, stopped briefly to absorb the changes and place her order, and then joined me at my table without even waiting for her drink. Her outfit caused a double take. She was wearing a pink quilted coat with an appliqué of a little girl in a bonnet.

"Is that Strawberry Shortcake?" I asked.

She looked down at the cartoon appliqué. "I'm not sure. It seemed cheerful, so I grabbed it."

She slapped a folder down on the table and then removed the overcoat, revealing a thermal shirt under Mork from Ork suspenders, and pants that were both high-waisted and baggy. Even though they were made for children, she had to roll them at the ankles. She wasn't wearing sneakers, but some kind of clogs with chunky toes like Birkenstocks. If they'd ever been in fashion, they certainly weren't now. "Are those comfortable?"

She looked down at her feet. "Not really. They're so strange—it's like my toes are just swimming around in them."

"Where did you find all these clothes?"

"They were in the box of unwished for items from Santa's warehouse that were handed out this morning. I guess I'll be able to wear them if it's not for long. It's fun. Do I look human?"

Before I could answer, Trumpet brought over Juniper's mug and laid it on the table. "Maple eggnog latte."

Juniper took an experimental sip. "Mm . . . that's good!"

Trumpet sent me a victorious glance, but I shook my head.

"It's nice and sweet," Juniper explained.

As if all eggnog in Santaland wasn't toe-curlingly sweet.

"I'm glad you had time to meet me," she said after Trumpet left us. "I was worried you might be busy with the reindeer this morning."

"No, I convinced Lucia to talk to them. She made a good case last night that suspecting reindeer of stabbing that man is all nonsense. Reindeer aren't homicidal."

Juniper looked as if she might speak, hesitated, then took a long drink of eggnog.

I leaned forward. "What?"

Her eyes widened. "What?"

"You were going to say something, but then you did that awkward looking-away thing like everyone did last night. As if there's this big secret I'm not supposed to know."

"It's not a secret," she said. "We Santalanders just don't like to talk about it."

My curiosity ramped up another notch. "About what?"

She looked around furtively, then lowered her voice. "Adolph the Naughty."

This was a new name to me. "I take it he was a reindeer?"

"An extremely naughty reindeer. He had serious anger management issues."

"When was this?"

"Almost a century ago. See, during a big reindeer obstacle relay contest, one of the reindeer, Adolph, went berserk and gored several competitors during a jump competition. Three of the other reindeer subsequently died of their wounds. Adolph also killed a snowman."

"That's awful!" I exclaimed.

"Well, the snowman was sort of collateral damage—he got squished when one of the wounded reindeer fell to earth."

Wrong place, wrong time.

"You mean that one incident has traumatized all of Santaland to the point that no one can speak of it a hundred years later?"

"Reindeer are central to Santaland identity, April. If they go bad, the whole world feels askew."

"But that was just one reindeer, a hundred years ago. If you think about it, one psychotic reindeer out of the however many millions that have lived here throughout history really isn't a bad percentage."

"It was so horrible," she said. "Adolph was permanently exiled to the Farthest Frozen Reaches, and he became the last of his name. Adolph the Naughty has spoiled the name Adolph forever."

"Well, he wasn't the only one." I drummed my fingers against my mug. "I wonder if we just found proof that Adolph the Naughty managed to survive his exile and produce offspring."

"I doubt Adolph has anything to do with our current situation." Juniper set her latte aside and opened the folder in front of her. "*This* is why I wanted to talk to you. I went to the library early this morning and did an internet search to see what I could find out about the visitors."

I scooted forward in my chair. I should have done a search last night, but my brain had been distracted by my husband's flying around the world.

"I started with the photographer's name. Sam Bradford. On the whole, he gets good reviews online, although two separate customers complained that he was late getting wedding pictures to them." She shook her head. "He can't be very conscientious. Do you think *he* could have stabbed that man?"

"From tardy photographer to murderer is a big leap." I doubted Juniper had called me into Christmastown to tell me about a couple of bad Google reviews, though. "What else did you discover?"

"Sam Bradford's a pretty common name, so I had trouble sifting through all the hits I got that didn't involve his business. Then I remembered what Boots told us about Sam saying that he and the two others were in a shipwreck. And sure enough, when I added 'arctic plus ship plus wreck' to my search, I got several hits. Sam was listed as a member of a team going to join a scientific expedition on a ship called the *Arctic Grayling*."

"Did the *Grayling* sink?"

"No, it's still in the Arctic. But the Twin Otter aircraft that the additional team members were flying in on disappeared during a blizzard earlier this month. A search was made, but the plane wasn't found. It was assumed that everyone on it died. The search was called off two weeks ago, to be resumed after the spring thaw."

Two weeks. And that was just when the search was called off. "How did they survive for so long?" I wouldn't have lasted two days out in the elements at the North Pole on my own.

"I guess some *didn't* survive. Five flew out to relieve the *Grayling*. Well, four plus the pilot. And of course, even the three that were found almost died."

I wondered how far they'd wandered from the plane crash. "Do you have any idea who the other two people with Sam are?"

She turned her pages toward me. "One article included little thumbnail pictures of the people on the science team who disappeared." She tapped one of those thumbnails. "I think this is the woman—Elaine Foskett."

I frowned. In Elaine Foskett's headshot, her sharp green eyes drilled into the camera with a confident gaze. Her dark hair was pulled back in a no-nonsense clip, and she wore a turtleneck under a tweed jacket. The overall impression the photo conveyed was sharp intelligence. Steeliness. Of course, it was hard to say for sure that this was the same woman whose vulnerable form I'd glimpsed last night under the dirty blankets on Boots's sleigh.

Foskett's thumbnail bio was impressive. Harvard under-grad, and then a master's and her doctorate in mineralogy from Stanford.

"Who was the other man?" I wondered. I couldn't tell from the pictures; then again, last night I'd been more focused on that antler in his back than on his face.

"Maybe David Perino, the pilot." She leaned in to look

at the pictures with me and tapped one. "Or this man—Eric Lynch?"

Maybe . . .

"Eric Lynch is *very* handsome," Juniper said. "A dreamboat, actually."

I nodded. Short, curly brown hair, piercing dark eyes, chiseled jaw. Both men last night had scraggly, ice-covered beards, though. It was hard to be sure.

"Do you mind if I take this folder with me to the infirmary this morning? Maybe I can match the photo to the man."

She shook her head. "Not at all. I made copies."

"I wonder what those scientists were researching," I said.

"It said that they were there to study the sea ice." She took a long sip of her drink. "I wonder if we need to send a search party out for the two others who were on the plane."

"Boots asked about others," I said. "That man told him that there were only three survivors. Of course, he was delirious."

"We should ask them again when they've recovered a little."

I nodded. "I wonder how they survived the crash." To say nothing of the frigid journey through the Farthest Frozen Reaches. They'd all been in such bad shape when they were found.

I studied the pictures and bios again that had been written up on the journal *Scientific Frontiers Today*. Sam the photographer did not have an impressive academic pedigree. The article did mention that his photographs had been published in *West Coast Naturalist* and *Bride*. I'm assuming that the former was the one that got him a job on a scientific expedition. No relatives were mentioned, but I didn't suppose they would be in such a short bio.

Meanwhile, Elaine Foskett's achievements went on and

on. She'd published papers in prestigious scientific journals, focusing on something called igneous petrology. She'd racked up more grants and fellowships than Santaland has gumdrops. She'd taught at Stanford, San Francisco State, and Pomona College.

I drank some of my coffee and read a little more from the articles. The search for survivors of the plane crash had gone on for weeks but the efforts were hampered by blizzard conditions. After two weeks, it was decided that the people on the plane couldn't possibly have survived.

But they had. How?

I needed to talk to Sam Bradford. Of the three, he seemed the most likely to be up and able to divulge information to us today.

I gathered my things. "I'm heading to the infirmary now. I'll call you if I find out anything."

"Or just tell me about it this afternoon."

I frowned. "This afternoon?"

"The Tiny Gliders concert?"

Omigosh, I had almost forgotten. The Santaland Concert Band was playing *The Nutcracker* for the Tiny Gliders show.

Juniper finished her drink, then looked at me with concern. "Be careful, April."

"I know—I need to get my head screwed on. I can't miss Tiffany's class's big show."

She shook her head and tapped the photos. "I meant be careful at the infirmary. We might be able to learn these strangers' names now, but it takes more than a thumbnail sketch to understand who someone really is. Or how dangerous."

Chapter 6

The word *Santaland* chiseled into the stone of the Santaland Infirmary's edifice had been discreetly covered over with evergreen boughs and red ribbons. The same decoration had been put on the other side of the word *Infirmary*. The impression was of a tastefully Christmassy hospital.

I'd just stopped to admire the camouflage—Butterbean's handiwork, I assumed—when the front door to the hospital opened and Audrey Claus came speeding out. Her long blond hair streamed over her shoulders, and always seemed to have a perfect curl at the ends, like shampoo commercial hair. She was in the process of shoving a knit hat on her head. The pom at the top was conspicuously big and sparkly.

Distracted, she nearly slammed into me. For someone Carlotta and Clement told me was eager to help at the hospital, she seemed in an all-fired hurry to get out of there.

"Oh, April!" She hopped back a step. "Any word from Cousin Nick about the sleigh's progress?"

"They seem to be right on time," I said, keeping the inner turmoil I'd felt for the past twenty-four hours out of my voice. "We missed you at the send-off."

"Really?" Her eyes bugged. "Do you think Nick noticed that I wasn't there?"

I suppressed a laugh. Nick had been so preoccupied before takeoff, I doubt he would have noticed if *I* hadn't been there. "No—it's okay. You had an emergency—I heard about the snowshoeing mishap."

She relaxed only slightly. "I wanted to be there, of course."

I tilted my head, studying her. "Is everything all right?"

"Oh! Yes!" Beneath her lingering Florida tan, her cheeks reddened. "Actually, no. I seem to be as hopeless with sick people as I am at everything else. Thank goodness I didn't want to go to nursing school. I would have failed at that even faster than I did at college, retail work, and yoga certification."

"Yoga?"

She sighed. "I mean, yoga *sounds* cool. But all that stretching and breathing—so tedious. It's misleading."

I felt some sympathy with her. In my twenties, I'd bounced around from job to job for a while until I inherited my inn and felt I'd found something I really loved doing.

"Anyway, I've got a million things to do today, so I'd better run," she said. "I still haven't wrapped all my gifts."

Her words caused a tightness in my chest. Wrapping. I would have to stay up late tonight and do that. Maybe put on a Christmas movie and make a marathon of it.

And then I was reminded that I still was short one gift. Pamela's. I absolutely could not leave Christmastown today without buying something.

Before I could voice my late-wrapper solidarity, Audrey was already down the infirmary's front steps and on her way.

"Thank goodness you're here." Nurse Cinnamon buttonholed me as soon as I crossed the threshold of the infirmary's main building, where the patients' rooms were. The ER was located in a newer wing at the side of the building, but it was only opened as needed. Nurse Cinnamon was dressed in her usual crisp white uniform dress but tottered in chunky white platform shoes unlike her usual white elf booties. Her stiff nurse cap perched on a scarf wrapped like a turban around her hair and ears.

Her appearance wasn't the only odd thing in the infirmary. Over loudspeakers, Celine Dion belted "My Heart Will Go On," which told me that Butterbean had been here. And several carts piled high with fruitcakes, cookie platters, and peppermint stick bouquets stood in the hallways, giving off vibes that were more hospitality than hospital.

"What's all this?" I asked, pointing to the trays of goodies.

"Everyone's sending get-well gifts to the three strangers. There were some balloons, too, but most had holiday decorations. I've been ordered to downplay Christmas ornamentation."

Butterbean again. He was confusing disguising Christmastown with obliterating Christmas itself.

"That's totally unnecessary," I said. "It's Christmas everywhere. The patients won't see anything too unusual with holiday decorations." I gestured up to the speakers. "And I don't think Canadian hospitals pipe pop music into their hospital hallways."

Nurse Cinnamon planted her hands on her hips. "Tell that to Generalissimo Butterbean." She lifted her shoulders and dropped them. "While you're at work, you do what you think is best. If you just happen to hit the off switch on that music player or accidentally hurl it off the rooftop, I'll never tell."

I laughed, until something embedded in what she'd said sank in. "While *I'm* at work?"

"Butterbean told me we should have a human on the floor at all times, so I've made a rota for all the Clauses. Well—except Lucia. No offense to your family, but I just don't think it's a good idea to have a woman who spends all of her time around reindeer in the hospital."

As if Lucia shed reindeer germs.

Although she *could* be pretty pungent at times.

"I ran into Audrey Claus on her way out just now," I said.

Nurse Cinnamon rolled her eyes. "*That girl*. She did one round of the patients' rooms and came out looking white as fresh fallen snow. She said she was sorry but she couldn't stand the sight of blood, and then tore out of here."

"I guess not everyone's suited for nursing." I didn't savor spending a lot of time in the hospital myself.

What I wanted didn't seem to matter much, however. Nurse Cinnamon took my arm and led me to a large supply closet. "But now you're here, so all is well. You can work until Mildred Claus's shift begins this afternoon."

Mildred Claus was Nick's old aunt. *It really must be all hands on deck.*

She held out candy-striped scrubs for me to change into. So much for my nice Mrs. Claus dress. I hoped the scrubs were made for male elves—otherwise I'd never be able to squeeze into them.

"You're just playacting, don't forget," Nurse Cinnamon said, turning her back to give me privacy as I struggled to wriggle out of my dress and into the scrubs. "If there's anything that requires medical expertise, you come get me or Doc Honeytree."

"Okay." The scrubs fit—barely—but there was nothing to be done about my boots, which were entirely inappropriate hospital footwear. I would never fit into anything in the little pile of human shoes—mostly children's—that had been left there. I had to hope that the patients who were awake would be so distracted by my candy cane–striped tunic and pants that they wouldn't examine my footwear too closely.

"You just want to make yourself seen," Nurse Cinnamon continued.

"I'll be hard to miss in this getup."

"You look fine," Nurse Cinnamon said. "All you have to do is fluff their pillows, and check that they have water and that they haven't fallen out of bed. Got it?"

"I think I can handle that." I didn't seem to have any choice.

"I have to go visit the emergency room at the other end of the building, but you should be fine here on your own."

Elves were hardy creatures, so Santaland's ER was usually even less used than the in-patient hospital wing. "Did something happen?"

"Our second sprain of the day. Elves are slipping all over town." She put a tray of mini muffins in my hand. Each muffin had a toothpick with a small Canadian flag sticking out the top. "You can take these to the patient named Sam."

"He's eating?"

Nurse Cinnamon blinked at me. "There's nothing wrong with him but exhaustion. He just needs to get his strength back."

That wasn't good. I'd been hoping for at least a day or two of all the strangers being out of it. Once Nick returned, he might have a clearer idea of what to do with them.

As Nurse Cinnamon marched off in the direction of the ER, I and my tray of Canadian muffins approached Sam Bradford's door. My nerves began to jangle strangely, like they did the one time I'd been foolish enough to take part in a school play. All I'd had to do was play an old lady sitting in the cemetery in the last act of *Our Town*. I'd fallen out of my chair on opening night. Actually, it hadn't really been my fault—the chair leg had broken.

But that was the problem with playacting, as Nurse Cinnamon had called it. A million things could go wrong, all of them unexpected.

At the door, I tapped lightly and peeked in. Wide-awake blue eyes stared back at me. The man scooched up a little, eyeing my tray of muffins. "Are those for me?"

I crossed to the bed. "I don't think your companions are quite up to muffin munching just yet."

He frowned. "Really? I heard rumblings coming from the next room that sounded like Elaine."

So it *was* Elaine Foskett.

He bit into a muffin and his face broke into an expression of pure bliss. "You have no idea how good this tastes."

I did, actually. "I can't claim many talents, but I consider myself a connoisseur of local baked goods."

He laughed. "You must have a lot of skill to be a nurse."

"Nurse assistant," I corrected.

He devoured the rest of his muffin. "There's this strange little woman who comes in sometimes," he said between swallows. "Is she a nurse too?"

I turned, smiling, and went to the sink to refill his water pitcher. Thankfully, Nurse Cinnamon wasn't around to hear her professional presence reduced to the label "strange little woman."

"Fresh water for you." After I put the pitcher down, I stepped back, hands clasped in what I hoped was a professional manner. "Is there anything else I can do for you, Mr. Bradford?"

"Sure, you can stop calling me Mr. Bradford. I'm Sam." Celine Dion started singing "All by Myself." "And you can maybe stop the music?"

I smiled. "All right, Sam. I'll see what I can do."

"And could you sit down and talk for a moment? I know it's selfish when you have so much to do, but I'm a little confused."

I lowered myself into the velvet upholstered visitor's chair by his bed. "What are you confused about?"

"This place, for starters." He lifted his hand and gestured vaguely around the room at the wood furniture, the old-fashioned shaded lamps, and the arrangement of gingerbread men and fruitcakes on the sideboard. "This is the weirdest hospital I've ever been in. It's got rugs, and weird wood furniture. This bed is smaller than the one I slept in when I was a toddler. And they don't seem overly concerned about patients having a healthy diet."

"It's an old building, and we're a small, remote town. We make do with donated furniture. Doc Honeytree—he's our principal doctor here—he thinks the homey touches help the patients recover. And the baked goods are just from towns-people who wish you well."

"Seriously?" He looked genuinely surprised, and touched. "That's extraordinarily generous."

"We don't get a lot of visitors."

"No, I don't imagine you would." Sam bit into another muffin.

"Where is your home?" I asked, feigning ignorance.

"Well, I grew up in Sacramento, but I moved to L.A. for college and never left."

"You're a long way from there."

"Where am I, exactly?" He looked at the little flags sticking out of the muffins. "I mean, I take it that this is somewhere in Canada, but I'm afraid I don't know my Canadian geography."

"Far north."

"Like, the Northwest Territories? Isn't that what it's called?"

"Mm," I said noncommittally. "Where were you intending to go?"

"The Arctic Ocean. There were four of us who were supposed to go relieve the crew members there on a research ship. Our plane took off from Yellowknife, but we hit bad weather and something went wrong and our plane crash-landed . . ." His expression darkened. "It was pretty awful."

"Three of you were found. Were you the only survivors?"

"Yes. Only three of us." He took a drink of water, and I detected a tremor in his hand. "Well, that's not true. Another woman survived for a day. We kept hoping for rescue . . . but none came. I don't think anyone knew where we crashed. We never even saw any search-and-rescue aircraft. That was . . ." He sent me a puzzled look. "What day is it now?"

"December twenty-fourth."

"We crashed on December third." He tilted his head. "It wasn't in your newspapers, or on television?"

"As I said, our village is rather isolated." *To put it mildly.*

"So it's Christmas Eve . . ." he said. "You don't know what happened to my phone, do you?"

"No, I haven't heard anything about a phone." Boots hadn't mentioned finding it. Would he have stolen a phone?

Sam's brows knit. "I wasn't carrying it on me. Eric had it—so it would be with his belongings."

"Why would he have had your phone?"

"Mine was the only phone that was working—well, it worked for a while, at least. And since Eric was our unofficial group leader, he kept it on him." His eyes brightened. "Could I borrow yours—or use the public phone here at the hospital?"

I had to think quickly. "Our lines are down. We had a storm."

Sam sighed. "Oh. That's too bad. I'd like to call home."

A wave of guilt washed over me. Of course he'd want to let his loved ones know he was okay. "Your parents?"

"No, my parents are both gone. I'd like to call my dog, though."

"You phone your dog?"

"Well, the guy who's pet sitting my dog. Peanut's with my neighbor."

I tried to change the subject back to the accident. "Are you sure we shouldn't send a search party out to look for anyone who might have survived?"

"There would be no point. Like I said, they're gone—the pilot, and Madison." He sighed. "It's weird that I made it. I was the last to be hired on. I'm not a scientist. I'm not even a college graduate. I dropped out after two years to pursue photography."

As if his lack of a degree made him less survival-worthy.

"Were you hired by the scientific team to photograph them?"

"To do a sort of photo diary for them, yes." He let out a half laugh. "Eric had this big idea that if they got coverage in a national magazine that they—or he—would be blessed with fame and fortune on their return."

"Eric," I repeated.

"Eric Lynch," he said. "Very ambitious guy. And not always the most practical."

"What do you mean?"

"Well, for one thing, would you go on a trip to the Arctic with your ex?"

"Ex-girlfriend?"

He shook his head. "Ex-wife."

"I guess if we got along . . ."

Sam barked out a laugh. "Those two are like feral cats in a small cage. I was only around them for a few hours before the crash, but in that short time I could see they were going to kill each other . . . if the plane hadn't tried to do the job for them."

"Tried."

"Eric and Elaine made it. Eric was in bad shape at first. I think he had a concussion, but he popped back after a day. Madison didn't, unfortunately."

I was struggling to keep them all straight. "Madison was the woman you mentioned, the one who died?"

He didn't affirm this, but he didn't have to. His face collapsed into an expression that was unbearably bleak. In his eyes, I could read the desperation those people must have felt while huddling in the wreckage of their downed airplane, trying to deal with the dead and dying, wondering and worrying if help would ever come for them. And then realizing they were on their own.

"Eric was right about one thing." He sent me a wondering smile. "He had this crazy idea about finding a hidden city in the snow. He kept saying we needed to find a valley between two mountains."

At those last words, I froze. Could he mean *our* valley, between Sugarplum Mountain and Mount Myrrh?

"Eric harbored some cockamamie idea that we'd find Shangri-la in the snow. Is this Shangri-la?"

"Ha." I shook my head, hoping to disguise my flushed cheeks. "He was probably hallucinating. That concussion from the plane crash . . ."

Seriously, though. How could he have heard where Santaland was located? Was our world more generally known to scientists studying the Arctic than we liked to believe?

"He seemed awfully sure for someone who was having a hallucination. That's why we finally went along with him. That, and because we didn't have any better ideas." He pulled up his blanket. "But next time someone asks me to fly to the top of the world, I'll say no thanks. I don't care if I do spend the rest of my life as a school picture photographer." He sank down against his pillows, his eyelids drooping.

I stood. "I should let you rest."

His eyes fluttered, then focused on me. "Have you ever seen a talking snowman?"

Nervous laughter burbled out of me. "What a question!" I backed away. "Get some sleep. You'll feel better after a nap. We'll wake you for lunch."

He closed his eyes. "I'm never going to miss another meal."

I tiptoed out of the room. Celine Dion was even louder in the hallway, so I closed his door and then hunted down the music player. It was in the little kitchen cupboard area where the mini fridge and the teakettle were. Butterbean seemed to have brought in a primitive kind of MP3 player—electronics in Santaland always lagged a little behind the rest of the world—and I had to squint to read the controls. I hit one button twice, which I thought would stop the music entirely. Instead, it returned to the first song—back to the love theme from *Titanic*. Over the song's opening bars, I heard a woman's voice.

"Hey, Nursie, come help me!"

Nursie? Incensed, I marched over and poked my head into the room. The patient, a woman with straight black hair falling over her shoulders and sharp green eyes I recognized from her thumbnail headshot, had swung her legs over the side of her bed. One of her legs and its foot were engulfed in a giant surgical boot intended to protect the bandage where her toe had been.

Her stance, poised to get out of bed, alarmed me. Was she supposed to be walking already?

"Should you be up?" I warned.

"Why not? Because one little piggy went to market and got chopped off? Screw that. I'm just going to the room next door."

"To see Sam? He's just fallen asleep."

Her lips twisted into a wry smile. "So Sam's here? I might have known. God takes care of fools. But it's not Sam I want to see. It's Eric."

"Uh . . ." I hadn't been in that room yet. "I'm not sure if he's in any shape to have visitors."

She glared at me. "I'm his wife."

"Ex-wife," I said.

She eyed me with amusement. "So Sam's been gossiping. Of course he has. What else can people do but gossip when they don't have any actual ideas in their heads?"

Good grief. Was she always like this?

She rolled her eyes. "Don't look so panicked. I only want to peek in for five seconds to see if Eric's really alive. Just give me your arm for a minute and I promise I'll be a good patient and go back to bed."

I nodded toward the crutch left by the bed, which was wood with a dark patina from years of use. "Do you want to try your crutch?"

She scowled at it. "That antique? It looks like it was made for Tiny Tim."

It was a little on the short side. I saw no real harm in doing as she asked—until she put her booted foot down on the ground and winced in pain.

"Maybe we shouldn't—"

"It's fine," she said through gritted teeth.

Obviously, it wasn't. But she had an iron will to go along with the iron grip she held my arm with. Her hand clamped down on me like a claw, and together we hobbled out of the room and made the short trip down the hall to the next door. Elaine's room was between Sam's and Eric's.

"Honestly, how can a toe cause so much pain when it's not even there?" she asked, glaring down at the dressing peeping out of her surgical boot.

"In my experience, the things we miss can cause the *most* pain," I said, thinking of Nick. Ever since his sleigh had taken off the night before, a sick flutter had taken up residence in my chest. "It's the loss of—"

Elaine cut me off. "I wasn't asking for a philosophical treatise. I just wish my foot would stop hurting." She glared at the offending appendage encased in its orthopedic boot. "I wish I had *your* boots. Very cool. Fully toed within, too, I'll bet."

I was torn between preening over the compliment and worrying that I was giving away my imposter nurse status.

"Of course, I'd rather cut off my entire foot than be seen in that outfit you have on," she said. "Is there some reason why a hospital would make its nursing staff walk around looking like barber poles?"

I couldn't think of a good answer aside from *Because we're in a world that loves candy canes.* "These scrubs are very comfortable."

"They ought to be. They're certainly not doing your hips any favors."

Inside the next room, Eric Lynch was lying in the bed on his side, the thick bandage around his torso visible through the open collar of his pajama top. The dressing was neat and clean, and the skin beneath his dark beard was a healthy golden-brown hue. He and Audrey Claus were probably the only people in Santaland with deep suntans. Overall, his appearance was a vast improvement over last night. His wild hair had even been trimmed and combed. He still had several tubes hooked up to his arm IV, however.

Elaine pointed to the tubes. "What's all that for?"

"A feeding tube, because he's unconscious. And I think that other going into his arm is some kind of antibiotic?" The doubt in my voice made me sound like the least competent nurse ever—which I was—but Elaine didn't seem to notice.

"So he's going to live," she said with no inflection.

"Doc says so."

"And do you know how he ended up with that huge bandage around his chest?"

I'd assumed she already knew. "He was stabbed."

That news seemed to surprise her. "Just stabbed out of the blue?"

For some reason, I hesitated to tell her about the reindeer antler. "We don't know the circumstances. We weren't there."

She looked up at me. "Neither was I. We split up. Sam and I followed Eric at first because he seemed so sure of himself, but when it became clear that we were probably all going to die if we didn't find help fast, we hedged our bets and separated. Anyone who ran into help was supposed to send a search party out for the other two. I guess *that* strategy worked, at least."

"Not really. Boots found you all by accident. None of you were in good enough shape to lead him to the others."

"Boots?" Her eyes brightened at the name. "Is that a person?"

"He's an"—I just stopped myself from saying the *E* word—"a backwoodsman. It's lucky he ran into you. He saved you all."

She looked down at Eric again, and bit her lip. "It's so strange to see him like this. Eric is robust. Very virile." She tilted a glance at me. "You don't know who stabbed him?"

"Boots said Eric told him it was an animal. But he was delirious."

"Sometimes men can behave like animals." Her disarming green gaze turned to me. "Women, too."

"There's an investigation underway." I didn't tell her that the suspects being interrogated were reindeer, and that the law in Santaland was a two-elf force more interested in baked goods and iceball than crime solving.

She put a hand on my shoulder to indicate that I should lead her back. Out in the hallway I realized Celine Dion was singing the love theme from *Titanic* again. Darn it. I didn't have the whole playlist on repeat, just that one song.

"By the way, what happened to our belongings?" she asked me.

"You didn't have much. Boots found forty-two dollars and Sam's business card."

"That's it?" The worried look in her eyes belied her nonchalant tone.

"Are you missing something?" I asked.

"No . . . not much survived the crash, or the long march through the snow. Eric insisted we leave most of our stuff back in the plane. And then, when we parted ways . . ." She shook her head. "We were mostly concerned with saving ourselves, not material possessions."

"Where were you all? How did you survive? You must have made some kind of shelter."

She hesitated. "We found a cave. Don't ask me where— I've been confused about directions since the plane went down. One icy crag looks just like another to me. We would have stayed in our cave longer, but we were out of food. We'd grabbed MREs we were bringing for the ship's emergency stores."

"MREs?"

"Meals ready to eat," she explained. "Like the military carries. Ghastly tasting but it was something. Of course, when the food ran out, we began to worry that we'd starve to death. Or that a polar bear would come into the cave and eat us."

"They're hibernating."

She smiled. "That's what Eric said, but I thought it would be just my luck that some confused polar bear would wake up early and bumble into our shelter."

We arrived at her door and she stopped.

"Don't you want to say hello to Sam?" I gestured toward his door just a few steps further on.

"Maybe later, when I'm not groggy from pain meds."

This was her when she was groggy? She seemed tack-sharp. I had a few more questions about that shelter they'd found, but I was supposed to be Nurse Assistant April, not a nosy Nancy Drew.

"Is there anything else I can get for you?" I asked.

"A phone. Or an internet connection."

"I wish I could help you, but I'm afraid all of our communications went out in the same storm that hit the night before you were all found."

She blinked at me. "*All* communication?"

"We're quite remote here in Centretown."

"You're telling me. What's this supposed to be the center of—nowhere?" She didn't wait for my answer, just reeled toward her bed. "I think I might have overdone it. I need to sleep. Can you please turn off that caterwauling woman? Her heart might go on, but my patience is about to snap."

"I'll see what I can do."

I scrambled to try to fix the music player. I couldn't figure out what mistake I'd made that had resulted in this Celine Dion nightmare loop. Unfamiliar with the player, I mashed a few buttons that looked as if they might make it stop.

A shadow suddenly loomed over me. It was Elaine, who had decided to use the Tiny Tim crutch. She grabbed the MP3 player, ripped the cord out, then dropped it to the floor and smashed it with her crutch until it was splinters of plastic and tiny metal parts.

"*That's* how you deal with an annoyance." She turned back toward her room.

As I watched her stump away, a disturbing thought reeled through my mind. If that was how she took care of an annoyance, how would she deal with an ex-husband?

Chapter 7

My three charges were quiet for the rest of my shift, so I did some light housecleaning chores. In between washing a few dishes and mopping the corridor, I checked for messages from Nick. Nothing.

Don't worry. Every year all my worries had turned out to be for nothing.

During the lull, I sent messages to Plummy and Butterbean to meet at my sister-in-law's tea shop when my shift as a fake nurse was over.

Then I looked in on Eric again to make sure he hadn't tumbled onto the floor. The infirmary's beds weren't typical hospital beds with guardrails. I approached him cautiously—he seemed so still. I really had no idea how to take a pulse, so I leaned in closely to detect any signs of breathing. As I was inches from his face, his eyes popped open.

I jumped back with a sharp gasp. He seemed surprised, too. Surprised but still groggy. "I expected Miss Mojito."

I frowned. "Elaine's right in the next room."

"Oh god." He closed his eyes and drifted away again.

When Nurse Cinnamon rushed back from her work at the ER to check on me, I told her my big news. "Eric Lynch woke up. He even spoke. He didn't make much sense, but . . ."

She cut me off with a wave of her hand. "He's been in and out all morning. I think he'd be more alert, but Doc's got him on sedatives and painkillers. How are the others?"

"Resting." I told her that Elaine had already been on her feet and walked down the hall. I didn't mention that she only wanted to walk down the hall to check that her ex-husband was still alive. Or maybe she'd wanted to see if he was dead.

Maybe she *wanted* him to be dead . . .

Nurse Cinnamon snapped her fingers in front of my face, bringing my speculation crashing back down to earth.

"What?" I asked.

"I asked if they'd had any lunch."

Was I supposed to feed them lunch? I looked over at the schedule. And there it was in big red letters. *LUNCH.* Oops.

"They did get mini muffins." At least, Sam did.

Nurse Cinnamon was obviously not impressed with me.

I wasn't impressed with me, either, but in my own defense, I said, "I wasn't expecting to be on my own for so long."

She bristled, but her irritation wasn't directed entirely at me. "I didn't expect to be so long away. But just as I had one elf bandaged up, another patient came in with a sprained ankle. I don't know what the world's coming to! I had to call for Dr. Algid Honeytree to help out."

Being ice skaters or at least ice walkers from an early age, elves developed strong ankles. Their lower center of gravity also helped them be more sure-footed on the ice. Apparently, elf booties made a difference, too.

She shook her head and lowered her voice into a confidential whisper. "Between you and me and those hundred fruitcakes over there, I'll admit that I've wished more than once that those people hadn't been found." She blushed. "Of course it's uncharitable of me to have thoughts like that, but the sooner those people are out of Santaland and we can return to normal, the better I'll like it."

"I understand." Elves weren't used to having their world turned upside down by unexpected visitors from afar.

So much seemed strange in Santaland at the moment. I thought of Pamela holed up in her room when she was usually such a huge Christmas presence. Then I remembered that we owed a bit of gratitude to Nurse Cinnamon on Pamela's behalf.

"By the way, I want to thank you for sending a nurse to the castle for Pamela Claus."

Her expression was blank. "What nurse?"

"Coco."

She rocked back on her platform heels. "You've got your lights tangled, Mrs. Claus. I've been a nurse for over twenty years, and I've never yet come across a Nurse Coco."

"I could have sworn that Jingles said she was a nurse."

"He's mistaken."

How odd.

Nurse Cinnamon nodded at Mildred Claus mousing her way along the corridor. "Here comes your relief."

Mildred was in her seventies, rail thin, and very unassuming. She lived in one of the oldest Claus chateaus on Sugarplum Mountain with her elf servant, Olive. In fact, Olive usually accompanied Mildred into town.

"Nothing's wrong with Olive today, I hope," I said.

"How kind of you to ask after her," Mildred said. "She's fine. I left her back at the house, chopping wood."

Olive was older than Mildred by at least a decade. "Is that wise?"

"Oh yes. Olive thinks it's imperative to have enough wood in case another blizzard hits."

"Chopping wood is rigorous work, I meant."

"Oh, you know Olive. She likes to keep herself fit as a flea." Mildred sighed. "I don't know where she gets the energy. We were up late last night making extra candied nut assortments for gifts. I held up okay through the walnuts and the sugar-and-spice pistachios, but the mixed nut brittle did me in."

She did look droopy, poor thing. Mildred's candied nuts really were to die for, though.

"It was doubly good of you to volunteer, then." I looked at my watch. "Gosh, I should go." And I still needed to change back into my own clothes first.

"Oh yes—don't let me keep you," Mildred said. "I'll check on the patients and see if there's anything they want. You run along."

I wasn't running back to the castle, but to Tea-piphany to meet Plummy and Butterbean.

My sister-in-law's tea shop, Tea-piphany, was several blocks away. I could have walked it, but Wobbler had already been standing still much longer than expected and looked antsy to stretch his legs. Christmastown was bustling with elves doing their last-minute shopping, and the streets were crowded with sleighs and snowmobiles. I saw more than one wearing sneakers slip and wipe out.

It was going to be a busy afternoon at the Santaland ER.

In front of the tea shop, Wobbler and another reindeer exchanged sharp words over a tight parking space.

"Watch where you're going!" the reindeer said when Wobbler got what he considered too close.

Wouldn't you know it was a Dasher. I could tell by the ridiculous rack of antlers he was sporting. They were obviously fake, and had been sharpened to points—the reindeer equivalent of a fancy power grille on a sports car.

"*You* watch your tone," Wobbler shot back. "This is Mrs.

Claus. If you don't scoot over, she'll barely have enough room to get out of her sleigh."

"Just because you're from the castle doesn't mean you own the road, you knobby-kneed misfit," the other reindeer sniped.

"Hey! That's enough!" I climbed off the sleigh. It *was* a tight squeeze. "There's no call for insults. There's room enough here for you both."

"Exactly," Wobbler said, tossing his head. "Don't get your antlers in a twist." He couldn't resist adding, "If they *are* your antlers."

I shot him a warning look. At the same time, I also couldn't resist a second look at those elaborate antlers. Given what had happened to Eric, their sharp, show-offy points now seemed more sinister than silly.

"I won't be too long this time, Wobbler." I lowered my voice. "Try not to get into any more arguments."

"Yes ma'am." He lifted his head and said, more loudly, "Someone should tell Mr. Meany over there that he's not supposed to be talking at all."

"Neither are you," I reminded him.

On the sidewalk, I passed three elves in red sweaters singing "O Canada."

Jiminy Cricket. This had to stop.

"You don't have to do this," I interrupted in a raised voice.

The Canadian national anthem went silent and three pairs of eyes blinked up at me.

One of them, a red-haired elf, asked, "*What?*"

He couldn't hear me. I leaned close to his earmuff and said in an even louder voice, "It's Christmas Eve. Sing Christmas songs!"

"But we spent a whole hour learning this one Butterbean gave us," the elf protested.

A fellow caroler bobbed her head, which was covered

in a hat from the Nordiques, a long-defunct hockey team. "Butterbean said—"

"Never mind what Butterbean said," I interrupted. "Christmas songs are fine."

The three elves exchanged doubtful looks, then began a hesitant rendering of "Good King Wenceslas."

Inside Tea-piphany, everything seemed comfortingly normal. No Celine Dion, no maple leaves, no earmuffs. I could have cried with relief. I'd never been so happy to hear Bing Crosby sing "White Christmas."

"Hi, April." Tiffany was leaning against the counter—almost slumped against it, which was not typical of her. She'd gone through a rough patch several years ago after her husband's death, but she'd long since bounced back and become a dynamo of positive activity. Tiffany still had the petite, lean lines of the competitive figure skater she had been in her youth, and in her store she was usually a blur of action behind the counter. In addition to the tea shop, she taught the Tiny Gliders. Also, she was Christopher's mother. Christopher would assume the role of Santa Claus on his twenty-first birthday, but for now he still answered to Mom. She took her role as single mother seriously, without ever devolving into helicopter parenting.

In other words, she was no slouch.

Yet here she was. Slouching.

"I thought you'd be out shopping for Pamela's present," she said.

I kept forgetting that present. Dread pierced me.

"I'm meeting Plummy Greenbuckle and Butterbean here." I looked around at the beautifully laid tables with red damask cloth over white, with gleaming place settings of beautiful old china cups, saucers, and dessert plates awaiting customers. "They haven't arrived yet, I guess."

"I haven't seen Plummy." Her lips turned down. "Butterbean came around early this morning, issuing orders about what music was supposed to be playing."

I nodded toward the speakers overhead. Bing Crosby had given way to a track from Ella Fitzgerald's *Ella Wishes You a Swingin' Christmas*, a personal favorite of mine. "I guess you decided to ignore the edict."

"Of course I did. I'm also going to ignore his recommendation that I change the music in my Tiny Gliders ice show from *The Nutcracker* to the greatest hits of Gordon Lightfoot."

Oh no. "He didn't actually suggest that, did he?"

"He gave me a list of prominent Canadian artists." She gave her head a ponytail-swinging shake. "April, has this town lost its mind? Three strangers arrive and suddenly my little elves are supposed to be skating to 'The Wreck of the Edmund Fitzgerald'?"

"There's always Nickelback," I joked.

She didn't laugh.

"I'll talk to Butterbean." I got out my phone and texted him again, reiterating that it was important that I see him.

After I shot off the message, my gaze switched from my screen to the scrumptious offerings in the display case. Muffins, scones, iced cookies, and little cream puffs dusted with powdered sugar. My stomach rumbled. I suddenly realized that I was starving.

Tiffany straightened. "Have a seat and wait. I'll get you your usual."

I sat down at my favorite table, which was close to both a large picture window and not too far from a toasty fire blazing in the hearth at the center of the room. Once settled, I remembered the printout Juniper had given me the night before with pictures of all the presumed victims of the plane crash. I felt as if I knew Sam and Elaine a bit now, but Eric was still an enigma.

I squinted closer at the impressive description of his achievements listed under his picture. Degrees in environmental science, awards in leadership, and recently a grant from a foundation for climate research based in Miami, where he was a visiting professor at a local university.

Tiffany came over with a Tower of Scones, my favorite of the offerings on her menu. The three-tiered tray offered savory scones on top, and plain scones with clotted cream and jam underneath. She'd also slipped in a couple of my favorite iced lemon cookies.

"Thank you," I said, reaching for a scone with rosemary and cheddar.

She stared down at the picture of Eric Lynch. "Wow— Greek god material there."

I nodded, buttering my already buttery scone. "He's one of the people Boots found last night."

She sighed. "He looks like Tommy Zane."

"Who?"

"The bronze medalist at the junior national championship the last year I competed. He had the most amazing triple axel but he fell on a flip. He broke my heart."

"Because he came in third?"

"No, because I thought he really liked me, but then I caught him kissing an ice dancer." Her mouth made a moue of disgust. "She wasn't even a medal contender."

The bell over the front door jangled and Plummy, bustling across the threshold, promptly slipped on the snow-dampened floor. Tiffany and I jumped up to help her, but she rebounded to her feet before we could reach her. She dusted off the back-side of her un-elfish beige puffer coat, which was probably a size XXS and still swallowed her.

"It's okay," she said, hurrying toward the table to put down her clipboard. "Just not used to these new snow boots." She lifted her too-long coat to reveal a pair of old-fashioned high-top sneakers.

I shook my head. "Those aren't boots. They're for playing basketball."

"Playing basketball in 1972," Tiffany clarified.

Plummy sank down in her chair, pulled off her ear coverings, and brought out her notepad. "Now what was it you'd like to talk to me about, Mrs. Claus?"

"Please, call me April." I nodded to the Tower of Scones. "Help yourself."

"I'll just have one." There wasn't an elf in Santaland who could resist an offer of baked goods. Carbohydrates kept the wheels spinning up here.

I poured her some tea from the pot Tiffany brought over. "I think there might be some misinformation going around, so I wanted to clear it up," I said. "I texted Butterbean, but he hasn't gotten back to me."

She drew back. "Butterbean's busy trying to get all the elves in line."

"That's what I want to talk about. I believe Butterbean is causing a bit of an overreaction."

"*Over*reaction? Butterbean's concerned that the elves aren't doing enough. And honestly, Mrs. Claus, we *really* need to do something about these reindeer. They just will not keep quiet, and I saw several young ones hopping over the library this morning."

I listened to her concerns as patiently as I knew Nick would have. "What I meant to say is that I might have steered you in the wrong direction last night about making the strangers believe that they're in Canada," I said.

She looked alarmed. "So we're *not* supposed to be Canadians? You'd better tell Butterbean. He's got an order at the Santaland Printing Works for a thousand maple leaf flags for people to put in their windows."

Maybe that was why he was a no-show for this meeting. I glanced at my phone to see if he'd responded to any of my messages. He hadn't.

Nor was there a new message from Nick, I couldn't help noticing with that now-familiar sinking feeling. *He'll be fine. Santa always comes back.*

And when he came back, Santaland would be wallpapered in Canadian flags.

"I don't want the town to think that it has to stop celebrating Christmas as usual. Other countries love Christmas, too. They still sing carols and enjoy the season."

"I'll make a note." She looked down at her clipboard. "The Little Gliders Nutcracker Ice Show will go on as planned tonight, but Butterbean did as you asked and canceled the sleigh return celebration. Evidently they're setting up a different site for the sleigh to land? But just so everyone won't be disappointed, we're arranging a Christmas night caroling procession through Christmastown tomorrow." She added quickly, "With no flying or singing from reindeer, naturally. But reindeer rarely do attend sing-alongs."

I thought about the two patients who were up and about at the infirmary. No doubt they'd feel even better tomorrow. The sound of the caroling would draw their attention. What if they looked out their windows? I didn't know if we could trust reindeer not to get overly enthusiastic with their hopping, or a snowman not to start belting out his favorite Christmas song at the top of his lungs. A distraction was needed.

"I think I'll have a castle elf bring my DVD player down to the infirmary. During the caroling we could show them movies as a distraction."

Plummy quietly drummed her stubby fingers on the damask tablecloth. "It's a shame that all three aren't well enough to simply ship home. It would make this week's activities so much less stressful."

I thought of Eric lying in that hospital bed with his bandaged torso. "The second man seems way too ill to travel."

"If he'd died, we could send the others back already and return to normal."

It was hard to know how to respond to that. Wishing a man dead so we could resume our regularly scheduled programming? These strangers seemed to have brought out some elves' less charitable impulses. "I'm glad he *didn't* die. Bad enough that he suffered such a terrible injury in Santaland. We still don't know who attacked him."

"Goodness gracious—I'm sorry. What must you think of me!" She let out a long breath. "They've just caused such a bother, and I *so* wanted to make a success of my first year being the Santaland Events Coordinator."

I tried to see the situation from her perspective. It was hard to take on a new role even under normal circumstances. "Everyone knows you're working hard and doing your best."

"Oh sure. But if something doesn't work out or gets canceled, who will they blame?" She thumped herself in the chest. "This elf, that's who."

"They'll be wrong. It's just an unfortunate circumstance. No one could have foreseen it."

She gathered up her things, put her napkin on the table, and stood. "Thank you for the scones, Mrs. Claus. I'll inform everyone that they can sing Christmas carols again—they'll be glad about that. And if I see Butterbean, I'll also tell him about our conversation."

After she was gone, I started in on another scone. Elves weren't the only ones fueled by carbs.

Tiffany had assumed that sunken look again as she leaned

against the counter dealing with a customer who'd come in while I was talking to Plummy. After the elf left, happily clutching the pink Tea-piphany box, I asked, "Is something wrong, Tiff?"

Her lips turned down as she dropped a gold Santaland coin into her ancient-looking cash register. She shoved the cash drawer closed and it dinged angrily. "The only problem I have is that my life is stagnant and probably will be forever."

Her words, and the real anguish behind them, took me by surprise. "How so?"

She looked at me as if I were being dense. "I'm sort of stuck here, April. I only moved here because my husband was Santa Claus—but Chris has been gone for three years now. I'm busy, but I feel alone. Do you know what I mean?"

I looked at her as I hadn't looked at her in a long time. She was a couple years younger than me, in great shape, and still as beautiful as she appeared in pictures from her figure skating heyday. And she had been a widow now for a long while. Of course she was lonely.

"Have you thought about dating?" I asked.

"*Thought* about it, sure, but date who? There's not exactly a big dating pool here. Most of the people here are my in-laws, and I'm just not attracted to elves. Your friend Claire snatched up the most eligible non-elf bachelor in all of Santa-land when she fell in love with Jake Frost."

"Of course, he also happens to be some sort of iceman-human mash-up . . ."

She tilted her head, considering. "Actually, maybe I should cast a wider net. Some of those snow monsters in the Farthest Frozen Reaches are virile looking, if you go for the hirsute giant type."

"And don't mind extreme halitosis."

She laughed. I was glad to see her smile, but I knew that what was bothering her couldn't be jollied away with one conversation. "Sometimes I think I should do something really terrible and get myself expelled from Santaland for good."

Like Adolph the Naughty.

There had also been cases of people and elves being expelled from Santaland for criminal behavior. I couldn't imagine Tiffany doing anything terrible enough to get her exiled to the Farthest Frozen Reaches, though.

"But of course I have Christopher," she continued. "He belongs here. I can't abandon him, even if he's not into hanging out with his mom anymore."

It was true that Christopher was rarely seen around the castle in his free time these days. He had a lot of friends in Christmastown and even over in Tinkertown, and he was now able to zip around on a snowmobile that had been a present for his most recent birthday.

I needed to have a sit-down with that kid.

She tilted her head. I must have been transparent, because she read my mind. "Don't you dare tell Christopher any of this. He's just a normal teenager—I don't want to guilt him into spending less time with his friends and more time around the castle out of a duty to me." She laughed. "Who knows? Maybe I'll head over to the hospital and nurse Mr. Heartthrob there in my free time." She nodded down at the picture of Eric Lynch. "Nurse Cinnamon's already left a message on my phone asking if I could do a shift."

I stood. "Okay, I won't say anything to Christopher."

She scooped up the leftovers from the Tower of Scones. "I'll box these up for you to take back with you. Pamela might like one with her tea."

Following her to the counter, I asked, "Have you talked to Pamela in the past day or so?"

She bit back a smile. "I haven't been able to get an appointment."

"What is *that* about?"

Laughter bubbled out of her. "I don't know. Maybe she doesn't want us to see her with a red nose. She's a little vain, you know."

That was like saying snowmen were a little chilly.

I remembered something Nurse Cinnamon had told me. "Jingles said that Pamela has a nurse caring for her."

"I think I saw her," Tiffany said. "A funny, mousy little elf?"

"Her name's Coco. But Nurse Cinnamon said she's never heard of a nurse in Santaland named Coco."

A hairline fracture of worry appeared between Tiffany's brows. "Then who is this elf?"

Good question.

I sighed. "I've been racking my brains trying to think of a gift for Pamela."

"I got her a framed portrait of Christopher."

"She'll love it," I said, feeling almost envious. "All I can think of is a Yarn-of-the-Month subscription from the Yule Love It Yarn Shoppe."

Tiffany's jaw dropped. "April, that's perfect!"

I tilted my head. "You really think so?"

"Of course. Pamela loves that place. Go for it." She handed me the box of leftovers. "You'd better get moving if you want to finish your shopping and still have time to get yourself ready for the Tiny Gliders show tonight."

I glanced up at her teapot clock. She was right to push me out the door.

I went straight to the yarn shop and signed Pamela up for her twelve months of yarn. The certificate announcing her gift was hand embroidered, so it looked slightly fancier than the usual gift card. After additional stops by Dash's Candy and Nut Shoppe and Wrapture, my favorite place to buy paper and ribbon, I headed home. Wobbler and I had just passed through the Christmastown arches and started on the path back up the mountain when a ping alerted me to a text. I pulled out my phone and looked down at the screen, hoping it was Nick.

It wasn't. Instead, I had received my first-ever text from Mildred Claus. It was a doozy.

Please come quickly. One of the patients at the hospital has died. I killed him.

Chapter 8

Sometime during the past couple of hours, the entrance into the Santaland Infirmary had become a disaster area. As I approached the entrance a frozen yellowish goo—was that *eggnog?*—had spread across the porch area and down the steps like slime from an old horror movie. Shards and smaller chips of glass protruded through the frozen ooze like tiny, treacherous stalagmites. A hand-printed cardboard sign strung across the front columns with red velvet ribbon announced, *This Door Closed. Please Use Emergency Room Entrance.*

No one had to tell me twice. No way was I going to navigate across that slushy, gooey minefield in my favorite boots.

I left Wobbler waiting at the curb and hurried around the side. The ER, which was housed in a newer annex, had a more clinical feel than the main section of the infirmary.

"Hi April!"

At the sound of the familiar voice, I turned in surprise. Juniper sat on a polished-wood waiting bench, cradling her left arm in front of her in a towel. Smudge was next to her.

I veered over to them. "What happened to your arm?"

"I slipped on a patch of ice."

Like elves all over Christmastown. They were used to

curled toes and special soles that gave them traction on frozen surfaces.

"Why didn't you call me?"

She shrugged. "I knew you were busy today, and Smudge said he'd meet me here."

"The candy cane factory's working at half shifts this week," he said.

I gave him a grateful smile before turning back to Juniper. "Can you walk?"

"Oh sure. My foot's fine. I just hurt my wrist when I reached down to break the fall. I'm lucky it's not my euphonium hand."

I smiled at that. "You can be forgiven for skipping the Tiny Gliders' *Nutcracker*."

"Oh, no—I'd have to be on my deathbed to miss the Tiny Gliders. They're always so cute." She looked into my face and must have read something there. "Are you okay, April?"

"Yeah, you look tense," Smudge said. "If it's about the concert, you shouldn't worry. You're not nearly as bad on percussion as you used to be."

"Thanks, but it's not the concert." Clearly, word of Eric Lynch's death wasn't out. I wasn't even sure what had happened, so I hesitated to say anything. Gossip and misinformation moved faster than avalanches here in Santaland.

I pointed to the sign that read *To the Main Building*. "Mildred just texted me. I need to run and check on something."

"Go," Juniper said. "We'll see you in a little while, at the concert."

I hurried through to the main hospital area. Mildred approached me the moment I stepped into the hallway. Her hands were flapping in front of her. "Oh, April—this is so terrible."

From her text, I'd expected that Constable Crinkles would be here, but at the moment she appeared to be all alone.

"What happened?" I asked.

"I don't know."

"But you didn't kill anyone, surely."

"You mean Mr. Lynch?" she asked, as if she'd come across more than one corpse today. "I might as well have done." Tears trembled in her eyes as she confessed with a wavering voice, "I fell asleep."

"He died while you were sleeping?"

Her head bobbed.

I blew out a breath of relief. Then she *hadn't* killed him.

"I never meant to nod off—I was just so tired from making all those candied nuts," she said. "Olive and I always like to do things properly, in small batches. The time and care makes them taste better, don't you think?"

"Yes, but . . ." Her nut assortments *were* tasty, but we were getting sidetracked. "When did you find Eric Lynch dead?"

"I didn't. Nurse Cinnamon found him, and she was furious with me. I woke up to her looming over me with such a scowl. She said I'd let the patient die."

"And where was *she* while he was dying?"

"In the ER, assisting Dr. Algid Honeytree," Mildred said. "I *was* the one responsible, but I swear he was just fine when I checked on him just before I nodded off at the front desk. He even spoke to me."

"What did he say?"

Her brow pinched a little as she took care to convey the exchange correctly. "I asked him how he was feeling, and he said, 'Like a billionaire, which is what I am.' And then he just closed his eyes and fell back to sleep."

I'd been anticipating significant last words—an explanation of what had happened to Eric out in the frozen wilds that would account for the fatal antler attack. Or some physical complaint that would account for his dying in the half hour after Mildred last spoke to him. *A billionaire?* That explained nothing. He was probably having a fever dream. "Was he delirious?"

"Oh no," Mildred said. "His temperature was normal. He seemed comfortable."

Nothing in his brief bio had indicated to me that Eric Lynch was a billionaire. Was he?

"Do you think Constable Crinkles will arrest me?" Mildred asked.

"The patient died from complications after being stabbed by a reindeer antler," I said. "You had nothing to do with that."

Now that I thought about it, that stabbing had just been elevated to full-blown murder. Which made finding whoever had wielded the antler all the more important now.

I convinced Mildred that the best thing she could do was go home. If anyone needed to interrogate her, they knew where she lived. I escorted her out through the ER—no sign of Juniper or Smudge, so hopefully Juniper's arm was being seen to. Outside, I instructed Wobbler to take Mildred home. She didn't look up to a sleigh bus.

"But what about you?" he whispered, mindful of the no-talking-reindeer edict. "Should I come right back?"

"There's no hurry. It doesn't make sense for me to go back to the castle now. I'd just have to turn right around to get back for Tiffany's Tiny Gliders show. I can catch a ride home with someone afterwards, or take the sleigh bus."

"The sleigh bus!" he repeated in horror, as if my riding public transport would be a personal affront to his professional dignity.

"Don't worry about it," I said. "Just get Mildred home."

Back in the hospital, Nurse Cinnamon had returned to the main floor. "I should have known something like this would happen with non-professionals looking after patients," she said in a low voice.

Not that I advocated for laymen replacing nurses, but I couldn't help pointing out, "People die in hospitals full of professionals all the time. It was the antler that killed Eric Lynch, not Mildred."

Her lips remained firmly pursed. "Doc Honeytree examined the man this morning and said he was going to live. He was improving." Her brow darkened. "I was hoping that we were going to get rid of these people soon."

"I wish they'd never been found." That's what Nurse Cinnamon had said earlier, when she'd voiced the wish to offload these patients somewhere else as soon as possible. "Maybe you'll get your wish now."

"No such luck." She drummed her fingers on the polished wood countertop of the nurses' station. "Doc told me that he wants the woman to remain longer for observation."

This was bad news.

"I don't mean to sound heartless." She bit her lip. "I blame myself for that man's death, too. I've had so many distractions today. You must have noticed the mess outside."

I remembered the eggnog and the glass. "What happened?"

She crossed her arms. "As requested, the Caroling Cow Dairy sent over an additional order of eggnog today, but Fuzzy the delivery elf was wearing silly Butterbean-issue shoes and slipped right on the front steps. He broke not only his wrist but four large glass containers. I had to cobble together a sign to close off the front entrance. Who knows when we'll get *that* taken care of. Butterbean sent my orderly home today. Said Jolly seemed too elfy. And then of course I had to see to Fuzzy's wrist and his foot."

"He broke his foot, too?"

"Just twisted the ankle. I also had to pick bits of eggnoggy glass out of various parts of him."

I winced in sympathy with poor Fuzzy. "You said Algid Honeytree is in the ER. Where is Doc?"

Her exasperation looked like it was going to boil over. "Seeing to an elf giving birth over in Tinkertown. Triplets." She shook her head. "He at least phoned in permission to give our female patient a sedative. Her hysterics were jumping on my last nerve."

I glanced over at Elaine's door. She hadn't struck me as the hysterical type. "She was upset?"

"Oh my golly gosh, it was terrible. There I was dealing with a death, and Miss Irritating decides to fall to pieces on me."

Huh. "*Mrs.* Irritating. She's the deceased man's ex-wife." I couldn't help remembering her demeanor when we'd been in Eric's room together, though. She had not seemed anywhere close to hysterical then. But this morning Eric had seemed to be better.

"What about Sam?"

"The other patient is doing just fine. Healthy as a horse, if you ask me."

"I'd like to talk to him."

"Of course you may."

We were interrupted by the arrival of Algid Honeytree. He looked exhausted. "I'm caught up on sprains now and thought I should come up and see the deceased for the death certificate."

My jaw dropped. "You mean Eric's just been lying there in his room?"

"He's dead," Nurse Cinnamon said. "I didn't need an MD to know that."

I trailed after them into the room. Eric's still form seemed to have sucked the air from the room, and I found it hard to breathe myself. He looked much as he had when I'd last seen him sleeping . . . only waxier in complexion.

His skin resembled Algid's, actually.

"What do you think, Doctor?" Nurse Cinnamon asked.

"He's dead, all right," Algid pronounced.

No one would ever confuse this place with Johns Hopkins.

"Can you tell *why* he died?" I asked.

Algid blinked slowly, reminding me of a lizard. "I'm an elf of science, Mrs. Claus, not a soothsayer. I see no signs of violence in the immediate vicinity here, so I'm assuming that his death had something to do with this huge honking antler wound."

Nurse Cinnamon sighed. "That's that, then. I'll send for the undertakers to retrieve the body. I'm not sure what directions to give them."

"His ex-wife is in the next room," I said. "She might know something of his wishes."

Algid nodded and filled out a death certificate. I leaned over to read it. He'd left the line next to *Cause of Death* blank.

He saw where I was looking. "I'll let my uncle fill that in."

"Good idea." *Huge honking antler wound* lacked the ring of officialdom.

I stopped two doors down and checked in on Sam, who was sitting up in bed looking understandably dazed. A trayful of demolished baked goods rested on the table near his elbow.

At my gentle tap, his gaze swung my way. "Oh, it's you."

I stepped into the room. "May I get you anything?"

He snorted. "A ticket home?"

I shifted uneasily. "I'm so sorry. We'll arrange some kind of transportation for you as soon as we can, but the doctor doesn't think that Ms. Foskett should travel quite yet."

"Right." He sighed. "Elaine and I are joined at the hip now."

Having my fate tied to Elaine's wouldn't have made me happy, either.

"Doesn't this place have television?" he asked. "Or at least a newspaper?"

My heart skipped a beat. One glance at the *Christmastown Herald* and it would be game over. "We have a book cart," I said. "I'll bring it in."

Before I could leave he said, "Wait—please stay a minute." He huffed out a breath. "I've never been a big reader. I wouldn't mind talking, though."

I edged back in and lowered uneasily into the armchair at his bedside. "Anything in particular you'd like to talk about?"

He narrowed his gaze on me. "Is there anything odd about this village?"

My hands started to sweat. I rubbed them discreetly on my coat. "Odd . . . how?"

"Don't get me wrong. I'm grateful to you all for saving my life. And *you* seem normal. But the others . . ."

"Before moving here, I lived in Oregon."

"Wow—small world." He brightened. "I was just in Portland last summer. Great town."

"It is." Cloudberry Bay was a hundred miles and often felt a world away from Portland, but it was nice to connect to someone who had passing familiarity with my old state.

"How did you end up here?" A trace of a smile touched his lips. "Hopefully not a plane crash."

"No, it was a good reason. I fell in love."

"That's not just a good reason, it's the best." His smile morphed into a hesitant frown. "Don't take this the wrong way, but is your husband on the short side?"

I laughed. "He's six feet tall."

"Oh."

"Unfortunately, he's"—I swallowed—"out of town right now. I'm sorry you can't meet him."

The only male Santalander Sam would have seen around the hospital so far would have been Doc Honeytree, and maybe Algid if he'd spotted him through the door. Neither had made a great effort to disguise their elfishness.

"People around here seem a bit different to me, but Elaine insists that people in remote communities often seem different than what we're used to."

I sent out a silent thanks that obnoxious Elaine had been able to channel her inner Margaret Mead.

His mouth twitched, but he couldn't seem to quite manage a smile. "I suspect all those days of cold exposure and not enough food affected my brain. I could have sworn I saw . . ." He cleared his throat. "There was this snowman—"

I cut him off. "You were delirious when Boots brought you in."

He bit his lip. "True, but . . ."

"I'm so sorry about Eric," I piped up, hoping to get his mind off snowmen. "I should have said that before."

"That's okay. We weren't exactly close. I didn't like the man, to be honest. I was grateful to him for hiring me, but I hated the way he treated Madison."

"Who?"

"The woman who died," he reminded me. "Eric was ready to leave her, even before she stopped breathing. She was the sweetest person, too. How could he just abandon someone like that?" He added, "A woman he was involved with."

I blinked. "*Involved*—meaning, sleeping together?"

His lips turned down. "I shouldn't gossip, but that's what Elaine told me."

I tried to get this straight. "So Eric not only invited his ex-wife to join the research party, but his girlfriend, as well?"

"Well, Elaine's an expert at ice core analysis. And Madison was somewhat qualified. She'd been a graduate student assistant of Eric's."

I found this all hard to take in. "She was his girlfriend-student"—ick—"and yet he wanted to leave her to die in the middle of the frozen nowhere all alone?"

"He said it was obvious that she wasn't going to make it. It was true—she barely had a pulse. Eric's argument was that we were all putting ourselves at risk by waiting on her rather than going to find this place he was sure was nearby. You know— the needs of the many outweigh the needs of the few."

Holy moly. That was cold.

"Of course, in the end he was probably right. She was doomed and we were going to be, too. After several days, it didn't seem like the expected rescue plane would ever come, and the plane wreckage didn't provide much shelter at all from the snow squalls."

"It was brave of you all to leave there."

"That was all Eric. Elaine and I probably would have stayed put. But Eric was so sure he could lead us back to civilization. He and Elaine had shouting arguments about it. In the end, we loaded up all the provisions we could put in one carry-on bag. A box of horrible dehydrated meals survived the crash. For days we sucked on those disgusting things like Popsicles, until we could find a shelter."

That word caught my attention. "What kind of shelter?"

He looked away. "Just a cave. It . . . wasn't much."

"Where was it?"

He laughed. "Somewhere in the snow. There was a mountain. I think we were walking along its lower ridge. The weather was terrible. By the time I reached the cave I felt snow blind and half-delirious."

It was probably in the frozen crag foothills at the base of Mount Myrrh. A bad place to be lost. There were leopards, snow monsters, and wild elves in those parts. "How long did you stay there?"

"A week? Maybe more. It's hard to judge days up here. They're so short. One nap and you've missed Tuesday."

I smiled. "I'm surprised you left the cave."

"That was down to Eric and his wild ideas." He shook his head. "Maybe not so wild, given how things turned out. And

Elaine's foot already looked bad—she obviously needed help. I'm surprised she just lost the one toe."

Eric had known there was a town here. Did he know it was Christmastown? I couldn't think of a way to ask Sam for more details without giving too much away.

He sighed. "We followed Eric for several days, but Elaine was having terrible trouble walking and I'm no hiker, either. Both of us thought Eric was off his rocker. Finally even our Popsicle food ran out. We decided to split up to have a better chance of finding someone to help."

"That must have been a difficult decision to make."

"It did occur to me that I was probably walking off to die, but Eric told me that dying of hypothermia isn't the worst way to go. Apparently you go numb and conk out before your heart gives out."

Eric sounded like a real gem of a group leader. "I can see why you're not too broken up about his dying."

He crossed his arms. "To be honest, he seemed exactly the kind of guy somebody might want to kill someday."

I drew back. "You think he was killed?"

"That antler didn't spontaneously lodge itself in his back, did it?"

I couldn't argue with that. "What were you doing this afternoon?"

"While Eric was dying, you mean?"

"I just wondered if you noticed anything unusual."

He shook his head. "Elaine and I were in this room most of the afternoon, playing chess. The old lady nurse found us a game." He nodded to the set on a side table. "Very peculiar board and pieces."

The old hand-carved and painted Santaland chess set was one I'd seen before—the king and queen were actually modeled after Nick's parents. I'd never met Nick's father, but Pamela was recognizable in her chess piece, with gray hair pulled back in a ballet bun, spectacles, and a frilly red velvet cap that I recognized as one she wore on special occasions. Other Santaland residents were also represented—the snowmen were bishops, the knights were antlered reindeer, and the pawns were elves.

Nice going, Mildred.

"We played several games." He laughed. "Well, more than several. I'm not a good player, so it never takes long for Elaine to demolish me."

"So . . . an hour?"

"More like an hour and a half," he said. "And then we heard the commotion outside of the two nurses running in and out of Eric's room. Elaine stumped out to find out what was going on, and when she saw Eric, she collapsed in hysterics."

"Really?" I asked, unable to keep the skepticism out of my tone.

"Surprised me, too," he said. "I mean, I know they'd been married, but I never would have known it by watching them together these past few weeks."

"She seemed genuinely upset to hear he'd died?"

He nodded. "She hobble-ran into his room and practically threw herself on him. And then she kept asking, 'Are you sure? He's still warm!'" His body shuddered at the memory. "I'll never forget that last part. 'He's still warm.'"

Like Juliet, I thought, in *Romeo and Juliet.*

Very theatrical.

"She kept repeating it until the smaller nurse yanked her out of the room and gave her a chill pill." He stretched. "It must be late. I'm exhausted."

I gasped. "What time is it?"

"I don't know," he said.

It had to be close to six. I needed to hurry over to Peppermint Pond for the Tiny Gliders show. When I looked up,

Sam was tugging at the heavy brocade drapes. "It's hard to have any sense of time in this room with the curtains always closed." He yanked a panel hard enough to pop the center pins and give him a view out the window.

Instinctively, I rushed over, but just stopped myself from throwing myself bodily between him and the window. *Nothing suspicious about that.* I had to trust that Butterbean's camouflage work had paid off by now and there was nothing to give away the fact that we were right in the middle of Christmastown, Santaland. It was just a picturesque, snowy village with—

Looking down at the street, I froze in shock. My sleigh was back, but instead of Wobbler, Cannonball was now hitched to it. And he was hopping from leg to leg, doing some kind of reindeer calisthenics.

"What is *that*!" Sam cried out.

I gulped, wondering how I was going to explain the odd gyrations of the tubby reindeer below, when I noticed that Sam's eyes were focused up at Sugarplum Mountain in the distance. My heart swelled at the sight of Castle Kringle, lit up and looking like something out of a fairy tale.

"That's"—happily, I stopped the words *Castle Kringle* before they left my lips—"my house."

"Your *house*?" He laughed. "What are you, a princess? Do cartoon animals speak to you?"

No, real ones do. "My husband's family has owned it for a long time. He . . ." I bit my lip. "I mean, his family, um . . ."

"Runs a hotel," blurted a voice behind me.

We turned. Mildred stood by the door with a basket on her arm.

"What are you doing here?" My astonishment at seeing her made the words come out more harshly than I'd intended. I added more gently, "I thought you went home."

She came forward. "Would you believe it? I got all the

way there and then remembered that I forgot to leave candied nuts for the patients. I told Olive that I'd probably forget my head if it wasn't glued on."

She handed Sam a large jar filled with three types of nuts. It was topped with a big gold bow.

"Thank you." He glanced over at the side table of cupcakes, muffins, fruitcakes, and gumdrops that had been brought into his room from the trolleys in the corridor. "I'm guessing this hospital doesn't keep a dietitian on staff."

"I was going to give a nut jar to Miss Foskett, too," Mildred said, ignoring his comment, "but I peeked in her room and she's still asleep. Maybe I'll just set some on the cart outside."

"Good idea." I twitched the curtains closed and put one of the pins back in. Talk about bolting the barn door after the horses had escaped. "I'll show you where the goodie cart is," I told Mildred.

"But I know—"

"This way," I said, dragging her out of the room.

When the door was closed, she pointed to the overflowing tea trolley that now had even more stuff on it, including a pyramid of boxes from Puffy's All-Day Donuts and a citrus fruit basket. "I'll just put my nuts over there."

I followed her. My voice a low growl, I said, "A *hotel*?"

"Oh dear, did I say the wrong thing?" Mildred's face was a study in anxiety. "I just blurted it out—I'm sorry. I thought I was helping. You'd drawn a blank."

Given my own propensity to stick my foot in my mouth, I had no room to criticize her. I let out a breath. "You're right. No harm done."

"I hope not," she fretted.

I looked at the wall clock and groaned. "I'll have to run to Peppermint Pond to make Tiffany's show."

We passed Nurse Cinnamon in one of the supply rooms

inspecting her medicine cabinet and told her that we were going to be leaving for the night. A look of relief washed over her face.

"I'm sure I can manage," she said. "Even though I've been here all day. And *awake* all day."

Mildred flinched a little. It seemed an unnecessarily harsh barb.

I practically sprinted to Peppermint Pond and barely got into place in time. Smudge looked exasperated as he noted my lack of uniform. As if anyone was going to be looking at me when there were tiny elves in costumes skating on the ice. He shoved the castanets and a triangle in my hands and nudged me over to the glockenspiel. "I thought I was going to have to be a one-elf percussion unit back here," he said.

Smudge usually covered bass drum, snare, and timpani. This was a good thing, since—unlike me—he actually had an excellent sense of rhythm.

"Sorry," I said. "There was an emergency."

His expression softened. "There's a lot of that going around today."

Juniper, who was seated right in front of me engulfed by a brass euphonium, swiveled in her chair. Her left hand was in a brace. "Is everything okay?" she whispered.

The band conductor, Luther Partridge, tapped his baton on the stand to silence everyone. Instead of answering Juniper, I made do with an eye roll. Word about Eric would spread around Christmastown soon enough, but I didn't want the grim news to ruin this event for anyone.

Luther counted us in with his hand and with those first iconic staccato notes the show began.

I had planned to use my fairly light percussion duties to try to piece together what I knew about Eric's death so far. But I missed a triangle cue, so I made myself concentrate on the show and was soon swept away by the amazing cuteness of the

Tiny Gliders dressed as gingerbreads, toy soldiers, and snow-flakes. The whole ballet was not performed, just excerpts, but the pond illuminated both by footlights at ice level and from the surrounding trees laced with white strings of Christmas lights created a more magical stage for the young performers than they could have found at Lincoln Center. The whole crowd was swept up by the spectacle.

And I will say this for Santaland—they don't skimp on imagination when it came to costumes. The snowflakes glit-tered, the rats were furry and energetic, and the Sugarplum Fairy was no stiff chocolate box figurine in a tutu, but a rav-ishing teen elf in pink and purple tulle with a sugarplum wand and sugarplum tiara. She glided across the ice and tossed candy to the young elves in the audience.

In the middle of her number, a text came in from Nick. Luther flicked a disapproving look as I stared down at my il-luminated phone, but I didn't care.

Wish you were here.

Attached to the message was an aerial shot of Paris, with the Eiffel Tower ablaze in red and green lights.

I snapped the phone closed, my heart full. Suddenly, I was as ready for Christmas as any kid on Christmas Eve. I didn't miss a triangle cue for the rest of the performance, and if I do say so myself, my glockenspieling never sounded better. Joy made a difference.

This time tomorrow night, I told myself, Nick would be back, and we'd be settling in for the holiday. I could already taste the champagne bubbles.

Chapter 9

I bounced out of bed the next morning full of holiday cheer. My outfit was a red wool sweater dress lined with white faux fur. Over-the-top Mrs. Clausy, maybe, but it suited my mood exactly. Nick would be home soon, and—save for that small matter of the death at the hospital—joy seemed the order of the day.

I gathered the gifts I'd stayed up too late wrapping last night. The pile was stacked up to my chin so that I had to walk downstairs carefully and then use my elbow to lever the handle of the arched oaken door leading to the family salon. Our towering Christmas tree twinkled away in the corner and a fire was blazing in the great stone hearth, but none of the family were here. Just Quasar, nibbling at a Christmas tree branch.

"Merry Christmas!" I said.

I might as well have yelled "Gotcha!" The reindeer hopped back and gulped down his illicit bite of greenery. He'd already received admonishments about consuming decorations. "M-merry Christmas, Mrs. Claus."

Pretending not to notice the fir needles stuck to his muzzle, I gestured around the empty room. "Where is everyone?"

"Lucia went out early to get the new landing spot ready. She should be back by now." Quasar's nose fizzled red to black. "Jingles is serving the others in the b-breakfast room, I think."

"Of course." Felice, the castle cook, always put on a delicious continental spread on Christmas morning: fresh hot buns, Danish, and her special holiday strudel. I hoped I wasn't too late for the strudel.

My intention had been to arrange my gifts under the tree, but one of them was for Quasar—a batch of his favorite moss cakes. Given his impulse control problem and uncertain nose, if I left him alone with the presents he might chew the paper off half the packages to reach his treat. Better not to risk it.

"I'm just going to find the others," I said, securing my gift stack with my chin before reversing course and backing into the corridor again.

Halfway to the breakfast room, I nearly collided with Lucia, who was dressed in high shearling-lined boots, a long, quilted snow-dusted coat, and blond hair topped by what looked like a Russian Cossack hat. She was pulling off extra-heavy leather gloves.

"Any word from Nick?" I asked her.

"Merry Christmas to you, too."

"Merry Christmas," I said. "Have you heard from Nick?"

"No, but we're ready for him. The sleigh landing strip I set up west of town has smudge pots and flags to guide him in."

"When do you think he'll be here?"

"Hard to say. I've texted him the coordinates of the new landing spot. So far he hasn't responded."

My face must have been a mask of worry, because she hastened to reassure me, "He's up in the air, April. North America has lots of cell phone dead spots, especially when you're in a sleigh."

"Right."

She blew out a breath. "Or it could be he hit a patch of weather."

The possibility struck fear in my heart. "That's what worries me."

"He knows what he's doing. You know what Winston Churchill said."

Good grief. Him, too? " 'Santa always comes back'?"

She laughed. "He said your advance worrying should be advance planning and action . . . or something to that effect. That's what I'm doing. I'm just going to grab a sandwich from the kitchen and head back out there. I left Butterbean keeping watch at the landing strip."

That elf seemed to have his hand in everything. "When you go back, can I go with you?" I wanted to be part of her planning and action. Churchill had a point. Just fretting was useless.

"Why? There must be plenty around here for you to do today—Jingles said he got a call early this morning from a strange woman asking to make a hotel reservation?"

"Oh no." Elaine. It had to be. Sam must have told her about the castle-like hotel on the mountain.

"You need to deal with that," Lucia said. "I'll let you know if I hear anything from Nick, though."

How was I going to "deal with" people who wanted to discharge themselves from the hospital and come stay at Santa's castle?

"Have you seen Quasar?" Lucia asked me.

Distracted, I nodded my head in the direction I'd just come from. "Parlor."

Her blue eyes widened. "He's in there by himself? Is there any tree left?"

"Let's just say it's probably good that we got a fourteen-footer this year."

She groaned. "I thought he'd be better off staying in the castle with the reindeer flu going around, but I'll take him with me when I go back out to the landing strip."

She brushed past me and I continued on to the breakfast room. At the long family table I found Christopher and Tiffany sitting alone. When I entered, Christopher jumped up to help me with my load.

"Merry Christmas, Aunt April! Are these all for me?"

"Yup," I said. "A whole stack of elaborately wrapped lumps of coal."

He laughed and gave one package a discreet shake. "I'm glad you're here. Grandma's not even coming down this morning."

I looked over at the end of the table where Pamela usually sat. There was nothing at her place but a large citrus fruit basket. I frowned. Christmas morning was when Pamela distributed the matching holiday sweaters she knitted for the family. The wrapped bundles were usually waiting for us in our chairs so we'd have the sweaters to wear all during Christmas Day. This early distribution ensured that her knit creations would be immortalized in holiday pictures and videos. But now there were no bundles, and no Pamela.

An unexpected disappointment coursed through me. I chalked it up to you–don't–know–what–you've–got–till–it's–gone syndrome. "Is she still sick?"

Tiffany nodded worriedly. "That elf Coco sent a message through Jingles that Pamela won't be coming down for celebrations until Nick gets back."

I grabbed a plate and started filling it with goodies from the sideboard. Strudel or Danish? I cut off a bit of each. It was Christmas, after all.

"She must be very ill," I said. "Do you think we should send for Doc Honeytree?" Surely the Tinkertown triplets had made their appearance by now.

"She said she doesn't need a doctor, just Coco."

"Or so Coco tells us." I sank down in the chair opposite Tiffany. It was rare that I saw my sister-in-law at breakfast. She was usually up and at 'em far earlier than me, since she gave sunrise skate lessons at the pond before opening her tea shop at nine. "If Jake Frost were in town, I'd ask him to look into who this Coco is."

Jake ran Santaland's only private investigation business. But he and Claire wouldn't be back till after New Year's.

Jingles came in, dressed in bright castle livery. "Merry Christmas, Mrs. Claus." But he looked anxious, not merry. "A snowman's chorus is here."

The three of us at the table exchanged excited glances. When enough snowmen assembled to create a chorus, it was always something special.

"What's wrong?" I asked Jingles.

Jingles replied in a low voice, as if the walls had ears, "Snowmen aren't supposed to be singing."

"Oh." I'd forgotten. I looked over at Tiffany. I could tell she shared my reluctance to turn the snowmen away. "We're miles from the infirmary," she pleaded.

"And they've come all this way," Christopher added.

I hesitated, but then relented. "It's just this once."

We all jumped up and hurried over to the large window that looked out over the front yard. Sure enough, there were at least two dozen snowmen facing us. Their ranks were arranged in three curved rows.

Before we could so much as wish them a Merry Christmas, the snowmen began singing "The Holly and the Ivy." Their voices were great, and surprisingly resonant for coming from blobs of solid snow. They sang a collection of eight carols, including a rendition of "The Twelve Days of Christmas" which, let's face it, is long enough for ten songs. When they were done, we clapped heartily. They seemed pleased. Usually I'd offer carolers a hot drink, but that wouldn't work with snowmen.

"Please make yourselves at home here," I said. "Salty will provide you with new scarves or anything you need." Pamela always kept a box at the castle stocked with her hand-knit scarves, buttons, and perfectly shaped coal for snowmen in need.

It would be wonderful to have them all here for Christmas. Snowmen made the lawn and its decorated trees appear even more festive.

"Merry Christmas," the lead snowman called out before we shut the window. "And a safe return for Santa!"

As I strolled back to the table I glanced down at my phone. No new messages.

"What's the matter?" Tiffany asked.

"Nick—he sent me a message last night, but I haven't heard from him since."

She studied my face. "Is there something else?"

"We had an argument before he left," I confessed. "I was worried about sleigh safety and seat belts. It wasn't the warmest goodbye, and now I wonder if some part of him dreads coming back."

If anyone understood that anxiety, it was Tiffany. She craned to look at my screen and the message exchange from the previous evening. "*That* doesn't seem like a message from a guy who dreads seeing his wife again."

Christopher had broken past the cellophane on the fruit basket and was now attempting to juggle oranges. "When I'm Santa," he said, his face pinched in concentration as he tossed fruit in the air, "I won't want seat belts on the great sleigh, either."

Now it was Tiffany's turn to look worried, but she managed not to say anything. Christopher would be our next Santa, but he was still just barely a teenager. His first flight was nearly a decade away.

One of his oranges thumped to the ground. I managed to capture it before it rolled beneath the table.

"Carlotta, Clement, and Audrey brought this basket over early this morning," Tiffany told me.

"Audrey must have cornered the citrus market," I observed. "How many crates do you think she brought back?"

"I think it's a great gift." Christopher managed to catch three oranges without mishap this time and finished with a bow. "Mom, can I go over to visit Hal?"

His friend Hal's family ran the Wonderland Wok in Tinkertown, but they also had a chateau on Sugarplum Mountain not far from Mildred's.

Tiffany looked a little disappointed, but said only, "Are you sure Joyce and John wouldn't mind?"

"Why would they? There's nothing happening today. There's not even going to be a sleigh return celebration."

"There's a caroling procession in Christmastown this evening," I said.

He looked as unimpressed at the prospect of community singing as only a teenager could be.

His mother relented. "All right, but don't go empty-handed. Take them a castle fruitcake, and make sure you come back early this afternoon. Just because there's not going to be a big ballyhoo when your uncle Nick comes back, that doesn't mean that he won't enjoy seeing you when he gets home."

"Okay." He gave his mom the fastest of pecks before speeding out the door, nearly running over Jingles.

The steward flattened himself against the doorjamb. Then, trying to regain his dignity, straightened and cleared his throat. "Constable Crinkles and Red Firball are waiting to see you, Mrs. Claus."

I glanced at Tiffany. "Do you know who Red Firball is?"

"The name sounds familiar."

Jingles jumped in. "He runs Tinkertown Knife Sharpening. I bet this has something to do with the murder."

"Why?" I asked.

"Because it's the constable—and *knives*." There was an almost ghoulish tremor in his voice as he pronounced that last word.

"Eric Lynch didn't die from a knife wound," I said. "So just simmer down and send in the visitors."

"Oh, all right." He backed up a step and sent me a disappointed bow.

When he ushered the visitors into the breakfast room moments later, I was glad that I had stood up to greet them and could put my hand on the back of my chair for support. Constable Crinkles was decked out in a North-West Mounted Policeman's uniform, complete with scarlet coat, jodhpurs, and stiff riding boots that caused him to walk in an awkward waddle. He looked ridiculous, like something out of an elf operetta.

Behind me, Tiffany masked a choking laugh by gulping down a slug of coffee.

Accompanying Constable Crinkles was an elf wearing a plain wool elf tunic with a leather apron over it. His feet were clad in modest felt booties. He obviously hadn't gotten the no-conspicuously-elf-apparel memo. Twisting his tweed cap in his hands, he gawped at the spacious dining room like a tourist at Versailles.

The constable's eyes went wide as he took in the sideboard heaping with breakfast baked goods.

"Merry Christmas," I said to the visitors. "May I offer you both some breakfast?"

Crinkles had a hunk of strudel on a plate even before the other elf could murmur, "Thank you, no. I've had mine."

"At least let me offer you some coffee."

Jingles cleared his throat. Even Tiffany was staring at me with raised brows.

"Eggnog," I corrected, remembering that most elves much preferred eggnog over coffee.

"Well now," the elf said, "I wouldn't say no to that."

Elves rarely said no to eggnog.

Jingles crossed to an insulated carafe on the sideboard, poured a mug for our guest, and sprinkled nutmeg on top. Then he pulled a chair out at the table for Red Firball. The elf had to hop a little to hoist himself into the human-sized chair. His shoulders and head and not much else cleared the tabletop.

"Thank you, ma'am," he said, lifting his mug. "Merry Christmas to you all, and a safe return to Santa."

We all raised mugs and cups and repeated the toast.

This visit still had me puzzled. I turned to Constable Crinkles for enlightenment and caught him in the act of shaking one of the gifts I'd brought in. *As bad as Christopher,* I thought.

Red-faced, he dropped the wrapped package and hurried to the table with a plate heaping with strudel and Danish. He took a nibble of the latter. "Delicious! Almost as good as Ollie's cinnamon rolls."

That was high praise. The cinnamon rolls at the Christmastown Constabulary were legendary.

"Does this visit concern the death of Eric Lynch?" I asked them.

"You've pinned the bow on the package, Mrs. Claus," Crinkles said, licking sugar glaze off his fingers. "Naturally I don't like to bother anyone with crime on Christmas, but Red here has information that's very important to my investigation."

So Jingles had been right.

With all eyes on him, the elf straightened in his chair. "I'm a knife sharpener, ma'am. My business is over in Tinkertown, so I don't get much of the castle trade."

"We take our sharpenables to the Knife before Christmas, in Christmastown," Jingles said.

Red nodded curtly. "They do a decent job. Of course, I don't get nearly the amount of work they do, so I need to run a small enterprise on the side."

"He's the Dasher-Habber," Crinkles informed us, as if cutting to the chase.

The title meant nothing to me, though. "I beg your pardon?"

Red explained, "Tailors are called haberdashers, but my side business is with reindeer. Specifically the Dasher herd."

Hence, Dasher-Habber. Understanding dawned. "*You* make reindeer toupees?"

"I prefer to call them reindeer headdresses, ma'am. They're one of several accoutrements for ruminants that I offer my clientele." His side hustle was obviously a source of pride. "You might say that I'm in the vanguard of reindeer head coverings. I have a loyal following. In the winter, after the reindeer lose their antlers, Dashers especially like to have something to cover their heads. And of course this season the pointy look is in."

"Tell her about Dandy," Constable Crinkles prompted him between bites of strudel.

Red took a sip of eggnog before continuing. "I don't like to cast suspicion on loyal customers, but this morning I heard about that man's death in the hospital and it seemed like my duty to come forward. A certain reindeer client of mine, a Dasher familiarly known as Dandy, visited me a few days ago. He said he needed a new antler headdress because the one I'd made for him earlier this fall had been lost."

Now we were getting somewhere. "Lost how?"

"That's what I wanted to know," Red said. "I thought maybe his old set of antlers might be repairable. But he told me that they were permanently, irrecoverably lost." He paused for effect before adding, "Somewhere up north, he said."

"I showed him the antler weapon." Crinkles looked at Red. "Tell them what you told me."

"The antler bears my mark."

Silence fell around the table. I looked at Tiffany, then Jingles, who raised his brow. Evidently the prime suspect in the suspicious death of Eric Lynch was four legged after all. And missing his antlers.

I rarely approached reindeer herds without Lucia by my side, but she had already left for the sleigh landing strip when Constable Crinkles and I set out to question Dandy about his conspicuously missing antler toupee.

The herd, like all reindeer herds, was nomadic and rotated around Santaland. It took some asking around and a long drive via snowmobile to locate the Dashers. Once the reindeer came into view, there was no doubt that we were in the right place. No other reindeer herd displayed so many antlered heads this late in December. In other herds, female reindeer were the last to shed their antlers, but here male Dashers sauntered around sporting full racks. All fake.

"I hope my coming to you doesn't kill my side business," Red had told me, and now I could see why he was worried. This herd alone probably paid his rent.

The head reindeer, the leader who bore the official title of Dasher much like Nick carried the name of Santa, approached us surrounded by a posse of young, fit reindeer. I felt glad that Constable Crinkles was with me, and that we'd asked a leader of the Comet herd to join us. He was actually the second

Comet in command. The leader, the reindeer I'd seen last night at the send-off, was down sick.

Dasher dropped his head in a polite bow to me. "Merry Christmas, Mrs. Claus. To what do we owe this honor?"

"We need to talk to one of your herd. A reindeer known as Dandy."

Dasher tilted his head, his large brown eyes regarding me curiously. "Why?"

I looked over at Crinkles. He piped up, "It's a constabulary matter. Mrs. Claus recommended that I speak to Dandy about the mur—er, the death of one of the people who were brought to the Santaland Infirmary."

More reindeer encircled us. All those pointy racks were unnerving.

Murmurs spread through the herd, and then the circle ripped and split like a zipper unzipping to let one of the reindeer in the back move forward. He was large, with a rich chocolaty hide. His head, as expected, was unadorned.

"I'm Dandy," he announced.

"Thank you for coming forward to speak to us," I said. "Did you lose your antlers—your headdress, I mean?"

"I did," he confessed. "It fell off during a half-marathon hop. Has it been found?"

He didn't sound anxious, or guilty. Just eager to get his fake antlers back.

"I'm sorry, the antler was the one that stabbed Eric Lynch, who's now dead. The maker, Red, identified the headdress as one he'd made for you."

The lead Dasher raised his head with a jerk. "You think Dandy is responsible for that man's death?"

Whites showed in Dandy's eyes. "*I* didn't do anything. I told you, I lost the whole rack. If the so-called Dasher-Habber had done his job better, they would have fit securely."

Comet had had enough. "We've warned you Dashers not to wear those bloomin' things during reindeer games."

Crinkles lifted his hands. "Now, now, let's stay civil. It's Christmas, and this is an inquiry, not an accusation."

"You could have fooled me." The lead Dasher stepped forward. "Lots of participants in that race can tell you that Dandy lost his antlers. There were witnesses."

A host of pointy-antlered heads nodded.

Crinkles looked at me. "Witnesses—that's a good thing, right?"

"What's more," the Dasher leader continued, "I find it notable that this persecution of one of us comes during the one year in a century that a Dasher hasn't been on Santa's sleigh team. A century!"

Oh, for heaven's sake. "We don't mean to persecute—"

I was interrupted by Comet, whose lips were curled. "The reindeer council decides who draws the sleigh based on results of the reindeer games. Your herd lost fair and square."

Dasher's hide twitched with defensiveness from ears to rump. "To a Muncher? It was a travesty of judging. And if our lead reindeer hadn't come down with the flu—"

"The Dashers lineup was weak," Comet said. "If you cared less about how you look and more about how you fly, maybe you'd be on Santa's team right now. The Muncher herd fielded a stronger team."

That statement was met with snorts of derision. "Cracker crumbs! They had Moose Muncher and a lot of second raters. I think the reindeer council should be ashamed of putting a reindeer named Moose anywhere near the Great Sleigh."

"It's just a name."

"It's an insult to reindeer!" someone else called out.

Things were getting out of hand. I tried to get the discussion back on track. "We just wanted to know how the antler was lost," I said.

"That's right," Crinkles interjected, bobbing nervously on his heels. "Now that we know there were witnesses, we won't need to worry you anymore."

"Oh sure," the lead Dasher said. "Now that the accusation is out there, you'll just walk away. Meanwhile everyone will now associate Dashers with this man's unfortunate death and call us murderers. We'll be the new Adolphs."

"It's a Muncher conspiracy!" one of the other reindeer called out. "Everyone is against us."

"They hate us because they ain't us," a particularly fancy-antlered Dasher said.

Comet rolled his large eyes. "This herd should change its name to the Drama Divas. For your information, no one is thinking of you at all today. Most reindeer are concerned with the return of the Great Sleigh, which is late arriving."

An abashed hush fell over the herd, except for the lead Dasher, who couldn't help muttering, "Maybe if a Dasher had been on the team, it would be on time . . ."

My phone vibrated in my pocket and I stepped away, hoping this would be good news from Lucia. Instead, a message bubble from Nurse Cinnamon popped up on my screen.

Trouble brewing here. You'd better get over to the infirmary ASAP.

Chapter 10

Sam had shown Elaine the luxury hotel on the mountain, and now she didn't want to spend another night in the hospital.

"But we've arranged entertainment for you tonight," I said. "Movies."

Elaine sent me a Medusa death stare. "That's what the shrimpy nurse was telling us. Apparently we get to choose between three creaky Christmas movies."

"I like *It's a Wonderful Life*," Sam said, trying to de-escalate the conflict. "It gets my vote. Or maybe we can do a double feature with *Home Alone*."

Elaine groaned.

I tried to take Sam's enthusiasm and run with it. "Totally. Or a triple feature. We're bringing in a television and DVD player especially for you."

"I don't care if there's an IMAX theater hidden behind the nurse's station," Elaine insisted. Whatever sorrow she'd felt about her ex-husband's death had been quickly displaced by her concerns for her own safety and comfort. "I want to leave here. It's dangerous."

"The hospital is the safest place in"—I swallowed before I could blurt out the word *Santaland*—"the land. Especially for you. You've had a serious operation and the doctor thinks you need to stay here."

She tapped her too-short crutch impatiently. "That old country quack? He probably has a jar of leeches in his office."

"He's well respected here. And he saved your foot."

"He didn't save Eric's life though, did he?" she shot back.

I didn't have a reply for that. Every fiber of my being wanted to leap to Doc Honeytree's defense, but Eric's death was a puzzle to me. And apparently to Elaine as well.

Or maybe she was purposefully deflecting blame.

"He was supposedly getting better," she insisted. "Then all of the sudden in the time it took to play a chess game, he was just gone?"

"It was several chess games," Sam allowed. When his fellow patient glared at him, he added, "To be fair."

She huffed in exasperation. "What difference does it make? The point is, I'm not going to die because of my toe. I might as well recuperate in luxury."

"The hotel is closed for the season," I said.

She eyed me skeptically. "And you can't open it up for two measly guests? We wouldn't be any trouble."

It was difficult to keep a straight face. I'd spent the better part of a decade running a small inn, and in my experience the guests who insisted they would be no trouble were the very ones who would plague you with a million demands and complain about everything from the thread count on their sheets to the jam options at breakfast.

"It's the holidays," I said. "Our family celebrates Christmas."

And how.

A too-bright smile broke across her face. "I *love* Christmas! I even brought little bottles of prosecco to give everyone on the research ship." She sighed. "All got smashed, of course."

"I could use one of those little bottles right about now," Sam said.

Elaine's lips twisted. "I could down about five of them, plus a Valium or two."

Oh boy.

She noted the look on my face and laughed. "It was a *joke*. I don't have a drug problem. Although I wouldn't mind another dose of that knockout drug the doctor gave me yesterday." Her smile flattened. "As long as I could guarantee I wouldn't not wake up, like Eric."

"Elaine, come on, don't be harsh." Sam bumped her arm. "I liked your idea of the IMAX. That'd be awesome."

It was his turn to have the death stare turned on him.

Sam was a conflict avoider. It didn't mean that he didn't agree with everything Elaine was saying, though. The Sam kind of person could be more unpredictable than an aggressive type like Elaine, because you never knew what he was thinking.

Although I hadn't said anything to anyone, I was now looking at these two people as possible murder suspects. We knew how the antler had been lost, and it was clear that no animal had stabbed Eric. It had to have been someone with a motive. And who else could have had a motive other than his two fellow survivors?

Sam admitted he didn't like Eric. Elaine was Eric's ex and didn't seem to like anybody.

Of course, everyone had people in their lives that they didn't like. And exes. Very few could stick an antler in someone's back. There had to be a deeper motive. To find it I'd need to watch these two more closely. Something was going on with them. Right now I couldn't tell if they were conspirators or just keeping an eye on each other.

I looked out the open window at Castle Kringle. Ferreting out a killer hadn't been how I wanted to spend my holiday. Then again, nothing about this Christmas so far could be labeled normal.

"A hotel?" Lucia gaped at me. "Has your brain turned to walrus blubber? We've got enough problems without dragging a bunch of strangers into the mix."

"Not a bunch. It's just two."

She planted gloved fists at the waist of her wool coat. "Two strangers who aren't supposed to know they're in Santaland. How easy is that going to be when they're let loose in Castle Kringle, Santa's home?"

"I know it's going to be a challenge . . ."

She hooted. "That's an understatement. That's why I want to be here to warn Nick."

We were standing out on the flat, icy plane where the alternate landing field was set up. A line of torches and orange flags stood out in the blowing snow. Representatives of the nine herds pulling Santa's sleigh had started to gather, ringing the landing strip. The gathering was sparser than I would have expected, though.

"Is this all the reindeer?" I asked.

"Two of the leaders said quite a few reindeer are down sick. The vet, Dr. Snowball, has been making the rounds."

On the far side end of the strip, I could just make out the short, round figure of Butterbean dressed in some kind of Day-Glo jumpsuit with LED marshalling sticks like airport crewmen used on the tarmac to guide planes in.

Unfortunately Nick hadn't been heard from since last night. The great sleigh was now officially, concerningly late.

I'd texted him twice in the past hour with no response. The gnawing in my stomach was back. "This may sound weird, but I think the distraction of these two strangers is the only thing keeping me from utter panic."

Lucia studied me for a moment, then stared up into the

gray sky. "I don't know why you're asking my opinion. I don't run the castle. Talk to Mom."

The thought of trying to get Pamela's blessing for this scheme didn't thrill me. Then again . . .

"Maybe having guests at the castle will bring Pamela out of her room," I said.

"If so, that's about the only upside to this stunt I can think of."

We stared out at the landing strip again.

Minutes ticked by.

"What could be holding up the sleigh?" I asked.

"Any number of things could have slowed him down. It's treacherous out there."

"Thanks, that's comforting."

"I'm not your therapist. And if you're going to carry out this nutty hotel scheme, you should get busy. I'll text you when the sleigh's been spotted."

She had a point. No amount of standing in the snow, watching the sky, and wishing would hasten Nick's return.

On the way back home I worried about the opposition I'd face at the castle. But I needn't have worried how Jingles would react. He was thrilled.

"Will I get to wear a tuxedo?" he asked when I warned him of the upcoming invasion.

"Um . . ." I frowned. "I don't think we're going to fool anyone that this is the Ritz."

Disappointment flashed across his face, but only briefly. "But as hotel manager, I'll get a jacket or something, right?"

Jingles loved a costume.

"I'll see what I can do," I said.

For the next hour, we put our heads together and came up with a plan—what rooms the two strangers could stay in, what areas would be off-limits, and who would be allowed to wait on Sam and Elaine. Maybe Clement and Carlotta could help out. We also figured out how to make the front hall seem like a hotel reception area.

"I've told them that the hotel is usually closed during the months of December and January," I said, "so hopefully they'll accept some of the family wandering around as just the normal state of affairs for a hotel in the offseason."

By the time I had to head to Christmastown for the caroling ceremony, we had a semblance of a game plan: elves would work on fixing up the guest rooms, Salty would mock up a believable front desk from old furniture in storage in the Old Keep, and Jingles would work on locking off areas we didn't want the guests bumbling into. There could be no phones, cell phones, or computers in evidence. Nick's office would need to be locked and off-limits at all times.

Jingles remained hung up on the question of his outfit. "I think I should at least wear a jacket with a Castle Kringle crest."

"Hotel Kringle," I corrected. More than anything, to make this scheme work I needed Jingles on board all the way. "I'll see what I can do."

All during our planning, I kept checking my phone. *Come on, Nick.* A few times my heart had raced at the sound of a text coming in. But it was always Lucia telling me that there had been no word from Nick yet.

Before I left for town, I stopped by Pamela's room to inform her of what was going on. Usually Pamela had her hand in everything during Christmas, so it was a little odd to have to go seek her out. But this was beginning to seem like the weirdest Christmas ever.

When I knocked at her door, I was left standing in the hallway for several minutes. Finally the door cracked open and a small face with big blue eyes stared up at me.

"Yes?" the elf asked.

"I need to speak to the dowager Mrs. Claus. It's urgent."

She appeared to absorb this for a moment and then shut the door. From the other side of the thick wood came frantic whispers, scurrying, cabinets slamming shut. After a moment of relative silence, the door was pulled open.

"Please come in," Coco said.

Pamela's room was not quite as big as Nick's and mine, but it was sumptuous in ways ours wasn't. The stone walls had been plastered and painted the color of fresh cream. The floors had thick rugs in shades of blue, gray, and white, and the drapes, bed canopy, and bedclothes were done in complementary floral and bird patterns. Above, the same delicate twinkle lights graced the ceiling as the ones in my own bedchamber. The lights were not just reminiscent of Christmas, they could also be programmed to go on and off gradually in a simulation of a day with a longer sunrise and sunset. In winter when real daylight was short-lived, this could be a lifesaver.

Pamela sat straight in her bed, bolstered by a mountain of satin pillows. Her ruffle-collared bed jacket gave her the air of a grand dame in a classic movie. The icy gray color exactly matched the gray hair that even in her illness she'd taken the time to roll into a perfect bun.

She regarded me calmly over her bifocals, her hands folded neatly on the bedcovers. Yet I had the distinct impression that I'd interrupted something. A conspicuous lump bulged under the covers next to her.

"Merry Christmas," she said. "Lucia's already informed me that the sleigh isn't back yet. I hope you're not here to fret about that."

"Aren't you worried?"

"I am," she allowed, almost as if this were a shameful thing to admit. "But you know what they say. 'Santa always comes back.'"

"They certainly do say that."

My sarcasm soared clear over her ballet bun. "I remember one year my husband was two days late," she said. "Turned out it was just sleigh trouble. Nothing serious."

It would be serious depending on where the sleigh was when the trouble was discovered.

"Another year the sleigh had to land on Mount Myrrh and the entire team hiked back in a blizzard. This was before the days of cell phones, so during all that time we here were in the dark."

"Apparently even having cell phones is no guarantee against being left in the dark," I grumbled.

"My advice is, let Lucia worry about the sleigh. Your job is to be Mrs. Claus and keep a calm demeanor. Focus on something productive."

That was my opening. *Here goes nothing.*

"About that . . ." I explained the circumstances of the strangers Boots had found, and told her my plans to turn the Claus ancestral castle into a hotel for the two remaining survivors.

Pamela's lips pressed into a thin line as I spoke. "Once an innkeeper, always an innkeeper," she said on a sigh when I was done.

I folded my arms. "I'm proud of running an inn. It's not something everyone has the talent and patience for."

My experience running the Coast Inn in Oregon was what made me reasonably certain that I could make a success of this charade. Of course, I wasn't telling Pamela or anyone that my real motive for opening the castle to the strangers was to decide which of them was a murderer. That wouldn't endear anyone to the scheme, except perhaps Jingles. And I couldn't risk him giving the game away.

"You act as if no one else could manage being hostess," Pamela said.

Have I mentioned that my mother-in-law is just a wee bit

competitive? I could see in her eyes that she thought she would make a better Castle Kringle hotel manager than I would.

I didn't take the bait.

"You seem to be feeling a lot better now," I observed. In fact, she didn't look sick at all. "Coco's taking good care of you?"

She tilted a smile up at me. "Why do you ask?"

"Well, Nurse Cinnamon at the hospital said that she'd never met a nurse named Coco."

"I never said Coco was a nurse. I said she was helping me."

I looked around. "Where did she go?"

"She had an errand to run," Pamela said brusquely. "And I'm sure you have more important things to do than stand there engaging in idle chatter."

In other words, I was dismissed. But at least she hadn't freaked out at the idea of bringing the visitors to the castle.

I asked Salty to get my sleigh ready, and ten minutes later Wobbler trotted up to the side portico to pick me up. "Merry Christmas, Mrs. Claus!" he whispered.

"Merry Christmas," I said. "It's safe to speak. Where's Cannonball?"

"He wanted to visit with family, so I volunteered to be on duty today."

"That's generous of you."

"Well, I'm an orphan. My family are the friends I make in life."

His words brought tears to my eyes.

"Please don't be upset, ma'am. Salty told me that what with talk of the Great Sleigh's lateness, I'm supposed to be extra cheerful and enthusiastic in order to take your mind off the many calamities that might have befallen Santa and his team, any one of which could be tragic for you." He pawed the ground. "So climb aboard—I'm ready to go!"

"Great. Thanks." I'd checked my phone five times in the past five minutes. So far, there was still no word of the sleigh.

"Where to?" Wobbler called out cheerfully.

"First, to Clement and Carlotta Claus's chateau."

"Excellent." Without further warning, he tossed his head back and bellowed, "On, Wobbler!" and bolted forward.

I fell backwards on the seat and grabbed my hat. "I wasn't expecting that," I said over his ears.

"Another of my resolutions for the New Year is to be more self-motivated!" he called back.

At Carlotta and Clement's, I got out and knocked at the door. Their butler, Baubles, greeted me warmly but told me that the siblings were all out. "Miss Audrey wanted to distribute Christmas hampers to needy elf families."

"That's good of her."

"Indeed it is," the butler said. "Miss Audrey suggested making it a new tradition."

"Well, please tell them I stopped by."

I handed Baubles the fruitcake I'd brought. It seemed a rather mundane offering in comparison to the citrus basket Audrey had sent to the castle.

Back on the sleigh, I had to think for a moment. I'd been hoping to talk to Carlotta and Clement before my next stop, but I decided to push on anyway. "To the Order of Elven Seamstresses," I said, and this time we tossed our heads back in a unison cry of, "On, Wobbler!"

The Order of Elven Seamstresses was housed in an ancient stone pile at the end of a long, snowy drive. The building dated almost as far back as Castle Kringle's Old Keep. The seamstresses were apprenticed young—many of them from the local orphanage—and lived lives apart from most Santa-landers. They were also prodigious needleworkers and viewed working for Madame Neige as an almost sacred calling.

Madame Neige reigned over the Order like a pint-sized Edith Head in a black tailored tunic and skirt, polished black elf booties, and black hair cut in a pageboy. Her no-nonsense appearance belied a genuine creative flair. She designed all sorts of clothes for the denizens of Santaland, from servants' uniforms to fanciful holiday costumes.

After I was ushered into her workroom, I told Madame Neige what I wanted. Usually she could capture whatever you described with just a few swift swipes of her pencil in a sketchbook. But as she listened this time, her pencil remained still.

"I can give you maid uniforms," she said. "They're what the maids here wear. We must have some bigger ones around." She snapped her fingers, and one of her minions scurried off to fetch the uniforms.

When I described the suit for Jingles, she nodded. "I can have that to you tomorrow. Sounds like a suit we made for a musical play for the Kringle Heights Players one year. *The Importance of Being Earnest*." In her French accent that was more cultivated than native, she added, "I could custom make, but it's Noel, you know?"

"Yes—I appreciate your help today."

"I will fashion a little patch myself for the suit and send it tomorrow." She gave the impression that fashioning patches was something she could do in her sleep.

When we were done, I was escorted back to the front door with an armful of surplus maid clothes. Before I could climb up onto the sleigh, though, I caught sight of an elf peering at me around a pillar. As soon as I looked over, the head ducked away and disappeared.

I knew who that was: Coco. I called out her name, but she scurried away toward the house.

Seeing her there gave me an uneasy feeling. What was going on?

I pulled Wobbler forward and looked around the pillar. She'd gone.

"Did you see that elf?" I asked him.

He gave his head an affirmative toss. "She arrived on foot just after you went in. Then, when she came out just a minute ago, she caught me looking at her and seemed alarmed."

But what had Coco been doing here to begin with? Was she running an errand at Madame Neige's too, or had she followed me here? If the latter were true, she'd no doubt had a directive from Pamela. The possibility of my mother-in-law spying on me made me *very* uneasy.

Because I hadn't been able to speak to Clement and Carlotta, it was still a little early for the caroling. I was debating whether to go back to the castle when my phone vibrated in my pocket. In a flash I was staring at the screen, amazed. It wasn't news from Nick. It was Claire.

I'm back. Merry Muffins before the caroling?

She wasn't supposed to be back until after New Year's. What had happened?

Faster than you can say cranberry streusel muffin, I'd replied: **M M in 10 mins!!!**

"On Wobbler—to Merry Muffins!"

Chapter 11

After we hugged in greeting, Claire sank back down in her chair and smiled as if it were the most normal thing in the world for her to be here when she was supposed to be in the Farthest Frozen Reaches with Jake.

Merry Muffins mostly did takeout business, but they did have several small bistro tables, and there was usually a good chance of finding one open, especially in the afternoon. Ours was already crammed with little muffin plates and mugs of steaming coffee, which the elf behind the counter had brewed especially for us.

"What are you doing here?" I said. "You're supposed to be in the Farthest Frozen Reaches."

"I'm having a muffin in the cozy warmth of a civilized cafe in the middle of a wonderful town, not an icy wilderness, and with my fun best friend instead of my certifiably nuts potential in-laws."

So I guessed the visit to Jake's family had not gone smoothly.

"Where's Jake?"

"As soon as we got back to town he said he needed to visit the constabulary." She lifted her mug to drink and a glint from something on her wrist caught the overhead light.

"Oooh, what is that?" I asked. "Christmas bling?"

She laughed, untied the bracelet, and dropped the pile of stones on the table. "My gift from Jake."

"Nic—" The word died in a moment of confusion. At first I assumed the little bracelet was porcelain or stone, but when I inspected the stones more closely I noted the bone-colored enamel's shine, and how the surface was rippled at one end and tapered to a point at the other, almost like . . .

I dropped the bracelet. "Are those somebody's teeth?"

"Close. They're some *thing's* teeth. A baby snow monster's."

From bling to *blech*.

She pointed to an irregularly shaped one. "See? That one had a cavity. According to Jake's uncle Jasper, it's the imperfections of tooth decay that make each piece of his artwork unique."

"Jake's uncle is a snow monster tooth artist?"

"A very talented one, according to the Frost family. And to give him his due, there's not a lot of raw material to work with up there. Just ice and dead body parts."

I squinted more closely at the object. Each tooth had tiny etchings, some quite intricate. "It reminds me a little of the artwork sailors used to make out of whale tusks."

"Only more disgusting, even," Claire said. "I can't decide what to do with it. I don't want to hurt Jake's feelings, but . . ."

I was almost afraid to ask . . . "So how was the trip up north?"

"Cold and weird." She took a sip of coffee. "And did I mention cold?"

I could only imagine. Santaland was colder than anywhere I'd ever been—albeit a dry cold, as the locals said. But the Farthest Frozen Reaches were said to make Santaland seem like Palm Beach.

"And Jake's family?" I asked.

"His uncle Joralamen is an icehouse builder who kept trying to convince us that we needed to move back to the Reaches. Said he could get us into an affordable starter igloo. I consumed so much walrus jerky that I'm probably going to sprout tusks. And then Jake insisted on visiting Uncle Jasper in his cave."

"Isn't a cave better than an igloo?"

She considered. "Warmer, but creepier. Apparently not too long ago the place had belonged to a snow monster family. It still bore the lingering odor of monster fug."

I shuddered. I'd only encountered one snow monster in my life so far, and the experience had been as smelly as it was terrifying. Hygiene was not a high priority with snow monsters.

"And then I kept wondering what would happen if the snow monster family decided that this was the Christmas they were going to return to their ancestral home and find us sitting there by a fire," Claire said. "Instant holiday roast feast."

I laughed.

She shook her head. "When I voiced that fear to Uncle Jasper, he said, 'Oh no, snow monsters prefer their protein raw.' Like *that* was comforting."

"Sounds like Jasper knows a lot about snow monsters."

"Knows about them? He's practically a snow monsterologist." She sighed. "I'm just not sure. Maybe there is too much of a cultural divide between Jake and me."

"Jake's not a snow monster fanatic."

"It's his family, though. You know what it's like to have oddball in-laws."

That was a contender for understatement of the century.

"Jake seems willing to meet you more than halfway," I pointed out. "He even moved his business to Christmastown to be closer to you."

"But is that good, really?" she wondered aloud. "I mean, sure, it seemed generous and romantic of us both to make such big gestures to be together, but it sort of puts pressure on the relationship, you know what I mean?"

"Like you both feel obligated to make it work now."

"Even if it's not working," she said. "It's like that movie, *Double Indemnity*. Remember? Once Barbara Stanwyck and Fred MacMurray kill her husband together, they keep reminding each other that they're bound together 'clear to the end of the line.'"

I loved that movie. "I'm not sure I'd compare Jake moving his office to spouse murder, though."

She laughed. "Well, no—but it does feel like we've invested too much at this point to turn back. I mean, I moved from Oregon, he moved from the Reaches." She waggled her brows in comical deep thought. "Hmm . . . I gave up a temperate climate, he gave up wild elves and snow monsters. I'm not exactly coming out on top here, am I?"

"All relationships are give and take."

"And Jake is wonderful, if a little oblivious," she said. "I'm not sure what happened, to be honest. All that snowy wilderness started to wig me out. I just know I never want to go back there. How much ice can a woman take?"

The bell over the door tinkled and Juniper appeared in her nylon pink puffer coat. She greeted us excitedly with a wave from her arm that wasn't in a brace but then tiptoed carefully over to the table. She sank down in the chair we'd saved for her. I helped her unzip her puffer coat and hung it on her chair back. Then she reached down with her good hand to undo the crampons she'd buckled over her shoes.

After her initial excitement to see Juniper, Claire couldn't keep her utterly confused gaze off Juniper's coat. "Is that Strawberry Shortcake?"

"I'm not sure," Juniper said. "It's growing on me, though. It's very warm, and so cheerful!"

"Where did you get those crampons?" I asked.

"Walnut's Bootie World is selling them now. Walnut's got his sales elves hocking them on the street corners. And lifts, too, to make elves look taller. He's calling them elfevators."

I pushed the muffin and eggnog I'd ordered for Juniper toward her and her eyes brightened. "What a great idea to fuel up before the caroling procession." She smiled at Claire. "I'm so glad you made it back in time for at least a few festivities."

"It took me a while to realize I *was* back in town," Claire said. "What's happened to Christmastown? There are Canadian flags all over the place, and elves in earmuffs, old human clothes, and elfevators."

Juniper and I tried to catch her up on all that had transpired in the past few days.

Claire looked shocked. "So now Nick's sleigh is late and you've got these two strangers in town, one of whom you think is a murderer?" She shook her head in amazement. "Meanwhile, everything's maple leaves and Anne Murray."

"And Joni Mitchell," Juniper said. "I like her. I suggested we sing 'Clouds' during the caroling."

Claire considered this. "Well, it's in that Christmas movie with Emma Thompson and Colin Firth, so technically it could be considered a Christmas song."

"But will people at the caroling know the words to 'Clouds'?" I asked.

Juniper nodded. "Butterbean's printed up lyric sheets."

"That elf sure gets around. The last I saw him, he was waiting on the makeshift sleigh landing strip." Like a tic, I checked my phone for the umpteenth time. Nothing. *Come on, Nick. Where are you?*

"How was your trip?" Juniper asked. As Claire told her

about it, the downsides of the vacay didn't seem to make an impression. Juniper actually sighed. "I would love to go on a romantic vacation with someone. Or just a vacation."

"I wouldn't exactly call freezing in the Arctic 'romantic.'" Claire thought for a moment, and seemed to adjust her attitude in the face of Juniper's words. "Although maybe I was a little too cranky while we were at his uncle's."

I recalled something she'd said earlier. "What's Jake doing at the constabulary?"

"He found something on the way back from the Reaches that he thought he should turn in."

"What?" I asked.

"A phone."

My antenna went straight up. "I bet it belonged to one of the three people Boots found."

"Much good it will do them now. The thing was smashed to bits."

I sat back, wondering about that. Why smash a phone?

Maybe because it contained evidence. But of what?

Juniper downed the last of her eggnog. "We should get going or we'll be stuck at the end of the line of carolers."

"Does it matter?" Claire asked.

"Of course! It's always more fun to be in the middle of things."

We stood, and Claire and I helped Juniper zip into her coat and hat before we put on our own.

Judging from the voices ringing in the streets, the caroling had started. We followed "God Rest Ye Merry Gentlemen" to Festival Boulevard and fell into the procession. Smudge waved us into his row and the elves made room for us. Many elves seemed taller than normal, if a little wobbly. Those elf-evators worked.

I hadn't gone two blocks when an instrumental refrain of

"A Holly Jolly Christmas" sounded in my pocket. I extracted my phone, expecting an update from Lucia. My heart nearly stopped when Nick's name flashed on my screen.

"That's not the right song," someone behind me groused, taking exception to my ringtone.

"It's Nick!" I couldn't help it—I was nearly shouting. All at once, the elves around me stopped, their voices quieting.

"Nick?" I said into the phone.

"April! It's so good to hear your—" His words stopped abruptly. "Is that 'Clouds'?"

The carolers in front of us had mostly continued on, and switched to the song Butterbean had printed out for them. Behind us, carolers too far away to have heard what was going on were getting annoyed by the unexpected bottleneck my stopping along with Juniper, Claire, and Smudge had created.

"What's going on?" one of the elves called out.

"Sh! Mrs. Claus is on the phone with Santa!" Smudge yelled back to them.

Nick's voice sounded a little thin and far away, but still I asked hopefully, "Are you at the castle?"

"No, no," Nick said. "I can't talk long. Vixen flew me around until we found a place with a signal. It's mountainous here."

"Where?"

"We're in northern Greenland."

"Greenland!" I repeated.

"*Greenland?*" the crowd echoed.

Murmurs of "Santa's in Greenland!" rippled up the procession line.

This wasn't quite the private conversation I'd hoped to have with my husband this evening. Of course, when I'd imagined speaking to him again, I'd thought we would be together, cozy in our castle room, popping open that bottle of champagne. Instead of looking into Nick's dark eyes, I found myself locking gazes with Biscuit, a clerk I recognized from the Christmastown Cornucopia, Santaland's largest grocery store. In his elfevators, he came up to chin level on me. His eyes were saucer sized with curiosity and not at all shy about eavesdropping.

I lowered my voice, but Biscuit and the other elves just leaned in closer. "What happened?" I asked Nick.

"Several of the reindeer fell ill," he said. "I decided it would be best to stop for a day or two."

"That's terrible."

"What's terrible?" came an alarmed chorus.

I held the phone to my coat, and explained, "Reindeer have fallen ill. He's stopping for a few days in Greenland."

Dismay hummed through the crowd.

When I held the phone closer to my face again, Nick's laughter came through the speaker. "I take it we're not alone."

"There's a caroling procession tonight on Festival Boulevard. I wish you were here."

"WE ALL DO, SANTA!" Biscuit projected toward the phone.

Further back in the crowd, someone called out, "Ask him when he'll be back!"

"Did you get that?" I asked Nick.

"We're going to stay until all the reindeer get their strength back to fly again."

"But what about food?"

"We have extra provisions," Nick assured me, although I detected something I didn't like in his tone.

"What did he say?"

I hesitated, but then with Nick's permission put him on speakerphone. Much as I longed to speak to Nick privately, it made no sense pretending that this was an intimate conversation anymore.

"You can't be having much of a Christmas dinner," I said.

Of course, neither were we. The Castle Kringle Christmas feast was always held back until Nick got home.

"Walrus jerky," he said. "Lucia put a whole box of it in the sleigh. The elves and I are sharing it."

"Good source of protein," one of the elves piped up.

"But not exactly comfort food," I observed.

"Any food is a comfort," Nick said.

I wanted to ask more about the details of where he was—what the conditions were—but I didn't want to force him into giving upsetting details to the entire crowd. Although I was equally upset *not* knowing the details.

By this time, word had spread up to the front of the caroling line that Santa was on the phone, and now they had turned and doubled back so that I found myself at the center of a tight crush of elves that sprawled for two blocks.

"I need to go soon," Nick said. "I've texted the details of where I am to Lucia, but I wanted to hear your voice, April. And I'm glad for the chance to wish everyone a Merry Christmas."

Biscuit gave a hop. "Let's sing a carol for Santa!"

Before I could warn against draining his cell phone charge, the elves broke into a chorus of "Silent Night." I couldn't help joining in—and then I heard voices joining in through the little speaker. It was Nick and the reindeer with him—the member of the Vixen herd that was chosen to draw the sleigh.

I finished the song through tears. Claire and Juniper held on to my free arm and squeezed.

"Merry Christmas!" Nick boomed.

"I love you, Nick!"

If he answered, it was impossible to hear over the chorus of well wishes and echoes of "We love you, Santa!"

It was like being married to a rock star. Of course I'd known going into my marriage that I was marrying Santaland's first citizen. I couldn't complain too much now about the lack of privacy.

After the call ended, the caroling resumed, but I was too numb to do much more than stumble along with everyone, moving my lips. Good thing I was flanked by both Juniper and Claire, who locked arms with me and kept me going while my thoughts raced. Was Nick really okay? How long could he, his elf helpers, and the reindeer survive in Greenland? What if Nick fell ill, too?

I needed to get back to the castle and talk to Lucia. She probably would have gleaned more from texting Nick than I had gotten out of him during that phone call.

The trouble was, I was Mrs. Claus, and I couldn't very well duck out on the Christmas night caroling procession. The elves were determined to sing their way across town, even if it meant repeating much of their repertoire. We were on our third "Clouds" when we finally reached Peppermint Pond and the crowd broke up. They would all be going back to their cozy homes to sit by the hearth, drink eggnogs, and maybe sing more songs. I would be going back to an empty castle.

Well, the castle was never empty. But it wouldn't have Nick.

Starting tomorrow, though, it would have two strangers in it. I couldn't say that I was looking forward to that.

Claire suggested swinging by the Santaland Scoop, for a nightcap. "I've still got one tub of ice cream in the freezer. I could do a frozen toddy for us."

I jumped at the idea. We were wending our way back up Festival Boulevard when a shadowy figure caught my eye. Coco? She was walking furtively, carrying a shopping bag full of something.

Before the others could stop me, I sprinted after her.

"April, where are you going?" Claire yelled from behind me.

I waved an arm. "I'll meet you at the Scoop!" I hadn't slowed my steps, but Coco was still a block ahead. "Wait!" I called after her. "I need to talk to you!"

The little elf turned. Seeing me gaining on her, she pivoted and tore off in the opposite direction, her little legs moving as fast as pistons. I called after her to hold up, but she kept running until, turning to see how close I was on her heels, she missed seeing the large snowman who shoved himself onto the sidewalk in front of her.

"Stop in the name of the law!"

Pumblechook's command came too late. When Coco looked forward again, she was running headlong into his solid snowy mass. I cried out in alarm. Coco locked her legs and looked as if she were trying to put on the brakes, but the result was just her skidding the rest of the way into the snow policeman.

Pumblechook grunted and Coco fell to the snowy sidewalk. I kept running and grabbed the shopping bag that Coco had dropped during her collision.

"Are you all right?" I asked Pumblechook.

"I've lost a button and several fistfuls of snow, I think."

It was true—his lower section now bore the vague imprint of Coco's torso.

I reached down and helped her up. She sputtered at me, "Why were you chasing me?"

"Why did you run?" I asked.

"Because you were chasing me!"

"I chased you because I thought you were following me. I saw you earlier at the Order of Elven Seamstresses. Who are you?" I raised a hand. "I know you're not a nurse."

She raised her arms in exasperation. "I never said I was.

That's just what Mrs. Claus—the dowager Mrs. Claus—let everyone believe."

"Why?" I asked.

She opened her mouth to answer, then checked herself. "I can't say."

I held up the shopping bag. "You dropped this. Do you mind if I look inside?"

"You have no right."

"She's Mrs. Claus," Pumblechook told her sternly. "Of course she's got the right. The law is clear on that."

Coco snorted. "It is not. Anyway, what do you know about the law? You're a snowman. You're not even supposed to be talking."

Pumblechook looked offended. "I'm a snowman with a constable hat, young lady. Don't tell me about regulations. I know as much about the law as Constable Crinkles."

Well, he wasn't wrong about that.

"What's in this bag?" I said, beyond caring whether the law was on my side or not. I wanted to know what this shady elf was up to.

"None of your beeswax!" She grabbed one of the shopping bag's handles and yanked it to her. The bag ripped, sending skeins of colorful yarn cascading onto white snow. She let out a cry of distress, dropped to her knees, and began to gather them all up again.

I helped her. "Yarn?"

She glanced up defensively. "Your mother-in-law invited me to the castle to knit. Is that so strange?"

It was, frankly. Pamela was a great knitter. "Why would she need you to help her knit?"

"We're trying to finish a big project before her son— Santa—returns."

That was also hard to believe. Pamela had been knitting

her Christmas sweaters for everyone for decades. "She's never had trouble finishing the sweaters before."

"These aren't sweaters."

Not sweaters. Something bigger, then. "Afghan?"

"I can't say. I shouldn't have even told you they weren't sweaters." She assured me, "We're almost done, and then I'll go back to the Order of Elven Seamstresses."

"Was she ever sick?" I asked. "Or was that a pretext to give her more knitting time?"

She bit her lip. "I think she had the sniffles one day." Getting up, she whacked snow off her torn shopping bag. "Now you know. And now I'll probably be dismissed for letting her secret out."

"I won't tell a soul."

She cocked her head curiously. "Really?"

"Of course not. Pamela will never hear anything from my lips."

Before she could scurry away, Pumblechook called out, "You dropped an eyeball, miss."

I glanced down. A glassy eyeball stared up at me from the snow-packed ground. Coco swiped it up, dropped it into her yarn bag, and hurried away at a clip.

"Looked like a nice eyeball, too," the snowman observed.

But why would Coco—or Pamela—need one?

I turned my attention to patching up Pumblechook. He was ticklish and couldn't help rumbling as I tried to reshape his belly. I couldn't find his button, unfortunately.

"I'm so sorry about this," I told him, arranging the other two so that the missing one wasn't so noticeable.

"Maybe I can find some new buttons. I like those brass ones Constable Crinkles has on his dress coat."

"If I see him, I'll ask." Although I imagined if he got the constable's buttons in addition to his hat, he'd never stop trying to police everyone in Christmastown.

"Snowmen aren't supposed to be talking, you know," I told him as we parted.

"Tell me about it! I had to give Chuzzlewit a stern talking-to early tonight after I caught him singing."

I headed back up the street toward the Santaland Scoop. I'd hoped that I would be able to go home soon. The castle needed to be ready to receive our "guests" tomorrow.

But the second I opened the door, I could tell by the looks on everyone's faces that something was wrong. Juniper and Claire stood behind the long glossy red counter that ran three quarters of the width of the room. Claire was pouring drinks from the blender into tall milkshake glasses, while Juniper waited next to her with a pitcher of newly whipped cream to dollop on the top. Their pinched expressions were out of place in the bright, shiny red-and-white decor of the ice cream parlor. Even Smudge, perched on a stool across from them, looked more disturbed than expectant.

Then I noticed a second seated figure: Jake Frost, Claire's boyfriend and Santaland's foremost private detective. His head-to-toe black garb often made him look like a harbinger of doom, and from the grim set to his mouth, I could tell he had news.

Some news about the sleigh? I'd just talked to Nick, though.

"What is it?" I asked, heart in throat. "Was there any more news from Nick?"

He looked confused for a moment, then shook his head. "No. I just came to tell you that there's been a murder."

Another one?

"The man named Eric Lynch," he explained.

I breathed a sigh. Bad news, but old news. "I know. He was stabbed with an antler."

Jake shook his head. "Turns out that he was killed while he was in the hospital. I just got a message. Algid, Doc's nephew, is going to the constabulary in person to explain it so Crinkles can understand. The constable said he has trouble thinking on the phone."

On the phone and everywhere else at times.

Claire handed out hot drinks with chocolate sprinkles. The blended ice cream, coffee, and dark rum looked silky smooth and so good.

Juniper, who had traded her Scandinavian-style wool cap with earflaps for the pointy, candy-striped paper hats the Scoop's clerks wore, handed around the tall milkshake glasses. "Does this make the two surviving strangers murder suspects?"

"I already considered them that."

Smudge's dark eyes bulged with surprise. "Juniper told me you invited them to the castle. What about the safety of everyone up there? Didn't you say that the dowager Mrs. Claus is ill in bed?"

Malingering in bed, it turned out. After my encounter with Coco, it was hard to know what Pamela was up to, but the image Smudge was trying to convey of her being a helpless little old lady made me laugh. "Even if there was a cage match between Pamela and a wily murderer," I told him, "I'd have my money on Pamela every time."

When we all had drinks in our hands, we leaned in from both sides of the counter and clinked glasses. "Merry Christmas!" we said before we each tackled the delicious shakes. I used a parfait spoon on mine—just until I worked my way through the layer of whipped cream.

I twirled the spoon in the thick, delicious concoction. It was rich, not overly sweet, and that little kick of rum was very welcome.

Jake's dark brows drew together until they were almost a solid, brooding line. "If you're going to have those people up at the castle, you'd better come with me to hear what Algid has to say. He was going to visit the constabulary once Ollie and Doc finished their Christmas dinner."

Claire stilled. "You're going back to the constabulary *tonight*? Christmas night?"

"You're welcome to come, too," Jake told Claire.

The room tensed in a collective wince. Jake didn't possess the most finely tuned romantic radar.

"I was thinking more along the lines of cuddling up next to a cozy fire," Claire said. "Not sleuthing in a winter wonderland."

"I'd like to hear what Algid has to say," I said. "I'll go."

I'd intended the statement to be a high lob to Jake, giving him a perfect excuse to stay here with Claire. He let the ball drop.

"I'll walk you over," he said. "You can also come, Claire. There's usually a nice fire at the constabulary." After a hesitation he added, puzzled, "If you like that sort of thing."

Claire sent me a look that said *See what I mean? Oblivious.*

I was beginning to see what she meant.

Chapter 12

Jake and I arrived—without Claire—at the Christmastown Constabulary just after Crinkles and Ollie had opened their presents. A fire glowed in the hearth of the constabulary's main room, where the lawmen's stockings hung on either side of the fireplace. The mantel was also decorated with evergreen boughs and several candles. Their woodsy scents competed with the mouthwatering aromas of apples and cinnamon wafting from the kitchen.

"You're just in time for cinnamon rolls," Ollie said, directing us to places set at the dining table. "My second batch today. These have apple in them."

Once we were all seated, he brought out a warm platter with rolls dripping with cinnamon-sugar icing. Having just gulped down a chocolate shake, I wasn't a bit hungry. And yet at the sight of those cinnamon rolls, I knew there was no way I would turn down one.

"Look at the potholders Unc gave me," Ollie said, holding up his hands. On each was a potholder decorated to look like a snowman.

"Nice," I said.

Crinkles beamed, pleased. "I thought they looked a little like Pumblechook."

That reminded me . . . "Pumblechook had an accident tonight. He lost a button."

"I have some extra buttons that I can wrap up this evening," Ollie said.

"That would be perfect," I said.

"We just got him a new scarf, but that didn't seem very exciting," Crinkles confided in a low voice, as if the snowman were listening somewhere nearby.

How a snowman was supposed to unwrap a package was something I didn't have time to contemplate at that moment. Doc and Algid came in the front door, stomping snow off their boots on the carpet mat by the door.

"It was murder, all right," Doc Honeytree announced with no preamble. He didn't even seem to notice the cinnamon rolls.

"Overdose of painkiller," Algid said. "A large enough dose to knock out a snow monster. For a normal-sized human man, it was deadly."

"What made you check?" I asked. "Everyone just assumed he'd died of infection after his wound."

"I wasn't going to let those two other survivors assume that I hadn't taken sufficient steps to save their friend," Doc said. "Why, he'd been getting better. I was sure of it."

"This changes everything," I said. "It certainly makes it less crucial to figure out who stabbed him to begin with, if the antler wasn't the cause of death."

Jake looked thoughtful. "Unless the stabber and the person who administered the overdose were one and the same."

"You think someone decided to finish the job they started?" Crinkles asked.

I contemplated this possibility over a gooey bite of cinnamon roll. Only two people I could think of could easily have been at the scene of the stabbing and at the hospital when Eric died: Sam and Elaine. As of tomorrow, they would both be guests at the castle.

"Or it could be someone who was put out that the strangers were staying here," Jake said.

That possibility threw a net over a much larger pool of suspects. Lots of elves didn't want the strangers here and had said so: Nurse Cinnamon. Plummy. Even Mayor Firlog. "Put out enough to murder one of them, though?" I wondered aloud.

Algid cleared his throat. "The elf or person you're looking for also had to know where the frankincense was kept."

"Frankincense?" It was a word I only associated with the story of the Three Wise Men.

"Frankincense is a very effective remedy for pain and swelling," Doc explained. "We often use it in combination with morphine."

Now I understood. "So the murderer would have needed access to the nurse's supply closet."

Jake added, "And some knowledge of how much would be needed for a deadly dose."

Doc shook his head. "An overdose could be caused by two drafts."

I looked to Algid for translation.

"Approximately two hundred milligrams is a normal dose," he explained. "But from the blood test I ran on the victim, I discovered four times that."

"Overkill." Jake scratched his stubbly jaw.

"Diabolical!" Crinkles exclaimed. "Who could have done it?"

"Nurse Cinnamon would have known where to quickly get the drugs."

"Nurse Cinnamon wouldn't have done this," Doc Honeytree said with certainty. "Besides, she would have known that death wouldn't have required three extra doses."

"And what would be her motive?" Jake said.

The memory of Nurse Cinnamon's wish that the strangers could be out of her hospital as soon as possible crossed my mind. She would be getting her wish now.

Of course, others had expressed the same sentiment.

"Who else was at the infirmary when the man died?" Jake asked.

"Mildred Claus." I added quickly, "But she was asleep during most of her shift."

"That's convenient," Algid observed.

Jake thought about this. "Or maybe it was convenient for the killer that Mildred was asleep."

"They might have even helped her along," Algid said.

I shook my head. "She told me she was tired from making candied nuts all night."

"There's no getting around it," Jake said. "We'll have to talk to Nurse Cinnamon."

"One draft," Nurse Cinnamon declared, jutting her chin high. "I gave the man his one morning draft, just as Dr. Honeytree instructed."

"And where were the other two patients?" Jake asked.

"In their rooms."

"Are you sure there was just one draft?" I asked. "You couldn't have mismeasured?"

"Of course not. I've *never* mistaken dosages." She gestured to the door to a supply cabinet. "Besides, Doc delivered the doses for the next few days pre-measured, as he usually does. Each patient's room has a corresponding shelf where that patient's medicines are kept."

That seemed sensible.

"Who has the key to this medicine cabinet?"

My question was met with a blank, blinking stare. Four of them, actually. Doc, Nurse Cinnamon, Crinkles, and even Jake all looked at me as if I'd started speaking in tongues.

"You *do* keep the medicines locked up, don't you?"

"Why would we do that?" Doc Honeytree asked.

Oh boy. It was another of those not-in-Kansas-anymore moments.

"Who'd want to steal frankincense?" Crinkles looked honestly perplexed. "If anyone wants to get inebriated, it's not hard to find a grog shop."

The others nodded as if this were just common sense.

"I think we'd better see how many of those doses that Doc gave you are left. Unless you've already checked?"

Nurse Cinnamon thought about this. "Well, no. I haven't needed any doses for him since . . ."

Since the patient died.

Our group trouped to the supply closet. Upon opening the cabinet—as easily accessible to anyone walking down the hallway as any bathroom medicine cabinet in a private home would be—we found only gauze on the shelf that corresponded to Eric's room number.

Nurse Cinnamon's mouth dropped open. "I don't know what happened."

I did. So did she, once the initial shock wore off and she began to understand the gravity of her position.

"I swear to you." She held her right palm out as if she were in a witness box, "I never would have given the man more medicine than what was required. I wasn't even here."

For Jake's benefit, she explained about the eggnog spill at the front of the hospital that day, and how she had been forced to leave Mildred in charge while she patched up Fuzzy the delivery driver in the ER. "If you suspect foul play from inside the infirmary," she concluded, "the one you should be talking to is Mildred Claus." She pointed to the front desk. "I left her in charge of the ward, and when I returned, she had her head down on the reception desk and was fast asleep."

"Well, if she was fast asleep, she probably wasn't killing anyone," Jake pointed out laconically.

Nurse Cinnamon folded her arms over her chest. "I don't know how long she was asleep for. It might have been minutes, it might have been an hour."

I understood how upsetting it could feel to have the finger of blame pointed in one's direction, but still. Her blatant deflection of blame by trying to make Mildred look guilty annoyed me.

"You can't honestly suspect Mildred Claus of murder," I said to all of them. "You know her. She wouldn't harm a fly."

Crinkles and Jake seemed swayed by my character reference, which riled Nurse Cinnamon. "I wouldn't harm anyone, either. I've spent my whole adult life helping people."

Doc Honeytree stood by his nurse. "We know you didn't kill anyone. We just need your help in finding out who might have stolen those doses and injected them into the patient while you were in the ER."

Nurse Cinnamon frowned in thought. "The other two patients were here the whole time, of course. And Mildred, as well as any visitors who might have stopped in."

"Is there a visitor book they have to sign?" The question sounded ridiculous even as I spoke it. Santaland wasn't a signing-in sort of place.

"Most of them just drop off their offerings and leave," Nurse Cinnamon said.

"Offerings . . ." As I repeated the word, I turned in the direction she was nodding toward. Down the hall near the reception desk where Mildred had been napping stood three carts loaded with fruitcakes, candy cane bouquets, and a fruit basket.

That was how we were supposed to figure out who was here? "Are there cards included on all the goodies?" I asked hopefully.

"No, but you can usually tell who left what by the looks of them."

By their fruitcake tins shall ye know them. But I'd lived in Santaland for several years, and I wasn't yet used to deciphering everyone's fruitcake fingerprint.

"Maybe we should start by asking Sam and Elaine if they noticed anyone hanging around," I suggested.

The two surviving patients were in Sam's room. The TV and DVD player that were supposed to distract them stood in the corner, turned off. Both patients were dressed in the clothes they'd been found in, which had been washed in the infirmary laundry. I made a mental note to go through my closets tonight to find some more clothes for them.

"Notice anyone hanging around?" Elaine repeated when we asked her. "It's a hospital. Who would hang around? *I* didn't want to be here, even before I knew there was a killer on the loose."

"We don't think you're in any danger," I said.

A laugh sputtered out of her. "How do you know that?"

Because you're the likeliest suspect. I bit my lip.

She answered her own question for me. "You don't. Why can't we leave right now? I don't like to be pushy, but how hard is it to get two hotel rooms ready?"

Jake broke in. "April tells me that you and Sam were playing chess yesterday afternoon."

They nodded in unison. "For about an hour and a half," Sam guessed. "Around one forty-five to three o'clock or three fifteen."

Elaine clucked her tongue in irritation. "There's literally nothing else to do here. I've never seen a hospital without at least a landline to call out."

"I wish I had my phone," Sam complained.

"It was found," I said.

Jake confirmed this. "It was in the snow, badly smashed up. I doubt it'll ever work again."

Sam's forehead wrinkled. "Why would it have been smashed? It survived a plane crash. I mean, the charge ran out while we were still waiting by the wreckage of the plane, hoping for rescue. But it wasn't smashed up while I had it."

"We can't explain it," I said. "I'm sorry."

Elaine and Sam exchanged a glance I couldn't decipher.

"Are you sure you never heard anything yesterday afternoon?" Jake asked them.

Sam nodded. "We had my door closed. This place is built pretty solid. You can't hear anything."

"Except Celine Dion," complained Elaine.

"That was just the first day," Sam reminded her.

"It doesn't matter. I still want out of here."

"Did Doc say you could leave?" I asked.

"Why would he object?" She thumped her crutches. "I just have these. I'm not even on serious painkillers anymore, which apparently is a good thing in this death house."

"I resent that," Nurse Cinnamon declared from the doorway.

"And I resent my ex-husband being murdered. If you ask me, it had to have been somebody who worked around here. Who else would have known where the drugs were kept?"

Anyone who'd been watching Nurse Cinnamon's movements. *You, for instance,* I thought, eyeing Elaine.

Nurse Cinnamon reddened like something about to erupt.

I lifted a hand. "I just need to step out for a moment."

I didn't know who had killed Eric, but given the tension between Elaine and Nurse Cinnamon, clearing Sam and Elaine out of the hospital might prevent a second murder.

I headed out of earshot of the room, to the reception desk, and dialed Jingles.

After one ring, he answered. "Castle Kringle Hotel and Resort. This is Leopold. How may I help you?"

"Leopold?"

"How many people named Jingles do you know outside of Santaland?"

Point taken. "I'm not sure we should be calling the place a resort, though. It's false advertising. There are no resort activities."

"I'm having Salty clean up some spare snowshoes and skis."

"The woman is on crutches," I reminded him, "and after what they've been through, I doubt either of them would relish the prospect of wandering around in the snow."

"Hmm . . . I hadn't thought of that."

But if he was already working on the entertainment for the guests, it gave me hope that the basics were covered. "Are the rooms ready?"

"All taken care of. And the front desk is in place. Salty unearthed a side table that was cast aside in the castle remodel of 1722. It works quite well."

"Good. Sam and Elaine want to move to the castle tonight."

Jingle's gulp traveled across the phone line. "Oh dear, our maid's not here yet."

"Maid?"

"Audrey Claus volunteered."

Of course she did. I wasn't sure how reliable she'd be when it came to making beds and cleaning bathrooms, though. Squeamishness had prevented her managing even an hour of hospital work. From what I'd heard, hotel maids often dealt with more gruesome things than nurses did.

Jingles added, "I didn't think we'd need her till the morning."

"We probably won't," I agreed.

Idly, I glanced at offerings on one of the trolley tables in the corridor, surprised to see that Tiffany had dropped some

scones by at some point. The Tea-piphany box sat nestled between the citrus basket I'd noticed yesterday and some fruitcake tins. So many fruitcakes . . .

"Mrs. Claus?" Jingles prompted.

I pulled my attention away from the goodies. "I think
we're okay for tonight. I doubt these two will want to do
much more than go to their rooms and sleep." I know I was
ready to collapse into a soft bed. It had been a long day.

In the next moment, guilt pierced me. Wherever he was,
Nick didn't have a warm bed to fall into, and I could just
imagine how long his day had seemed.

I needed to talk to Lucia and see if she had any new details
about him.

"Is Lucia around?"

"She might be—I haven't seen her since this afternoon."
Jingles reminded me, "I've spent my entire Christmas creat-
ing Hotel Kringle."

"I know, and I appreciate all you've done. You and Salty
and all the elves helping you today will get extra time off after
New Year's."

I dearly hoped that Sam and Elaine would be gone by
New Year's.

But that thought raised another question. Once they were
installed in the castle, how were we ever going to get rid of
them?

Chapter 13

As I predicted, "we won't be any trouble" was just an empty phrase to Elaine.

Imagine, if you will, being tucked into an open sleigh, swaddled in cozy pashminas and lap robes, and chauffeured up Sugarplum Mountain on a gorgeous Christmas night. The crisp, clear air was redolent of evergreens that lined our path and graced the yards of the chateaus of Kringle Heights. The great houses all beamed out a holiday glow in the darkness, some in delicate white, others—like Clement and Carlotta's—in garish multicolored twinklers. Overhead, the northern lights ribboned across the sky in faded pink and vibrant green, as if even the heavens had gotten the memo about what day it was. The air was still, with no sound but the muffled trotting of reindeer hooves against the snow, and the faint jangling of Wobbler's harness.

At last, we turned up the curving driveway leading to Castle Kringle. The castle might have been an illustration on a magazine cover. Warm lights outlined the walls, towers, and windows. The trees in the snowy yard had been decorated like a Christmas tree, too, and mingling around them were many of the snowmen who had come up the mountain to serenade us on Christmas morning. The castle and its grounds were a dazzling Christmas vision I never tired of.

When the sleigh stopped, Elaine kept her bored gaze focused on the door to the castle. "I hope this old place has room service," she grumbled.

"And Wi-Fi," Sam added.

I took a breath. "We can bring you anything from the kitchen, but we don't have Wi-Fi."

The two gaped at me.

"Here, either?"

Sam's disappointment sent a wave of guilt through me. I was glad there was just a dog waiting for him at home instead of a worried family. "The whole region was hit."

"Can't they get it fixed?" Elaine asked.

"Well, it's Christmas week."

"Canada!" she said in disgust as she balanced on her crutches. "I never knew that they were *this* backward."

Sorry, Canada.

"No kidding," Sam said, "if I were you, I'd write to the president."

She leveled a withering gaze on him. "There is no president of Canada."

"Well, the viceroy or whatever you call the top guy here."

"I believe the title you're looking for is prime minister," she said, sneering at his ignorance. "Prime Minister"—her brows knit—"Whosit."

While they were talking, a gentle rendition of "Still, Still, Still" had started out in the yard. I froze in shock. The snowman's chorus. They had forgotten about the edict—but why wouldn't they? I'd overlooked it on Christmas morning, and praised their talent.

Sam's eyes widened. "Listen to that!" He pivoted toward the yard. "They're singing."

Elaine looked at him as if he were cracked. "Who?"

"The snowmen!"

She laughed and made *Twilight Zone* sounds.

"Well then, how would you explain it?"

"It's a recording, you nincompoop," she said. "They've obviously set up speakers out there—although I can't imagine why." She turned to me sharply. "Please tell you that you don't pipe that through the hotel hallways."

"We don't," I said.

Salty, in a long trapper cap whose flaps covered all but the very tips of his earlobes, took Wobbler's reins from me. I almost thanked Wobbler as usual, but remembered myself and gave him a pat. He huffed out his impatience through his velvety nostrils. Clearly, he deemed being patted instead of talked to condescending.

"Apologies," I muttered in what I thought was a low voice.

Elaine overheard, but luckily misunderstood. "Never mind—as long as I don't have to listen to it inside. Right now I just want a hot beverage and a soft bed."

At that moment, the large, arched front door swung open and Jingles, decked out in a tuxedo, stepped into the light. His hands were covered in white gloves, even. Heaven only knew where he'd gotten the idea that hotel managers were supposed to dress like Fred Astaire. Behind him stood Pamela, looking exactly like what she was: a model Mrs. Claus. She wore a red wool dress with a white apron, low black pumps with buckles, and round wire bifocals. Her gray hair was pulled back in its usual tidy bun.

I groaned inwardly. She'd picked a great time to play hostess with the mostest. She might as well have a neon sign saying *Welcome to Santaland* across her chest.

"Welcome to Castle Kringle." She even spread her arms in greeting, unable to resist playing the grand dame of the castle.

"The finest *hotel* and resort in the greater Centretown area," Jingles added quickly. "I am the manager, Leopold. Your rooms await you."

He was laying it on thick, but it at least distracted our guests from the person who was very obviously Mrs. Claus standing behind him.

"Let me assist you, ma'am," he said to Elaine.

"I can manage." She thumped up the wide entrance steps. "What I need from you, Leo, is a brandy, a sandwich—turkey club if you have it—and a fresh green salad sent up to my room, stat. I practically OD'd on muffins and fruitcake at that nutty hospital." She barely spared Pamela a glance. "And I'll need extra pillows on the bed. Bring some to the room as soon as you can."

Pamela, unused to being ordered about this way in her own castle, blinked at the woman in astonishment.

At my mother-in-law's dumbstruck reaction to her command, Elaine flicked a sympathetic glance at me. "I guess good help's hard to come by everywhere, huh?"

I had to bite back a laugh. She thought Pamela was the housekeeper.

"Excuse me, young woman—" Pamela, reddening, looked like she was gearing up to put Elaine in her place.

I intervened, stepping between them. "Of course, we'll make sure that you have extra pillows and anything else you need. Right now Leopold will show you to your rooms and relay your orders to appropriate staff."

Jingles gestured toward the sweeping staircase. "Please follow me."

"Nice place." Sam turned around in the palatial foyer, which had been scrubbed and polished within an inch of its life. A fully decorated tree stood in the center, just underneath a chandelier dripping with snowflake-shaped crystals. To the side, the "front desk" seemed wildly out of place to me, but apparently it looked believable enough that the guests barely spared it a glance.

"I guess we can check in later?" Sam asked.

I nodded. "Plenty of time for that tomorrow."

When they'd climbed enough stairs to be out of earshot, I turned to Pamela, who was still smarting from Elaine's snub. Her outrage made me fear she'd march upstairs and give the whole game away.

To smooth over her ruffled feathers, I said, "Very smart of you to dress up like that. You fooled them."

Her brows rose like theatrical curtains over surprised eyes. "Did I?" She looked down at her outfit, which had been hand sewn in the finest wool by the Order of Elven Seamstresses. "Maybe it's the apron."

"And don't worry, I'll round up the extra pillows for her highness," I said. "I'm sure you'd like to go back to bed."

She looked as if she didn't understand at first.

"Although you seem to be doing *much* better," I added pointedly.

"Oh! Yes!" She cleared her throat. "I took a turn for the better this afternoon."

"Is Coco still here?" I asked.

"Yes, she's with me for a little while longer."

She was still determined not to give me any clues about what she was up to.

At any other time, the mystery of the malingering mother-in-law would have preoccupied my brain until I winkled out the truth. This week it was so far down on the list of Santa-land crises and quandaries that I didn't the mental bandwidth for it.

I descended to the laundry and storage room to see what I could round up for the guests. The area, which usually hummed with machines whirring and elves singing and talking their way through their work, now was so empty that my footsteps echoed. Christmas night, I realized. Jingles had released the castle elves to go spend the holiday with their families.

I stacked three pillows and some extra towels in my arms and headed back upstairs. On the first landing, I passed Jingles. "Salad," he grumbled, "at midnight."

"I'm sorry. Would you like me to go to the kitchen and help you?"

He looked horrified by the idea. "It's bad enough seeing you fetching and carrying for those two like a servant."

"For the next few days, you'll have to get used to it." I smiled at his formal wear. "Nice tux, by the way."

"Do you think so? I ordered it when I tried out for the role of Henry Higgins in the Kringle Heights Players' summer production of *My Fair Lady*. I thought I was a shoo-in for Henry Higgins."

"What happened?"

A trace of lingering bitterness could be heard in his tone. "Mayor Firlog got the part."

"Well, your official uniform is being sent over in the morning."

"Good. I try to wear my tux sparingly."

"Do you know if Lucia has spoken to Nick?"

His lips twisted. "I believe she's in his office now, making plans for a rescue trip to Greenland."

I gulped. The office was supposed to be locked. "Do you think his situation is so dire that he needs immediate rescue?"

"You'll have to ask Lucia about that," he said.

I would. Just as soon as I delivered the pillows.

Before we parted, I added, "We have got to get those snowmen to pipe down. Seriously. Not one more peep."

He nodded. "I'll tell Salty to give them a strong talking-to."

I continued on to the wing the guests had been given.

It was on the upper floor of the newest section of the castle, one floor above Tiffany and Christopher's quarters. The more modern wall sconces in addition to the twinkle lights in the ceiling made it not quite as dark as some of the other areas. There was also a thick runner carpet on the stone floor, which explained why Elaine and Sam didn't hear me as I approached their rooms.

I didn't yet know whose room was whose, but they were huddled in one of them, arguing.

"I just wish I had my phone," he complained. "Or better yet, my video recorder."

"Would you shut up about that phone? I don't understand why you need it so much—and don't tell me it's to talk to your dog. You're not *that* stupid."

"I am, actually. Dogs have souls, and understanding."

"Spare me. Of all the things to worry about, phones would be the last on my list."

"Because you have no one to call. No friends."

"Shut up," she said sharply. "Eric was my friend."

"You called him an idiot."

"He was—but I loved him." She added, "As much as I can love anyone."

"He was right about some things," Sam said. "You have to admit that."

"Oh yes, there was a town out here." Voice dripping with sarcasm, she added, "Stop the presses! The earth is inhabited!"

"But he said—"

She cut him off. "I know what he said. It was ridiculous."

"You didn't see the snowman that first night, but you saw all those out in the yard tonight."

"What is it with you? Were you traumatized by Frosty the Snowman at a tender age?" She laughed. "Mind you, I always thought Frosty was kind of creepy myself."

"I'm telling you, they were *singing*. Who puts speakers in trees in their yard?"

"Christ on a cracker, Sam, if you don't drop the singing snowmen I'm going to pull my hair out. Better yet, I'll tear yours out. I've already lost a toe—I don't see why I should lose my hair, too. You are the poster child for why laymen don't belong on scientific expeditions."

"Eric was a scientist."

"He also fancied himself an impresario. He thought he saw a chance to exploit a place and make a buck. 'North Pole Adventures.' It was all lunacy, though."

Another pause ensued.

"Do you really think he was murdered?" Sam asked her.

"Of course he was. He had an antler in his back."

"Attacked by an animal," Sam reminded her. "That's what he's reported to have said."

"He could have meant someone armed with an antler."

"Whoever tried to kill him with that antler could have found Eric in the hospital and decided to finish the job."

"But why?"

Her voice lowered. "You know why . . ."

"Are you accusing *me*?"

I leaned in to find out, but in the process one of my towels dropped. The soft *plop* as it hit the carpet might as well have been a bomb going off. I froze.

"What was that?" Sam asked.

"I hope it's that guy with my sandwich and salad," Elaine said.

After bending to scoop up the towel, I decided to tap at the door and announce my presence. Elaine's eyes narrowed with suspicion.

"Here are the extra pillows you requested," I said breezily, moving efficiently into the room and dropping them on the bed. This had to be Elaine's room. Neither of them brought luggage to the castle, of course—they no longer had anything to put in a suitcase. But Elaine had made herself at home and put on a thick red robe Jingles had pinched from my closet to give the castle the air of an upscale resort hotel.

"Leopold will be bringing up your turkey club as soon as it's ready."

"Thank you—" Elaine stopped herself. "I'm sorry, what's your name?"

"April."

"I'll also need an extra blanket or two, April." She sent me a tight smile. "If it's not much trouble."

"No trouble," I lied.

I hurried back downstairs, grabbed some blankets from the supply room, and then delivered them. When I entered the room, she and Sam were conspicuously closed-mouthed, as if they'd agreed not to converse while I was in the room. Darn it. A thick, awkward silence descended on the room as I delivered the towels to the en suite washroom and left again.

It had been what felt like the world's longest and least Christmassy Christmas Day in Santaland history, and right now I just wanted to go to bed. But I knew I would find no rest with worries about Nick troubling my mind. I slipped over to Nick's office to see if Lucia was still up.

Of course she was. She'd been around reindeer so much that she could probably lock her knees and take standing naps during the day. When I went in the room, Lucia, Jingles, and Quasar were all studying a map of Greenland on the new wall screen. Lucia was wearing the clothes she'd had on all day, and Jingles was still in his tuxedo. The intensity of their focus frightened me.

"Has something happened to Nick?" I asked.

Barely taking me in, Lucia shook her head curtly. "No,

not that we know of. He sent me his coordinates as best as he could manage."

"He told me that their camp is out of range," I said. "That must mean that it's very rough country where they put down."

"Yes. It's bad."

No one could ever accuse Lucia of sugar-coating anything.

"But it's the reindeer I'm worried about," she added.

No one could ever accuse her of putting her own family's welfare ahead of reindeers', either.

"Reindeer at least have thick hides," I said.

"We can't be sure what shape the sick ones are in," Lucia said. "That's why I'm going."

I gaped at her. "Going to Greenland?"

She nodded. "Nick's sleigh wasn't provisioned for a long emergency. And they might need medical help." She bit her lip.

Quasar's nose fizzled a bit as he ducked his head in thought. "Maybe you should take a reindeer doctor with you. Dr. Snowball might agree to go."

Dr. Snowball was Santaland's best veterinarian.

"I need to contact him." She looked at Jingles. "And could you get Salty to check over the spare sleigh and make sure it's in tip-top condition?"

Jingles practically saluted. "On it!" He turned and hurried out the door.

"Nick's everyday sleigh, you mean?" I asked.

The Claus family owned two great sleighs—the old, ornately carved sleigh used for the annual gift run as well as ceremonial occasions and official visits, and Nick's spare sleigh, which was a large sleigh but wasn't carved and painted as elaborately as the other one. Of course it was no doubt just as sturdy as the ceremonial sleigh.

She nodded.

"Do you have a list of what you need?" I asked. "I can start loading it up. Maybe we can even leave by dawn."

Days were so short, that gave us a big time window.

"*We?*" Lucia scowled at me. "You're not going."

"Why not?"

"We need supplies on the sleigh, not people. And you're not a doctor, or a vet, or somebody with icy outback experience. Plus you get sleigh sick on long rides."

I wanted to say *"Yes, but I'm Mrs. Claus,"* but in my heart of hearts I knew she was right. I loved Nick, but other than that, I wouldn't bring a lot to the reinforcement efforts.

"And from what Jingles was telling me about these visitors in the castle, you're going to have your hands full dealing with them. Just as well that I won't be here. The moment one of them barked an order at me I'd blow my stack." She hurried over to Nick's desk and took out a piece of paper. "We need to put together a team," she told Quasar. "Who do you suggest?"

At the question, the reindeer's nose glowed red briefly and then flamed out. "We sh-should go through the lists of runners-up in the reindeer games." The winners of those games, which were conducted all year long right up to December, were the reindeer who were with Nick now. "And then c-consult the leaders of the herds," he added. "A show of respect."

Lucia nodded. "We'll need eight names."

Quasar blinked. "B-but surely you'll want to take nine."

Santa's sleigh was traditionally eight reindeer harnessed in pairs, and then one reindeer—usually from the Rudolph herd—on point in front.

"*You're* nine," Lucia said.

"Me?" he asked, amazement in his low voice.

"I wouldn't make the trip without you, friend."

Quasar stood straighter.

The idea of everyone leaving started to panic me. "What if *you* need help?" I asked. "What'll I do then?"

"I won't need help."

I had to refrain from rolling my eyes. "Are you going to tell me that Santa's sister always comes back? Because that platitude hasn't worked out so well this week."

"Nick's coming back," Lucia said. "He's just hit a bad patch on the road."

A very unmirthful laugh escaped my lips. These Santa-landers were cracked in the head. "He's marooned in Greenland. He had to fly forty miles just to make a phone call."

"See? He's resourceful."

"He could be sick himself and just not telling us," I said.

"Hard to fly forty miles when you're not feeling well."

"Right. So if we don't hear from him, I'll be worrying that he's incommunicado on account of illness."

She shook her head at me. "Put some more brandy in whatever it is you're drinking. You need to calm down and stop worrying about catastrophes that haven't happened until you've dealt with the problem right in front of you. You over-think. It's exhausting."

I folded my arms. As much as I hated to admit it, she made a good point. I needed to find other ways to contribute to the relief mission. "Okay, I'll round up blankets, food . . . and what else?"

"Call Doc Honeytree and ask him what he thinks he'll need. That should take priority."

Now that I had my marching orders, I headed for the door. Before leaving the room, though, I turned back to her. "Thank you for taking the lead on this. It's brave of you to go out there."

She looked puzzled. "It's not a trip to the moon, April. Just a sleigh ride to Greenland."

She said it like a flying sleigh ride to Greenland was no bigger deal than a quick jaunt into Christmastown. Piece of cake.

If that were really the case . . .

"Are you sure you don't want me to come along?" I asked.

"Oh yes—very sure," she said with such deadpan certainty that I had to laugh.

Chapter 14

Readying the relief sleigh made for a long, exhausting night. What kept me awake was the hope that our work would bring comfort and a message of love and support from Santaland to Nick and his stranded crew. Yet as I gathered blankets and other items from the supply list Doc Honeytree gave me, I had a hard time believing blankets could possibly keep the team warm in what were probably flimsy tent shelters in Greenland.

Then I remembered that Christmastown had two wild elves in residence. Wild elves came from the Farthest Frozen Reaches and were expert icehouse builders. After consulting with Lucia, it was decided that room on the sleigh should be made for Ham and Scar. Lucia would go into Christmastown first thing in the morning and ask them herself. The iceball season opener would either have to be postponed or Crinkles would have to do without his star players.

I told Jingles not to bother bringing me coffee in the morning. I thought this would allow me to sleep in, but I had a restless night, troubled by nightmares of strangers wandering lost in the snow, sneezing reindeer, and menacing antlers. Most strangely, the image of Lucia loomed large in these visions. When I finally gave up trying to sleep, dim December light was peeking through the window shutters, and Lucia's voice rang clearly in my head: *"Deal with the problem right in front of you."*

She'd been talking about the relief mission, but this credo could also apply to the puzzle of what had happened to Eric in that hospital. Who were the obvious suspects? The people who had the means, and the motive. I didn't yet know Sam and Elaine enough to suss out what motivated them, but I did know that to have the means and opportunity the killer had to have access to that drug cabinet in the hospital. They must have been there sometime after I'd left to go to Tiffany's tea shop. That narrowed down the possibilities quite a bit, didn't it?

I dressed warmly and quickly and hurried downstairs to try to rustle up some coffee. Voices coming from the breakfast room gave me hope that I'd still find some coffee left in the urn on the sideboard.

As I walked into the room a flash of light blinded me. Belatedly I raised my arm to shield my eyes. The momentary blackness was temporary, and accompanied by a click and a two-second metallic whir. "What the heck?"

Elaine and Sam were seated at one end of the room. Elaine was at the head of the table, her booted foot sticking straight out to the side, her torso slumped in the wooden dining chair. She was messing around with some sort of toy. A Rubik's Cube?

"He's going to be a nuisance with that thing," she told me, nodding over a small pile of torn wrapping paper at Sam, who was holding a Polaroid camera. He smiled and held out the photo he'd just taken. The instant photo didn't have the best color—I was tired, but my face shouldn't have been *that* pale.

I sank into an empty chair, staring at the picture. Where had the camera come from?

"Oh yes, join us," Elaine said without enthusiasm, her attention focused on trying to get the colored squares to be uniform on each side of the cube.

Sam grinned like a kid with a new toy—which I supposed he was. "Isn't this fun? I didn't know these cameras even existed anymore."

"Who gave it to you?" I asked.

"Santa Claus!"

I sputtered in confusion before managing, "No, really. Who?"

"Okay, it was some kid in a Santa hat. I guess he's the bell-boy or something. When we sat down to breakfast, he and the housekeeper came in and put these presents by our places."

I swallowed. Christopher. He must have gotten his hands on some discontinued items. "Fun," I said, with less enthusiasm. We now had a photographer running around with an actual camera and film. He'd be able to take pictures of everything.

For some reason I hadn't thought to warn Christopher about the visitors. A key oversight.

I tried to think positively. Maybe the gifts weren't entirely a bad thing. For once the visitors seemed absorbed in something besides their own unfortunate predicament. They weren't asking about phones and Wi-Fi, at least. I just needed to think of a way to get ahold of all the pictures taken with the camera before Sam left Santaland.

And when would that be? More important, how would it be accomplished?

Crawling back to bed started to seem so appealing. Then I remembered that I was supposed to be the owner of this so-called hotel.

"Did you have a good breakfast?" I asked politely.

"Sure did," Sam said. "Very tasty scones. I told the waitress that the chef could open a store, and she said that the woman ran a tea shop in town. I'd like to go there."

Chef Tiffany? Jingles must have given the castle's real elf chef, Felice, a vacation for the duration of Sam and Elaine's stay. But Tiffany still had her business in town to tend to. She would probably be dashing out—if she hadn't already.

Soft footsteps approached from the direction of the servants' corridor. Audrey Claus appeared in the maid's uniform Madame Neige had provided, which looked like something a character in an Agatha Christie story would wear. The dress was high necked, black with a white collar and apron. She wore black stockings and shoes, a white cap on her head, and—when she spied me sitting at the table—a surprised expression.

"Oh, April! Hey!" she said, sounding very un-servantlike.

"Good morning, Audrey. Are there any scones left?"

"Oh god. More than you can shake a stick at." My steady stare finally penetrated, and she added, "I mean, yes ma'am."

"You can bring a plate for me," I said. "I'll pour my own coffee." I stood and headed to the sideboard.

"As long as I'm making the trip," Audrey asked the others, "does anybody else want anything from the kitchen?"

I sighed as I poured coffee. At least she *looked* like a model maid.

"I'll have another of those delicious cinnamon scones," Sam said.

Audrey glanced at Elaine, but Elaine kept twisting squares on her Rubik's Cube.

"I was never smart enough to figure those things out, either," Audrey said.

Elaine gave her a hairy eyeball stare.

"Thank you, Audrey," I said.

"Oh—okay." She backed out of the room.

"The employee situation must be *really* dire here," Elaine said.

"No kidding," Sam said. "I've never seen a place where nurses moonlight as hotel maids before."

Heat crept into my face. Another stupid mistake. Audrey had spent so little time at the hospital that I'd totally forgotten that Sam might have seen her there. She'd only done a partial shift the morning after they arrived. But of course Nurse Cinnamon told me that Sam had been awake and alert that morning.

"Audrey's not really a nurse," I explained quickly.

"She's not much of a maid, either," Elaine said. "I had to ask her three times to bring me some butter."

"She just volunteers at the infirmary sometimes."

"Man, this sucks," Elaine said.

"I beg your pardon?" Was she talking about the hotel service?

"This so-called toy annoys me." She tossed the Rubik's Cube onto the wrapping detritus on the table. "Who came up with that stupid thing?"

"Mr. Rubik?" Sam guessed.

"Thanks for the information, Mr. Smarty Pants." She puffed out a breath. "What are we going to do today? Didn't Leopold say we could take a sleigh ride or something?"

"No!" I said.

At my outburst, the two looked at me with startled eyes.

There were only two sleighs at the castle now: mine, and Nick's everyday sleigh. I needed mine for errands, and the latter was being loaded up to go to Greenland. Lucia and her crew would be taking off soon, too—so it would be bad to have the visitors wandering around outside.

"What I mean is, the weather forecast looks terrible today," I explained. "They're predicting snow squalls. You don't want to get trapped in one of those in an open sleigh."

"Never mind." Elaine fitfully reached for her cube again. "Going outside would just make my toe hurt."

"Maybe we could find some other games for you to play," I suggested. "You like chess, I believe."

"Sure," Sam said, unable to hide his lack of enthusiasm. "Losing builds character."

"In that case," Elaine said, "you're a paragon."

As they sniped, I finished my coffee. My scones hadn't arrived, but knowing Audrey, I might as well be waiting for the Great Pumpkin. For all I knew, she'd already fled the castle the way she'd bolted from the hospital after an hour.

I stood. "I'll have Pamela arrange some indoor activities for you." On my way out, a muttered "Oh goodie" trailed after me.

Where was Pamela? Where was *everybody*? I finally had to ask Salty when he handed me the reins to the sleigh. Wobbler was pulling today.

"Probably down at the runway, watching the relief sleigh take off," he said.

So soon? Then again, it was probably almost eleven o'clock. Staying up so late had made me lose track of time.

"That's where we'll go first," I informed Wobbler. "And then the Christmastown Constabulary."

I picked up the reins and waited. We didn't move. "What happened to self-motivation?"

His flanks puffed out, then deflated. "Oh, I don't know. I feel kind of silly. I was looking at Cannonball today. He went to the Dasher-Habber yesterday and bought a girth guard."

I looked at the windows to make sure neither Sam nor Elaine was looking out at us. "A *what*?"

"A corset that holds his innards in like a sausage casing. He thinks it makes him look more toned up so that he'll attract a doe at the Hop-n-Snort. But the truth is he's just kidding himself."

I frowned. "It's up to Cannonball to decide how he wants to look. What does this have to do with you?"

"But what if my resolutions are just as pointless? I've been anxious my whole life. What's going to be different this year?"

"It's about attitude, Wobbler. You have to believe in your-self and not let fear stand in the way of the reindeer you want to be."

"I guess you're right." He heaved a heavy breath.

This was not the moment for a reindeer existential crisis.

"Come on," I said. "We need to get moving. I'll say the words with you."

We "On, Wobblered" together and shot off down the path.

At the new runway, no crowd had gathered. The emer-gency mission had not been publicized. Pamela was there, and Christopher. Salty and Cannonball had come, too. Can-nonball did look a bit squeezed in his girth guard, I couldn't help noticing.

Nick's second-best sleigh was jam-packed with bundles of blankets, cords of firewood, and crates of provisions. Perched atop this mountain of provisions were Dr. Snowball the vet, Doc Honeytree, and the two wild elves. Ham and Scar were in their homespun wool tunics and wore no head coverings. Their shaggy hair seemed to provide enough warmth.

I was so grateful to them all, especially to Doc Honeytree. "You'll take good care of Nick?" My voice looped up with anxiety as I spoke to him. "I mean, if anything goes wrong with him. Which I hope it won't."

He looked at me as if I'd lost my mind. "What do you think I'm flying out there for—a vacation?"

Someone touched my arm. It was Pamela, bundled in a pink wool coat with a faux fur–lined hood. She handed me a steaming go-cup. "Hot cocoa," she said. "It sounds as if you could use some."

I took a sip and immediately warmth and the magic of cocoa rippled through me. "Thank you."

"Brave face, April," she admonished me.

Christopher joined us. "Hi, Aunt April." His face was a

mask of frustration. "Can't you talk to Aunt Lucia? She says I can't go to Greenland."

"You're thirteen," I said.

"So?" His chin jutted forward. "I'm a Claus. I belong on the sleigh instead of wild elves."

"Get back to me when you can build an igloo."

His full cheeks reddened. "But I'm going to be the next Santa."

"Exactly. We don't want our future Santa to be stranded, too," I said. "Besides, haven't you played Santa enough for one day?"

"What do you mean?"

"Those gifts you gave to the visitors."

"It was just old stuff. Granny said she overheard the man saying he wished he had his camera."

"I thought it would be a nice gesture," Pamela explained. "Little gifts from the hotel."

"It was nice, except now we've got a nosy guy running around with the ability to photograph his experiences in Santaland when we agreed that we didn't want word of this place getting out into the world. Why do you think we've gone to so much trouble to mask Christmastown from their eyes?"

Understanding dawned in Christopher's eyes. "Oh."

"One old-fashioned camera shouldn't cause too much trouble," Pamela said.

"It might not—as long as we can keep the pictures from getting out." I turned back to Christopher. "Here's your chance to redeem yourself. You need to keep an eye on Sam and make sure none of those Polaroids leave with him."

Christopher gaped at me. "How?"

"You'll think of something, I'm sure."

Pamela touched my arm again. "The sleigh's about to take off."

I hurried over to Lucia, who was making a last inspection of the harnesses. Quasar was in front of the eight other reindeer on the team. Though his lameness in one leg and his unfortunate fizzling nose had put him in the misfit category, neither of his defects affected his ability to fly.

"Keep in touch as much as you can," I told Lucia.

"We've seen how that works where Nick is." My disappointment must have shown, because she added, "But I'll do my best."

The same frustration that Christopher felt now coursed through me. "I wish I were going with you. Tell Nick I . . ." A glob of emotion in my throat prevented me from finishing.

"You can tell him yourself in a few days," she said with her usual gruffness. "Just try if you can to figure out how to get rid of the uninvited guests before then. That would be a huge Christmas gift to all of us."

It might also qualify as a Christmas miracle. So far I hadn't been able to work out how we were going to extract those two from Santaland and guarantee that they wouldn't go home and blab about Santaland to the world. But there had been a lot of distractions.

"Okay," I said.

Lucia climbed aboard the sleigh and took up the reins. The wild elves, Ham and Scar, seemed to have broken into the supply crates already and were gnawing on walrus jerky, making peculiar wild elf noises as they chewed—groans of delight mixed with the odd belch.

Suddenly I was full of doubts. Those two could eat their way through crates of food before the sleigh reached Nick and the others. Were we right to send them along?

"Maybe we should have put Nurse Cinnamon on the sleigh instead."

Lucia shook her head. "Will you stop worrying? It's just a short hop over there. What can go wrong?"

As if in answer to her question, one of the reindeer sneezed so violently that a wave of revulsion rippled across the whole harnessed team as the other reindeer tried to hop away from the sneezer.

"Eww!" called out the reindeer standing in front of the sneezer. "You got mucus on my rump!"

The answer came in the form of another sneeze.

Lucia hopped down from the sleigh, as did Dr. Snowball.

"You sound bad, Pearly," the vet said.

"I can make it," the reindeer protested. "I just—just—*atchoo!*"

Pearly, a reindeer of the Vixen herd, was taken out of the line.

Lucia was not pleased. "Great. Now we need to rustle up another reindeer—and I was hoping to take off while there's still light." She scanned the snow-covered field. Her gaze landed on Cannonball, who had his snout buried under some snow he'd pawed through to reach the lichen below. She squinted in confusion. "What happened to him?"

"He's wearing a girth guard."

I could see her mentally eliminating Cannonball from her list of substitutes. She sighed. "I'll have to go out to the herds on the other side of Christmastown. And these guys are ready to take off now." With a curt nod, she indicated the team. "Or I guess I could move Quasar into Pearly's spot and just do without a reindeer on point, but it's awfully handy to have a red nose at the front."

Like a headlamp.

"ON, WOBBLER!"

A jangling and the swoosh of sleigh runners against the snow grew louder as Wobbler—still attached to my small sleigh—trotted toward us.

"Reporting for duty!" he announced when he'd pulled to a stop.

Lucia gave him an up-and-down inspection.

"Are you sure?" I asked him.

Wobbler had to be terrified at the idea of taking on this job, but his knobby knees were locked so that his legs didn't tremble. "I'm able-bodied and healthy. In fact, I'm in peak condition after a month of doing calisthenics with Cannonball."

Lucia glanced over at Cannonball. She had two replacement reindeer immediately available to her. To her, apparently, the choice was clear. "All right," she said. "Let's get you harnessed to the right sleigh."

"Yes ma'am!" Wobbler could barely contain his excitement, but he did remember to turn back to me. "I'm sorry, Mrs. Claus. You'll have to ask Cannonball to accompany you on errands today."

"Don't worry about it," I said. "I'm proud of you—and grateful. Just take care of yourself."

"I will!" he said excitedly. "Would you take my picture?"

"Of course."

When the unfortunate Pearly had been led away, Wobbler stood in place on the team, and Lucia clambered back on the sleigh again.

I snapped a photo on my phone.

As soon as I was done, Pamela stepped up and handed Lucia a full thermos. "Here's some cocoa for the trip. Drive carefully."

"I will," she assured her mother.

She tucked the thermos into an oversized pocket, then made a noise between a snort and a honk to urge the team forward. Without any of the fanfare the great sleigh team had received when Nick had taken off, the reindeer galloped forward in a flurry of hooves and heavy grunts. My chest felt tight watching them all running and straining, and Wobbler and Quasar—two misfits—on the team. Lifting a fully loaded sleigh off the ground was no easy task, but by the end of the runway they were airborne. Lucia turned to us with a last curt wave.

Pamela sighed. "I wish I could have sent Nick's Christmas present to him, but Lucia wouldn't let me load it on the sleigh."

When I looked over at the snowmobile she and Christopher had driven over, I could see why. The package was very big, the size of a coat box. Certainly too big to be one of Pamela's hand-knit sweaters. Maybe it *was* a coat. It seemed odd that she would break with the sweater tradition.

"What is it?"

She gaped at me, aghast. "I'm not going to ruin the surprise." She turned to Christopher. "Come along. We need to get you back to the castle so you can keep an eye on those photographs."

"Okay." When his grandmother was out of earshot, he lowered his voice to me. "Don't get your hopes up. I already shook the boxes Granny put under the tree. They sound like clothes."

I laughed. "Someday, probably soon, you'll be grateful for new clothes."

"I'm not *that* old," he grumbled. "I don't know how grown-ups stand it. If Granny gave *me* a package as huge as the one she put under the tree for you, I'd be dying to open it."

How big *was* it? I was tempted to ask, but Christopher had already loped off to join his grandmother. Gift anxiety hit me again. I'd thought my last-minute gift idea for Pamela would be just the ticket, but on second thought it seemed sort of . . . last minute-ish. Would she notice?

Was her gift to me really huge?

Cannonball lumbered over to me as I picked up the empty harness Wobbler had left behind. "I would have taken Pearly's place," Cannonball said, "but Wobbler seemed to want to go."

"Yes, he did." He'd be talking about this adventure for years to come.

"Anyway, it's a lucky thing I'm here, what with Wobbler running off on you like that."

I nodded. I had my hybrid sleigh, so technically I didn't need a reindeer for my errands today. But I was glad for the company. Once you get used to reindeer driving you everywhere, motorized transport can feel a little lifeless.

Salty and I harnessed him up, and I set out for Christmastown.

At the constabulary, the aroma of fresh-baked cookies hit me the moment I opened the door. Ollie emerged from the kitchen holding a baking sheet filled with a batch just out of the oven. He wore an apron embroidered with the words *Baking Spirits Bright* across the bib.

"You're just in time for tea and almond shortbread," he said.

At the large dining table in the principal room of the constabulary sat Constable Crinkles, who was busy cutting tissue paper into narrow strips. I couldn't help noticing that the scissors he was using were the round-edged kind that I used in first grade. He smiled at me in greeting. "You're also just in time to help make pom-poms."

"I didn't come here for cookies and crafts," I said, but then I frowned and backtracked. "Cheerleader pom-poms, you mean?"

He held up a handful of the cut red-and-green strips and shook them. "For the Christmastown Twinklers pep squad."

"I didn't know there was a pep squad." Usually the entire spectator section seemed like a pep squad.

"There is now." His eyes widened as an idea occurred to him. "Would you like to join?"

"I'm in the pep band," I reminded him. A contingent of the Santaland Concert Band—those of us who rooted for the

Twinklers—always played at games. An equal number of band members played in support of the Tinkertown Ice Beavers.

"Shoot, I forgot." Crinkles picked up his scissors again. "Doesn't mean you couldn't make a pom-pom or two, though. It's lots of fun."

Ollie placed a plate of cookies in front of an empty chair at the table, indicating for me to take a seat. "And there's always time for a cookie."

There's Always Time for a Cookie would make a good Santaland motto, and one I would embrace wholeheartedly. I sank into the slightly too-small chair and took a bite of perfect shortbread—dense and buttery, and still warm. It didn't crumble into a sandy texture like so much shortbread I'd had before I came to Santaland.

"Get Mrs. Claus a cup of tea," the constable instructed his nephew.

"Yes sir." Ollie spun on his heel to return to the kitchen.

"I can't stay long," I protested. "I just came by to run an idea by you." Though Constable Crinkles was accustomed to my nosiness by now, I didn't like to take over investigations. At least not without giving him some warning.

"You know we've postponed our season opener," Crinkles said.

"Because of Ham and Scar?"

"Without them, the Ice Beavers would clobber us."

"Lucia says they'll be back by New Year's."

Ollie came back in with a dainty cup and saucer decorated with winter scenes.

"But to be honest, Constable, I didn't come here to discuss iceball."

Crinkles frowned. "Has something happened?"

"The murder?" I reminded him.

"Oh—that business at the hospital."

"That *murder*," I repeated.

Crinkles held up several sheets of crepe paper. "Sure you don't want to make a pom-pom while you're here?"

I took a breath for patience. "It occurred to me last night that we shouldn't overlook the most obvious suspect in Eric Lynch's murder just because Doc vouches for her."

"Nurse Cinnamon, you mean?" Crinkles's scissors stilled.

"Can you recall any other odd deaths at the Santaland Infirmary since she worked there?"

Crinkles frowned, then gaped at Ollie. "Remember Cousin Puddin? *She* died at the infirmary. Nurse Cinnamon was with her when she died."

I leaned forward. "Was there anything notable about Puddin's death?"

"Well, she never had anything wrong with her before that day."

"That is suspicious."

"I'll say," Ollie chimed in. "Suffering sugarplums, why didn't we think of this before? Never sick a day in her life, and then she just up and dies after ninety-eight years."

Ninety-eight.

I sighed. "Okay, maybe we shouldn't distract ourselves with past case histories just now. Nurse Cinnamon's alibi is that she was in the ER at the time of the murder. I want to go talk to Fuzzy, the elf who was in the ER being treated by her around the time the murder occurred."

"Fuzzy, from the Caroling Cow Dairy?" Ollie asked. "So that's what happened to him. He's our delivery elf, but he hasn't been by for two days now."

Interesting. "I think I'll go by the Caroling Cow and see why he's AWOL from delivery duty."

"That's a genius idea!" Crinkles had the bar set low to judge genius by, apparently.

"Are you coming, too?"

Crinkles eyed his stack of crepe paper longingly. "Well . . . I would, of course, but I've still got all this work to do here."

I turned to Ollie.

"And I'm supposed to go to the orphanage to make gingerbread houses this afternoon," Ollie said.

Right. What was a measly murder next to gingerbread houses and pep sticks? If someone wanted to get away with murder, Santaland during Christmas week was apparently the place to be.

But this killer was out of luck. I needed to know whether or not I had a killer hiding out at Castle Kringle, and until I did, I was going to be on the case.

Chapter 15

The Caroling Cow Dairy, a large complex of greenhouses, barns, and a factory, was about a twenty-minute drive south of Christmastown. Judging from the greeting I received, they weren't used to receiving visitors. Especially not from the Claus family.

"Fuzzy? What do you want to see him for, ma'am?" The manager of the Caroling Cow Dairy, a stocky elf with caterpillar brows beneath his cap, looked worried. "He's not in any trouble, is he?"

"Oh, no." I smiled, assuming my best Mrs. Claus noblesse oblige manner that I'd learned from Pamela. "I just want to see how he's doing. He was at the infirmary's ER recently, I understand."

"He certainly was." He breathed out a mournful sigh. "Five gallons of superior premium nog spilled across the pavement. What a waste."

"At the constabulary, they said Fuzzy hadn't been by for the past few days."

Those brows rose so high, his large ears seemed to go up, too. "The constabulary? Are you *sure* he's not in trouble?"

"No, I—"

"We sent a cleaning crew to the infirmary just as soon as we heard what had happened," he assured me.

"That was very good of you. I know Nurse Cinnamon was concerned for the safety of—"

The manager's hoot cut me off. "Nurse Cinnamon! That dragon was the one who called us. It was short and to the point—a full minute of tongue blistering."

"Really."

"She's got a temper, that one."

I bit my lip. *That* was interesting. "What did she say to you, exactly?"

"Just that we'd better get down there and clean up Fuzzy's mess or there would be some all-fired heck to pay." He ducked his head in embarrassment. "Excuse my language, Mrs. Claus—but those were her words."

"All-fired heck" didn't seem too out of bounds, given that she worried that another elf might have an accident in front of the hospital. "I'd better talk to Fuzzy."

I glanced around the factory floor. This is where the eggnog itself was made, with elves mixing up eggs and milk in stainless steel bowls. A series of vats seemed to hold the basic ingredients from the dairy cattle who were kept in special barns in back. Keeping elves supplied with eggnog was a vital concern, and the Caroling Cow Dairy was just one of many small dairies in Santaland.

"Fuzzy's still not able to make deliveries," the manager explained. "I've put him in the nutmeg room until his injuries heal."

I was shown to a small closet of a room where Fuzzy sat on a high stool and an equally high table, grating nutmeg. His bandaged hand braced the grater, which didn't seem ideal. But his ankle's being in a cast probably precluded his doing deliveries for several weeks, at least.

We'd never met, but he recognized me.

"Mrs. Claus!" Awkwardly, he started to stand up.

I held up my hand. "Stay as you are, Fuzzy. I just wanted to ask you a few questions about your visit to the infirmary the other day."

"I didn't mean to spill the eggnog," he said defensively. "It was the shoes—I wasn't used to them."

"No one's blaming you for what happened."

He looked as if he might cry. "No one except my manager here, and that crazy nurse."

"Nurse Cinnamon?" I said. "You think she's crazy?"

His eyes went wide with fear. "No, no—that just slipped out. It's an expression."

"But she seemed irritated when she was treating you?"

"Well, when she was picking glass out of my foot, she was *very* mad about the spilled eggnog and glass. Said it was going to mess up her schedule if any more elves wound up in the ER because of it."

So Nurse Cinnamon was concerned about her schedule. Was it because she didn't trust Mildred, or because she had something she needed to get done? Something like murder.

"How long did she spend tending to you?" I asked.

"All told?" He thought for a moment. "About an hour."

"And she was with you the entire time?"

He nodded—then frowned. "No, Dr. Algid set my foot. Nurse Cinnamon stepped out. She had to make a phone call, she said."

Maybe that was when she'd called the Caroling Cow's manager and given him . . . heck.

"How long was she gone?"

His lips twisted. "Fifteen minutes? Twenty?"

"Seems like a long time for a phone call." From the manager's description, the call had been blistering but brief.

"It did to me, too. After Doc finished with me, I was hoping Nurse Cinnamon would come back and give me a painkiller."

"She didn't?"

"She came back eventually, but all I got was a ginger tablet." He shrugged. "I guess it helped. I'm fine now—only I don't think they're going to trust me with deliveries again for a while. I'll be grating nutmeg till doomsday."

If Nurse Cinnamon's call to the manager of the Caroling Cow was only about a minute long, that left up to fifteen minutes or more for her to be absent from the ER. Could she have used that time to run upstairs, murder Eric, and then run back down again?

It was possible, but why would she have done it?

"Did you see anyone else at the hospital that day?" I asked.

"Well, there was another elf just arriving sitting down on the waiting bench when I left. She wanted to be seen for a sprained arm."

That was probably Juniper. I knew she didn't kill anyone.

"And no one else?"

"No one." He shook his head, but stopped when something occurred to him. "Except for Mrs. Claus."

That startled me. He wasn't talking about me. "You mean Santa's mother?"

"No, the other one. The tea lady."

Tiffany—the third Mrs. Claus. *She* was at the hospital that afternoon after I left her tea shop?

"You saw her go into the infirmary?"

He nodded. "Both in and out. She was leaving just as I got called into a treatment room."

I didn't like this. At all. "How long was she there?"

He tapped a nutmeg in thought. "About five minutes?" he guessed. "Not more than ten."

Why hadn't Tiffany told me about this?

★ ★ ★

Tiffany's eyes widened to the size of dessert plates. "You can't think that I had anything to do with the murder. I didn't even know the man."

She didn't know him, but I'd thought back on our conversation the afternoon just before he died, and a few things troubled me.

Her jaw dropped. "You *do* suspect me."

We were in the back room of Tea-piphany where Tiffany was piping custard into small cream-puff shells in preparation for an afternoon tea at Mrs. Firlog's house. From a little boom box on a counter, the Drifters were singing their bouncy doo-wop version of "White Christmas," which was jaunty, jarring music to discuss murder by. Right now, my sister-in-law looked like she wanted to squirt some of her custard in my face.

"Of course I don't suspect you," I said. "I mean, not really. But you did say that you sometimes thought you should do something awful that would get you booted out of Santaland forever."

Murder would fit that bill nicely.

"And you thought that would mean that I would kill someone? For no reason?"

"Well, you also said Eric looked like some skater who dumped you for an ice dancer."

A laugh bleated out of her. "Right—that would be a *great* reason to kill someone."

It did sound silly. I should have thought twice before coming here. But I'd been so surprised by what Fuzzy had told me, and so puzzled over Tiffany's not saying anything to me about her visit to the hospital that day. "But you can see why I would have to ask you about it, after Fuzzy told me he saw you there and once I remembered the things you said."

Now she just looked annoyed. "You've conveniently forgotten that in the next breath I told you that I never would get myself expelled from Santaland, because of Christopher."

She was right. I had forgotten that part.

"Why didn't you mention you were there, though? You had to know that I would be looking into the murder."

"Honestly? I just didn't think of it." She shrugged and inserted the tip of the pastry bag into a cream puff shell. "I'll admit that when I went over to the infirmary, I intended to get a look at the man who looked like Tommy Zane. But once I got there everything seemed so odd, I was in and out in just a matter of minutes. I was in a hurry to get to Peppermint Pond and set up for *The Nutcracker.*"

"Did you notice anything while you were there?"

"Yes—there was eggnog everywhere and the entrance was closed. So I had to go around to the side and enter through emergency. Then, when I did get to the main wing, it felt so quiet and deserted. Mildred was asleep and looked so knack-ered that I decided not to wake her. So I just dropped off my scone box next to a pile of fruitcakes and left the way I came."

"Mildred was asleep the whole time you were there?"

"I wasn't there more than two minutes, but yes, her head was down on the desk. I could even hear her snoring."

"Did you see Nurse Cinnamon?"

She shook her head. "No. I assumed she was down in the ER. There was an elf waiting to see someone."

"What did the elf look like?"

She frowned, trying to recall. "He wore a green coverall and matching cap, and the most ridiculous-looking pair of sneakers."

Fuzzy.

"And you didn't see anyone else?"

"No. Honestly." But even as she said that last word, more color rose in her cheeks, and she laid the bag down on her polished butcher block worktable. "Except that I did look in on Eric Lynch."

"You saw him? And you didn't mention that?"

"There was nothing to mention. Like you said, I wanted to see if he really resembled Tommy Zane."

"And?"

"Of course not. Tommy Zane was eighteen. This was a grown man. With a neck beard."

"What was he doing?"

"Nothing, of course. He was asleep." She bit her lip. "I never saw Tommy Zane asleep."

A terrible thought occurred to me. "Are you sure he was asleep?"

She lifted her shoulders. "I guess. He didn't hear me when I pushed open the door to his room and—" Her eyes went wide and her face blanched. "Oh no. Do you think he was dead?"

"I don't know. Could you tell if he was breathing?"

"How should I know? He was just lying in bed. I glanced once at him and then left when he didn't wake up . . ." She groaned. "I shouldn't have gone there. It was stupid."

"No—I'm glad you did. You might have been the last person to see him alive."

"Or dead." She swallowed. "I think I might be sick."

I tried to mentally retrace her steps. "So you went in through the side, passed through the hallway where Fuzzy was waiting, then entered the main building of the infirmary." At her nod, I continued, "You saw Mildred snoring, put down your box, peeked into Eric Lynch's room, and then left."

"No, I went to Eric's room first. If he was awake I was going to offer him a scone." She flushed again. "As an ice-breaker."

"But he was asleep—"

"Or dead."

"—and then you saw Mildred at the reception, also asleep, and decided just to leave your box on one of the trolleys, next to the fruitcakes."

She nodded. "There was a box from Puffy's All-Day Donuts there, too."

Something was scratching at the back of my mind. "And that was it?"

"To be honest, I was preoccupied with the Tiny Gliders performance—in fact, I was kicking myself for being so stupid as to try to talk to Eric Lynch at all. It was something a teen-age girl would do."

"And then you left the way you came in."

"That's right."

I nodded.

Her lips twisted. "So what are you going to do now?" she asked. "Ask Constable Crinkles to slap me in the pokey?"

I waved a hand. "No. Anyway, the constabulary is the last thing you have to worry about this moment. If he arrested Jack the Ripper, Crinkles would probably just put him to work making pom-poms."

She almost smiled then, but stopped herself and focused a serious gaze on me. "What I said before about wanting to leave Santaland . . . you know that's not true."

"I understand being homesick for another place, Tiff." I reminded her, "*I'm* the one who still goes back to Oregon every summer."

"It's just this time of year." She blinked back tears. "Usually I think I'm dealing pretty well with Chris being gone forever. But Christmas is hard."

"I know." I gave her a hug.

The holidays were difficult for everyone wrestling with grief. But how much harder was it when the person you were grieving had been Santa? By all accounts, too, Chris had been every inch the perfect Santa—"born to don the suit," as they say in Santaland—larger-than-life, jolly, and popular with everyone. Nick had struggled to fill his late brother's boots, which he would be doing until Christopher stepped into them in eight years and assumed his rightful place as Santa.

If Tiffany felt Christmas melancholy, it was possible that Pamela did, too. My mother-in-law had been a widow for longer, but did that kind of grief ever go away completely? I doubted it.

Maybe that was why Pamela had felt like staying in her room this past week. If that were the case, maybe we had the strangers at the castle to thank for snapping her out of it.

My phone vibrated in my pocket. I was coming to dread texts.

I pulled it out and read a message from Claire.

Emergency meeting at the Scoop. Jake has idea for getting rid of our unwanted visitors.

Chapter 16

The Santaland Scoop was located on Mistletoe Lane, which for Christmas this year was decorated with arches wound with white lights, fir boughs, and—of course—mistletoe. The effect was magical, and elves in sneakers, puffy coats, wool knit beanie caps, and earmuffs stopped to take selfies of themselves and their significant others kissing. They were so cute, I couldn't find it in my heart to remind anyone that cell phones and cell phone cameras were verboten at the moment. Besides, the stranger danger was halfway up Sugarplum Mountain now, safely installed in Castle Kringle.

Christmastown was secure. For the moment. But how long could I keep two people confined to the castle?

I was surprised that the Santaland Scoop still appeared closed from the outside, with shades drawn. It wasn't like Claire to remain shuttered while she was in town.

Inside the Scoop, though, the lights were on, Eartha Kitt was crooning "Santa Baby," and Butterbean was back in his uniform and behind the counter, busily making milkshakes.

Two of the Scoop's bistro tables had been pushed together to form a makeshift conference area. Claire and Jake sat next to each other. Juniper was there and greeted me with a cheery hello and a wave of her good hand.

The display freezers were still mostly empty. I looked longingly for the salted caramel ice cream that I'd been craving since Claire had gone to visit Jake's family.

"No salted caramel," Claire said. She knew me. "It's limited selection until we can make enough ice cream to restock."

"How long will that be?"

"A day or two?" she guessed. "But Butterbean's whipped up milkshakes for everyone."

From the other side of the counter, Butterbean pushed forward two tall glasses. "Eggnog or peppermint?"

There was no question. "Peppermint."

I narrowed my eyes on him. Something was different. The top of his head came almost to my shoulders. "Did you grow?"

He bobbed excitedly. "I got Walnut's elfevators."

I leaned over the counter to peer down at the platform sole his shoes had been buckled onto. "Are those stable?"

"Once you get used to them. I've only fallen twice this afternoon."

More potential business for the ER.

I carried my milkshake over to the tables and sat next to Juniper.

"How's your wrist?" I asked her.

She smiled. "Much better now that I have a medicinal eggnog milkshake."

I looked around. "Who else is coming?"

"This is it," Claire said.

"Shouldn't we get Constable Crinkles over here, or the mayor, or Algid?"

Claire looked puzzled. "This doesn't have anything to do with them."

I begged to differ. The visitors posed an existential threat to Santaland. Unless I misunderstood what we were doing here. "What is this plan you mentioned?"

"Not sure," Claire said. "Jake didn't want to lay it out before you got here."

I sat down at the table. "Well, I'm here and I'm milk-shaked, so lay it on me."

I expected that statement to bring at least a quirk of a smile from the laconic detective. It did not.

"I know a snow witch who can help us," he said.

The statement was met by a moment of stunned silence—at least from Claire and me. Juniper continued to suck on her milkshake straw as though nothing bizarre had just been said.

"A snow witch," I repeated, unable to keep the skepticism out of my voice. After a few years in Santaland, I was accustomed to a level of the supernatural that in my former life would have made my head explode. Snow witches were entirely new to me, though.

"I've never heard of a snow witch," Claire said.

"Understandable," he said. "They don't come down from the crags very often."

"Uh-huh." I couldn't help shooting a glance at Claire to see if she found this as odd as I did. Her arched brows practically brushed her scalp.

"And this is supposed to help our situation here how?" she asked Jake.

"Our large sleighs are off in Greenland," he pointed out. "A trip out of Santaland would be difficult for a snowmobile, especially in treacherous weather, and slow and equally hazardous for a reindeer team pulling a small sleigh. Unless they could fly."

"Flying reindeer would give Sam and Elaine a big tipoff about where they've been," I said.

Jake nodded. "Exactly. A snow witch might be able to fix that problem and get these people back to where they came from."

I struggled to see how. "Teleport them, you mean?"

"Something like that." His lips twisted. "Maybe. We'd have to ask."

Maybe. I couldn't believe I was even considering this possibility. "Have you ever talked to one of these snow witches?"

"Sure. There's an old crone up on Mount Myrrh I've dealt with a few times during the course of an investigation. She'll help us if she's able."

"How can you be so sure?" Claire asked.

"One time I rescued her daughter from a snow monster's lair." He shrugged as if this were all just part of a day's work. "She said if there was anything I could ever do for her . . ."

"What's this witch's name?" Claire asked.

Jake frowned. "It's something unpronounceable. Elves who know her just call her Imelda."

I supposed it was worth a shot.

"Can I go see her?" I asked.

"I don't recommend it. She lives up on Mount Myrrh, and she doesn't particularly like uninvited guests dropping by. If you don't watch out you can find yourself hexed into a lemming or woolly bear moth before you even finished knocking."

Claire crossed her arms. "I don't like this."

Juniper spooned an unblended blob of ice cream out of her glass. "I think it's a good idea. Snow witches are supposed to have awesome powers. Some of them can even change their own appearance so that they look can look like anything—an animal, a tree, or a beautiful maiden." She frowned. "Of course, they've also been rumored to turn elves to ice."

That last bit did nothing to soothe Claire's worries. "So how do you propose to summon this snow witch?" she asked Jake.

"I'm going to find her myself and bring her back."

"*Now?*" She gaped. "We just got back from there."

"Someone has to go in person, and I'll have the best chance of getting Imelda to come back with me."

Hysterical laughter burbled out of Claire. "Really? You'll just walk up to this old crone who can turn you into a caterpillar or an ice cube?"

"I told you, she knows me." He stood up. "I just wanted to get the thumbs-up from April. I'll be on my way."

"*Now?*" Claire's voice looped up. "Like, *right now?*"

Juniper and I exchanged uncomfortable glances. Personally I was all for Jake leaving ASAP, but I didn't want to side against Claire.

"Why wait?" Jake asked, pushing in his chair. "I'll do my best to bring Imelda back," he promised me.

"Thanks."

He only stopped to give Claire a kiss on the cheek on his way out. Unresponsive, Claire watched him go. When the door closed behind him, however, she let her fury flag fly.

"That's *just* what I mean. What business do I have being involved with an iceman who runs off to consult snow witches?"

In her quietest voice, Juniper said, "It *is* for the good of Santaland."

Claire stalked back behind her counter. Butterbean scrambled to get out of her way and lost his balance on his high shoes. He disappeared for a moment.

"Okay, forget him." Claire drummed her hands on the counter. "I need to get these freezers filled up so we can open soon. What flavor should we make next? Salted caramel?"

"I love salted caramel," I said. I wasn't sure she was in any shape to make ice cream, though.

Her fingers were still beating an angry rhythm on the counter. "Salted caramel and maybe gingerbread cookie dough."

Butterbean had resurfaced a healthy distance down the counter from her. "I'm on it."

Claire started dragging ingredients out of the pantry to make gingerbread cookie dough. It was the noisiest cookie prep ever.

Juniper and I sucked uneasily on our milkshakes. Juniper cleared her throat, groping for small talk to fill the awkward void. "Did I tell you that I taught Dave to fetch?"

Dave was her pet rabbit.

"That's amazing," I said.

"Well, he's the best." She smiled. "There's nothing like having a pet when you live alone."

Claire heaved a bag of flour onto the counter, and then, with a muffled curse, she yanked her Santaland Scoop apron off and tossed it on a wall peg. She reached under the counter and grabbed her purse. "Butterbean, you're in charge."

"I am?" The elf blinked. "Till when?"

"Till I get back from climbing Mount Myrrh to see some crazy old crone."

Juniper and I locked surprised gazes.

"I want to see these freezers fully stocked when I get back," Claire told Butterbean.

"Yes ma'am."

She headed for the door.

"Are you sure you want to do this?" I asked her. "You just came back from the Farthest Frozen Reaches, and you were miserable there."

"I came back because I wanted some alone time with Jake, apart from his crazy relatives. But now it appears that to get alone time I'm going to have to trek up Mount Myrrh to make sure he's not hexed out of my life." She reached for the knob, but turned back to me. "If I'm not back in five days, it probably means I'm a toad in a jar in this witch's cave. I've split the ice cream shop between you both in my will."

"Good luck," Juniper and I called out.

After Claire had slammed the door on her way out, Juniper leaned back in her chair and sighed.

"I think that's so romantic. She must really love him."

I nodded. "She was still wearing that tooth bracelet."

It was sometimes hard for me to square Claire from our carefree single days to the smitten one-iceman woman she'd become. I hoped that this trip up Mount Myrrh didn't doom their relationship.

Juniper leaned forward and took another tug on her shake. "You know I've never been out of Santaland? I'd love to go somewhere exotic."

"I wouldn't call Mount Myrrh exotic."

She nodded toward a basket of fruit that was a smaller version of the ones Audrey Claus had been dropping off all over. "It doesn't have to be Mount Myrrh. What about Florida or someplace like that? Can you imagine being somewhere you can just pick the fruit off trees, and they aren't even in a greenhouse?"

After a December like the one we'd had, it was hard to imagine that a tropical world still existed.

Juniper sighed. "And to think, Claire and Jake wouldn't have met if she hadn't come up here to visit you."

I looked again at that fruit basket. What was it reminding me of?

"Maybe if I went to visit you in Oregon, I'd fall in love with someone," Juniper said.

"Huh." Something about that citrus fruit set off an odd scratching at the back of my mind. I couldn't place it.

"Or maybe it would just change *me*," Juniper continued. "Traveling gives you a different air. A *je ne sais quoi*. Once you've seen a little of the world—well, it's like sugared crystals on a sugarplum."

I squeezed my eyes shut, trying to remember. I couldn't

recall seeing a fruit basket on the hall trolley of the infirmary when I was talking to Mildred before I left to meet Plummy at Tiffany's. But there was definitely one there when I came back after Mildred texted me. And Tiffany hadn't mentioned seeing a fruit basket when she left her scones . . .

"April?"

I gave myself a shake and tried to concentrate on what Juniper was saying, but it was difficult. A terrible suspicion was flooding through me.

"Please don't think I'm begging an invitation to Oregon," she said. "I was just using that as an example."

Could Audrey have left that basket and given Eric the fatal frankincense?

"I mean, yes, I would *love* to see Cloudberry Bay. Maybe the next time you go there, I could go, too. You and Claire have talked about it so often that I can almost picture it already. It would be so neat to see it in person, and I think I'd really love it there, don't you?"

"Of course."

But why would Audrey have done something like that? She had even less motive than Nurse Cinnamon.

"And if I went for a summer, I wouldn't mind working. I could do housework, or run errands . . ." Her voice trailed off and she asked again, "April?"

I stood up. "I need to go."

"But you haven't finished your milkshake," Butterbean said.

"I know—it's really delicious, but there's someone I need to talk to," I said, then turned to Juniper. "I'm sorry to duck out so abruptly." First Claire, now me.

"That's okay," Juniper said. "I'll see you tomorrow."

I froze. Had I forgotten something?

"The Hop-n-Snort's going to be at the Tinkertown Arena," she said.

"We can't go to the Hop-n-Snort." That affair was strictly for reindeer.

"The Swingin' Santas are playing, and you know how loud they are. A lot of elves are planning sleigh parties outside the arena."

"Cannonball is counting on attending. We could all go over together." I shrugged my coat back on and wound my scarf around my neck. "I'll give you a buzz tomorrow."

Outside, I found Cannonball practicing a few dance moves. When he spotted me coming up the sidewalk, he stilled self-consciously.

"Castle Kringle," I told him.

"Yes, ma'am," he said.

This time I remembered to activate the hybrid motor before Cannonball pooped out. It also made the trip much quicker. I directed him to the side portico and hopped out so that I could take the back way to the kitchen without risking being seen by the two visitors. From the corridor to the kitchen, I could hear the sounds of clinking china. Dinner hour.

But I didn't see Audrey anywhere. She wasn't in the kitchen.

I crept down the corridor to the swinging door that led to the dining room. It was closed, but I could hear Sam and Elaine talking.

"I'm telling you, they've moved."

"They're snowmen. Snowmen don't move."

"Look out the window—they're not in the same places they were last night."

I touched the door lightly, intending to crack it open just enough to peek inside, when it swung violently toward me. I jumped back just in time to avoid getting smashed in the face.

Holding a tray of used dishes aloft, Jingles scowled at me.

He was wearing his new "Leopold" uniform: a burgundy coat with tails, snowy white shirt, burgundy tie, and black pants. He looked very elegant. Elegant and annoyed.

His voice lowered to a hiss. "What are you doing skulking in the servants' corridor?"

"Looking for Audrey."

"You're not the only one. She just up and said she had to leave tonight and I'm having to serve at table." He shook his head. "It's hard to get fake help these days."

"Did Audrey say where she was going?"

"It's not for me to ask a Claus her business."

I drew back. "You always ask me."

"Well, yes, *you*," he said, as if this were a given.

"Okay, I'm going to try to find her."

He tilted his head. "Why? What has she done?"

"Nothing." Part of me hoped that wasn't a lie. Audrey seemed like a flake, but I didn't want her to be a murderer. Why would she be, when she was here trying to make a fresh start?

I hurried back the way I'd come in. Maybe it wasn't too late to catch Cannonball before Salty unharnessed him.

Sure enough, I was able to flag down the reindeer halfway to the castle's stable. "We have one more trip to make tonight," I told him.

A few minutes later we coasted into the circular drive in front of Clement and Carlotta's house, which was outlined in tasteful white lights. When I knocked on the door, their servant Baubles answered the door. He was wearing a little human suit with a clip-on tie. I guessed it was probably something Clement had worn when he was ten. And the pants still had to be pinned up.

"I'm sorry, Mrs. Claus," he explained to me, "Mr. Clement and Miss Carlotta are at dinner."

"Actually, it's Audrey I'd like to speak to."

Clement and Carlotta poked their heads into the foyer from their dining room door. "For whoopie's sake, Baubles," Carlotta said, "bring Mrs. Claus into the dining room. And set another place."

"I shouldn't . . ."

"Nonsense," Carlotta said. "Come in. At least have a glass of wine."

Clement added, "You're just in time for the cheese course."

Cheese? I stepped forward. I really hadn't eaten much today besides baked goods and ice cream. That might be a solid day of eating for an elf, but a little cheese would hit the spot.

The dining room was decorated for the holidays with a red and green cloth, candles, and sprays of evergreen festooning most surfaces. The chandelier over their table let off an amber glow. Clement pulled out a chair for me and then filled up a glass of wine, while Baubles started piling cheese slices, bread, and fruit on a plate.

I looked around. "Is Audrey here?"

Carlotta smiled. "She's at the orphanage, helping build gingerbread houses."

"Oh right. I was at the constabulary earlier and Ollie said he would be there."

"Audrey's been looking forward to it all week. She's got such a big heart."

Clement nodded. "That's what our mother always said—'Audrey's so sensitive,' she'd say."

"And since we were so much older, she was always our responsibility."

Hard to imagine growing up with these two as your spare guardians.

Clement cleared his throat. "What were you doing at the constabulary?"

"Talking to Crinkles about the murder of Eric Lynch."

Clement and Carlotta exchanged distressed glances.

"So awful!" Carlotta said. "And to think, we were probably there just before it happened."

"Or maybe after," Clement piped up.

Carlotta's mouth made a moue of surprise. "I hadn't thought of that—he might have been lying there, lifeless."

"Wait." I shook my head, confused. "*You* were at the infirmary the afternoon Eric died?"

"Not for long," Carlotta said.

Clement said, "We just ran in."

"With the fruit basket."

I was so surprised, I put down my cheese knife. "You both were there?"

The two of them looked at each other—I assumed because they had no idea why I found their having been at the infirmary so surprising.

"Yes. To drop off the fruit basket."

"Audrey had shopping to do. We left her at the Cornucopia."

"Oh." I frowned, staring at the two of them. "Then you saw Mildred there?"

"Yes, although I don't think she saw us. She was asleep, poor thing."

"Snoring, wasn't she?" Clement said.

Carlotta nodded. "Yes, she snores."

"Has sleep apnea, I wouldn't be surprised," her brother said.

This fact that it had been Clement and Carlotta at the infirmary threw me for a loop. I had been so sure I had zeroed in on a likely suspect. But I knew Clement and Carlotta. These two goofballs never would have murdered anyone.

"Did you see anyone else at the infirmary?" I asked.

"Not a soul," Clement said.

"What did you want to talk to Audrey about?" Carlotta asked.

I felt completely deflated. "Oh . . . nothing, really." If she was at the Cornucopia, someone would have seen her there.

"Is something wrong?" Clement asked. "You're very droopy looking all of a sudden."

Carlotta nodded at my plate. "You'd better have some of that Gouda."

"The Camembert," her brother contradicted.

Her eyes widened in surprise. "You prefer the Camembert? Do I know you at all, Clem?"

He grinned. "When it comes to cheese, I'm a sibling of mystery."

"And completely wrong," she scolded him. "That Gouda's been aged five years. So deliciously nutty!"

Deliciously nutty might be a good descriptor for these two. But homicidally dangerous? Not so much.

Chapter 17

"Mrs. Claus? Mrs. Claus?"

Jingles's urgent whisper pierced my veil of sleep. I grunted an incoherent response.

"Wake up, ma'am," he said. "We have an emergency."

That last word finally penetrated my brain. In nothing flat, I bolted from blissful sleep to waking panic. "What emergency?" I sat up in one frightened lurch. "What's happened? Is it Nick? What have you heard?"

Jingles, already dressed in his burgundy Leopold suit, stepped back in alarm. "About Santa? Nothing. I assume Lucia will call you if she has any news . . . and if she can find a Wi-Fi hotspot."

I exhaled in relief . . . until I remembered that there were other things that could be a potential source of panic. "Is it Sam and Elaine?"

"No, it's Lynxie."

I sank back against my pillows. "You woke me up and scared me half to death because of Lucia's cat?"

"I didn't mean to scare you," he said.

"My husband is trapped in Greenland with a bunch of sick reindeer and you said there was an emergency."

"An escaped wildcat in the castle *is* an emergency. What if he bites one of our visitors?"

Lynxie was supposedly a hybrid between a lynx and a housecat, but he was more the size of a lynx. After years in the castle, he still liked to lurk in hallways or behind furniture, pounce on the shins of passersby, and sink his incisors into the calves of his victims like a demented furry vampire. This was painful and terrifying for anyone, but might carry serious heath repercussions for someone recovering from a toe amputation.

I pushed the covers off me and swung my feet off the bed. "Where are Sam and Elaine now?"

"Breakfasting."

"Alone?"

"Audrey Claus is waiting at table."

"She's back?"

"Yes ma'am." His lips pursed. "I don't like to be a tattler, but she's not being very helpful. Last night Christopher managed to arrange for Sam's camera to be dropped from the upper landing to the foyer's marble floor below."

"Excellent!" I said. "I just told him to steal the photographs, but destroying the camera is even better."

"Yes, but when Audrey heard Sam complaining about his now unusable camera this morning, she told the man that she could find him a replacement."

I groaned. "We need to nip that in the bud."

"Exactly what I thought." Jingles straightened. "I took the liberty of sending Christopher back to the old toy storage to find something else that might keep him occupied. Something that doesn't involve collecting permanent photographic evidence."

"Good thinking."

"I hate to be a shirker, but I have my hands full looking after these guests. Sam was out front this morning shouting at snowmen."

I frowned. "Why?"

"The man's a lunatic," Jingles said. "He was walking right up to their faces, practically standing nose to carrot, and yelling at them to see if they'd react. Luckily Salty had warned the snowmen not to utter so much as a peep, and none of them did."

"That's good."

"But I can't keep an eye on the guests and look for Lynxie, too."

"Don't worry. I'll find him."

As soon as I dressed, I went down to the basement to begin the search. Unfortunately there was no sign of Lynxie down there in the rooms I poked into. Although, to be honest, I didn't perform the most thorough of searches. I assumed that if Lynxie were down there when I was by myself, the temptation to jump out of the shadows and sink his teeth into my leg would have been too much for the beast to resist. I managed to make it through the castle's lower level unpunctured by pointy teeth.

My intention was to work my way methodically through the castle, but after a while I realized it was pointless. If Lynxie were hiding near the guests, he would either have been spotted, or we would have heard the screams of his victims. I decided to go directly to the Old Keep.

I was no stranger to the oldest wing of the castle. It had been built many centuries ago, and abandoned in the last century after a ceiling collapse. The damage had been shored up, but rather understandably no one felt entirely safe there now. Whenever I found myself having to visit there, I tried to stay on the inner perimeter of the walls, where I supposed I would be less likely to have the roof come crashing over my head.

The Old Keep was built on simplistic lines like a medieval fortress. The structure was basically a rectangle, although there were a few chambers off to the side. I knew this because

the ceiling of one on the first floor formed a floor for an outdoor patio to the exit on the second floor above it. Thinking
that this ground-floor room might be a place Lynxie might
want to hide, I made my way over to it.

I'd never explored the room before and with just the
sconces outside lighting the interior of the small space, it felt
cold and creepy. I walked right into a cobweb and cringed as I
batted it off me, praying that the owner-occupier wasn't now
crawling on me, seeking vengeance for his destroyed home.
Hard to imagine even a spider living in this dark, frigid place,
though. When my pulse returned to normal and my eyes began to adjust, I could make out large antler racks mounted on
boards all over. Only half were hanging; the rest were leaning every which way, like a tangle of briars against the wall.
The Antlers of the Greats. I hoped the reindeer didn't know
that the antlers of their famous ancestors were stored in such a
higgledy-piggledy fashion.

I needed to speak to Nick about this. Something should
be done.

As I stood envisioning myself as the founder-benefactress
of a new antler museum, the great door between the Old
Keep and the new castle creaked open on rusty hinges.

"Oh god, look at this," Elaine exclaimed. "Dracula's castle!"

"Shh . . ."

"No one can hear us." Her walk was very distinctive—a
regular step and then the thump of the hard rubber end of the
crutch against the stone floor.

I guessed that it was Sam who had shushed her, and the
next words spoken in his voice confirmed it. "Don't be so
sure. Have you noticed how people around here watch us?"

"We were patients in the hospital. They were supposed to
watch us." She thumped further into the room. "Shame they
couldn't have watched Eric a little more closely."

"I'm not talking about the hospital. I'm talking about here

at this hotel. There's something about this place that just isn't right."

Elaine let out a groan. "Please don't mention snowmen again."

"I know what I saw," he insisted. "That night when we first arrived, that snowman was talking."

"You saw some weird decoration. One year for Halloween my neighbor had a talking skeleton that was set off with a motion sensor."

"It sure didn't seem like a talking decoration to me."

"You were delirious."

"Yeah, but—"

"What *is* this place?" Elaine asked, obviously tired of the subject of talking snowmen.

"It must be the old part of the castle."

"Why didn't they just tear it down?" Elaine wondered aloud. "I can't imagine it has much value. Look at those beams somebody put across the ceiling."

"You think that's what's keeping the roof from caving in now?"

"I think it's what someone hopes will keep it from caving in."

Suddenly I worried that their inspection would lead them to the oversized closet I was huddled in. I should have made myself known to them right away. Stepping out and greeting them now would be awkward. They would know that I'd been eavesdropping.

Also, I wasn't sure I wanted to stop eavesdropping just yet. They spoke more candidly to each other than they would in my presence. But as their footsteps came closer, I panicked.

There were no hiding places in my little room, but there was a bolted door behind me. I backed toward it and tugged at the bolt. Instead of being rusted closed as I expected, the bolt slid open with little resistance at all. I quickly opened the door and slipped outside . . . and nearly had a heart attack to find myself on an icy stone ledge overlooking Calling Bird Cliff, which the Old Keep backed right up to. A hundred-foot dead drop was mere inches away. I flattened myself against the castle wall. Mercifully, my hands found a finger hold in the stone's chipped surface.

Foolishly, I hadn't made the logical leap that if the Old Keep was next to the cliff face, an outside door might be treacherous.

So there I was, hugging as tightly as humanly possible against the stone outer castle wall. Despite the blast of cold, I was sweating bricks beneath my cashmere sweater. The heels of my decidedly ungrippy shoes were inches from a deadly fall. A breeze gusted through Calling Bird Canyon, threatening to carry me along with it. I'd left the door open a crack and now I couldn't decide what was worse—being exposed as an eavesdropper and not finding out what these two had sought out a secluded spot to talk about, or possibly crashing to the rocks below in a suitably Wile E. Coyote ending.

When a gust passed, I heard voices again and the decision was made for me. Curiosity killed the cat, and there was a good chance it might kill Mrs. Claus, too.

"This is an odd storage room."

I couldn't see her, but I could just imagine Elaine poking her head into the room. Hopefully she wouldn't notice the breeze coming from the slightly ajar door in the back.

"Bring that candle you had over here," she said.

Flattened against the wall, my ear as close to the door as I dared, I listened as Sam's footsteps moved inside the room.

Elaine thumped behind him. "You have to *light* the candle, genius."

"Oh. Right!"

A match struck and the two of them gasped in unison.

"What the hell?" Elaine said.

"Antler trophies."

"From deer?"

"Maybe reindeer."

Elaine made a clucking sound. "Look at those idiotic plaques the antlers are mounted on. Prancer the Fifth? Rudolph the Second?"

"Maybe Eric wasn't wrong," Sam said, causing a stab of fear in my chest.

"Oh please." Elaine clucked in disgust. "The people in this place obviously have a Christmas fetish, but that doesn't mean this is some sort of Santaland. It's just one of those weird Christmas villages like they have in Germany. It even looks like Bavaria, a little. Bavaria crossed with Siberia."

"I've never been to those places," Sam said. "Although I drove through Carmel, California, once in December. They decorate for Christmas in a big way." He paused. "I don't know if anyone there has a creepy Santa's reindeer antler fetish, though."

"I can't believe we're stuck in this icy hinterland—and for who knows how long," Elaine grumbled. "Another reason I'd like to kill Eric, if he wasn't already dead."

"If we hadn't listened to him, we'd probably still be back in that cave, dying of starvation. I mean, yeah, he was probably delusional—but we made it and we're fine."

"Says the man who *didn't* lose his toe."

"If I blame him for anything, it's Madison," Sam said. "He was just going to leave her."

"So was I—you can blame me, too."

"You weren't sleeping with her."

There was a hitch in the air. "Were *you*?" Elaine asked Sam.

"*Me?*" Sam's voice looped up in shock. "No. Madison and I were just friends. But she really helped me. She got me this gig."

"Yeah, that's turned out great for you." Elaine thumped her cane in frustration. "We should never have gotten on that plane. I told Eric the weather looked bad."

"Well, he's gone. No sense thinking about him now. You certainly don't seem heartbroken anymore."

"Leave my heart out of this," Elaine snapped. "What I'm concerned about is what they've done with our stuff. We can't leave until we find out."

"Maybe it wasn't found on us."

"Of course it was. Our pockets didn't empty themselves."

"Eric could have stolen it from us."

"How? That doesn't make sense. *He* was attacked."

"But we don't know when. You say you passed out in the snow. Maybe he found you before he was attacked."

There was a pause, as if Elaine were considering a new possibility. "Or maybe *you* found him."

Sam laughed nervously. "That's crazy. You can't think that *I*—" His breath caught. "What about that guy they say rescued us? He's the one who probably ransacked our pockets."

I leaned against the wall, feeling guilty. Boots *had* ransacked their pockets. Could he have stolen from them? He'd saved them, yes, but I remembered now that he seemed uneasy that night. He said he'd found the business card, and forty-two dollars. His returning the money had made it seem that he hadn't wanted to steal money. But perhaps he had found something even more valuable.

Listening to Elaine and Sam, I realized there was no perhaps about it.

"I just wish I had my phone," Sam said.

"Would you stop whining about your phone? You can buy another one."

"Easy for you to say. I'm not rich. And now I don't even have the money I was planning on getting from this trip."

There was a long silence, and I shifted, easing back toward

the door opening. They had to be communicating something in that silence. What?

"Okay, point taken," Sam said.

What point? What had I missed?

A flash of black passed before my eyes. I let out a cry of surprise and shrank back. Not that there was anywhere to go. I stumbled to the side, away from the door, and crouched defensively.

Grimstock!

Grimstock was a vulture that Butterbean had brought to Santaland by mistake during a mail-order turkey mix-up. Ever since his arrival, the hideous bird had tended to swoop in and out of my life at the strangest times. And right now was a particularly inconvenient time.

"What was that?" Elaine said from inside.

Oh no. I held my breath.

"It was outside, I think." A pause ensued, and Sam said, "Look—that door's open."

"No wonder it's so friggin' cold in here."

Footsteps and thumping hurried toward the door. I edged further away, but I needn't have bothered. As soon as the door was opened, Grimstock spread his wings and dropped his hooked beak open, releasing a menacing hiss. The big scary bird was all they saw. With his red, leathery bald head and sharp eyes, he looked like a harbinger of doom against the steep cliff drop.

Sam let out a primal scream. "It's a death bird!"

"Shut the door before it gets in."

They slammed the door and in the next moment the inside bolt dragged and chunked into a locked position.

Locking me out.

Grimstock turned to me and relaxed his wings.

"Thanks," I growled at him. "Thanks a lot."

I was talking to a bird. Of course, as I peered over the

edge of the slate ledge I was perched on, it occurred to me that the bird might be the last soul I ever spoke to.

Without so much as a hiss of goodbye, though, Grimstock flapped his wings and flew away.

Carefully, I straightened to standing and edged back toward the door. The outside handle was nothing but a pitted, rusted iron ring. Pulling it just confirmed that the weathered wood door was indeed locked, and that I was screwed. I pounded my fist against the door, but the result was just a muffled thump that probably barely penetrated into the interior. No response. No doubt the vulture had scared Sam and Elaine clear out of the Old Keep. I looked around, trying to figure a way out of my predicament.

After five minutes outside, I was freezing. I wasn't wearing a coat or gloves. My hands and feet were starting to go numb. If I didn't hurry, I might end up hobbling around without a toe or two, like Elaine.

If I had to shuffle sideways, I was more comfortable moving toward the right, but a sound to my left made me pivot in that direction. About ten feet away, seated on the ledge just at the corner, was Lynxie, blinking at me nonchalantly.

"I forgot about you," I said.

He answered with his usual grating meow, then did a quick turn and padded off out of sight, as if walking along the ledge were just nothing at all. Which for a cat it probably wasn't. As a not-very-agile human, I had to take it more slowly, creeping sideways inch by inch. I tried not to look down, but every once in a while I caught a glimpse of the deadly drop right beyond my toes. This caused a corresponding drop in the pit of my stomach.

I tried to take my mind off my immediate peril by mentally reviewing the conversation I'd just heard. Sam and Elaine were talking about something that had been taken from them. What could it have been that they were concerned about?

Something personal, or something they'd salvaged from the plane wreck? It was possible that someone on that plane could have been carrying something valuable. Money, or even jewelry.

But why would scientists take expensive jewelry with them on an arctic expedition. Money seemed more likely. And what had Eric said before he died? Something about being a billionaire.

That forty-two dollars Boots found could have been a clever attempt at misdirection, to throw us off the scent of taller money that he wasn't telling us about.

At the corner which Lynxie had navigated so deftly, I hugged the angle of the building as I edged my way around. The good news was that I was a mere ten feet or so from a place where the drop-off was not so steep. As this wall receded from the cliff, the snow-covered rock of the ground rose at a steady incline until at the end of the wall the ground met the ledge itself. Every step now led me closer and closer to safety.

"Mrs. Claus!"

I looked up. Salty stood just beyond the building in the yard between the side portico to the reindeer stables. "Mrs. Claus, let me help you!"

I held up a hand. "I'm okay."

But Salty was an elf dedicated in service to the Claus family, and he was determined to help. "I'll be right there!" He scrambled onto the ledge and started side-stepping toward me.

"That's really not necessary," I said.

He shook his head. "Glad to be of h—aaaaaahhh!"

He had seemed sure-footed, but the heel of his unfamiliar boots hit a patch of ice and shot out from under him. In horror, I watched him wheel his arms and begin to totter over the edge of the ledge.

If necessity is the mother of invention, panic must be the

mother of dexterity. I side-hopped toward the elf and just managed to grab his coat sleeve as he tumbled off.

Keeping hold of a hundred pounds of dangling elf while I myself was barely maintaining my own balance was a challenge that pampered Santaland living had not prepared me for.

"Golly doodle," Salty said, when he saw our predicament. His feet scrabbled at the side of the castle, but that just made it harder for me to hold on to him without pitching forward. My arm already ached. The initial fall to the ground wouldn't hurt him too much—it was just ten feet below his feet. But once he hit the ground, there was a good chance he would slide down the incline toward the cliff.

"Mrs. Claus!"

I glanced over. Cannonball was staring at us, panic in his eyes.

"Do you need help?"

This time I didn't hesitate. "Yes!"

I wasn't sure how Cannonball could get us out of this mess, but the reindeer plunged forward, picking his way carefully down the snowy jagged cliff with surprising dexterity. I felt sick watching him—he nearly lost his footing more than once—but I felt even more sick considering what would happen if he didn't reach Salty in time. Sweat dripped off my forehead.

"Get on my back," Cannonball instructed Salty when he was just close enough.

Salty managed to loop one leg over the animal. Cannonball then began backing up, a much more awkward, not to mention treacherous, operation than moving forward. Unfortunately, Salty had not yet let go of me. At the first hop, I toppled off the ledge. Now I found myself being held, barely, by Salty, whose short legs were only just able to straddle Cannonball's back.

"Grab hold of me," Cannonball said.

"I don't see how—"

But the moment my foot slipped on the cliff face, I lurched and grabbed hold of Cannonball's girth guard. The thing might have looked ridiculous, but right now it was saving my life. With Cannonball backing up and me holding on and scrambling with him, and Salty simultaneously hugging the reindeer's neck and keeping a grip on me, we made our awkward way back up. When we were just a few hops from level ground, the ominous sound of ripping reached my ears. I looked over to see the hook-and-eye closures of the girth guard starting to give way. *Pop-pop-pop-pop!*

Salty spotted the problem, too, and moaned in dread.

I was just a few pops away from doom. I mentally prepared a final goodbye to the beautiful world before the girth guard and I would begin the slippery slide down toward Calling Bird Cliff.

And then, in an instant, it was over. One last backward hop by Cannonball brought us all to level ground. I collapsed just as the girth guard plopped down to the snow, too. Salty slid off Cannonball's back. We were safe.

"Phew!" Salty hopped to his feet, then offered me a hand. "It's a good thing we were there to help you, Mrs. Claus."

I cleared my throat and brushed snow off me. "Yes, thanks." I was too relieved to be alive to tell my rescuer that he'd almost gotten us killed. As far as I was concerned, the real hero was Cannonball, and I turned to tell him so.

The reindeer was nuzzling his girth guard, still in a pile on the snow. "It broke," he said mournfully.

"It can be fixed," I told him.

"The Hop-n-Snort is this evening, though."

I sent Salty a pleading look. "I'll work on it," he volunteered.

I gave Cannonball a grateful hug around his neck. "Thank you so much—you saved the day."

He ducked his head modestly. "I just did what any reindeer would do."

"Well, we're lucky you were there. Otherwise . . ."

I hazarded a glance over my shoulder and shuddered. *This is what comes of eavesdropping.*

Of course, another thing also came from eavesdropping: information.

I turned to Salty. "Is my sleigh charged up?"

"Where are we going?" Cannonball asked.

"You're not going anywhere. You're going to rest up and get groomed for the big night tonight."

"But what about you?"

"Don't worry—I'm just dashing down to the constabulary."

It was only half a lie. From the constabulary I was going to set out for the outback snow drifts to have a talk with Boots Bayleaf.

Chapter 18

It took a little cajoling—as well as a personal promise to make ten spirit sticks before the iceball opening game—to convince Constable Crinkles of the need to interrogate Boots Bayleaf.

I could have gone myself to visit Boots in his remote cabin. I'd been there before, once. I didn't think the grizzled old elf posed any risk to me. But the old guy was ornery and could be tight-lipped. Constable Crinkles might seem like a joke to me sometimes, especially when he was still dressed as he was today in his Dudley Do-Right togs. But he was the elves' top lawman. His badge of office made them feel compelled to answer questions that, if posed by me, might be met with respectful yet stony silence.

When we arrived at Boots's remote A-frame log cabin, the little light the day afforded was already waning. When we knocked, from inside Boots turned on a floodlight on the porch where we stood. Above us, the front window of the second-story loft opened.

Boots poked his head out.

"What do you want?" he called down to us through snow flurries.

"To talk," Crinkles said.

"What about?"

Crinkles stamped his boots. "Couldn't we discuss that inside, over some eggnog?"

"I don't have eggnog."

Crinkles looked horrified. "Cocoa, then?"

There was more grumbling overhead, then the window slammed down. A few minutes later, Boots was ushering us into his cabin. The first floor was all one room—a combination workroom, seating area, and kitchen. The most notable feature was the large potbellied stove in the middle of the room, with a pipe that went straight up to the vaulted ceiling.

Boots was a taxidermist, and evidence of his trade was all around us: a wolf posed standing, showing his fangs. A polar bear towering in one corner on two legs. A white fox was posed on a kitchen counter. I was grateful that there didn't seem to be a work in progress at the moment.

Our host dutifully went about heating some milk for cocoa in an old copper saucepan.

"What do you want to talk to me about?" Boots asked, spooning cocoa into mugs the size of tankards.

"Mrs. Claus here has the idea that there's something you left out when you told us about finding the bodies in the snow," Crinkles said.

The grizzled elf looked up at me. "I told you exactly what happened."

"You were short a detail or two, weren't you?" I asked. "You didn't mention what you took from the strangers."

Instead of answering, he poured the heated milk into the mugs, stuck a tarnished spoon in each, and handed us each one. The constable stirred his eagerly. I was a little squicked out by the idea of eating anything in this place, to be honest. Nothing killed the appetite like the smell of formaldehyde.

"The two survivors know you took something from them," I warned Boots. "You can tell us now, or you can come back to town and tell them to their faces."

Boots tensed. "It wasn't anything worthwhile."

"So you did take something?" Uncomfortable, Crinkles turned to me. "Am I going to have to arrest him?"

Before I could answer, Boots blurted out, "You can't take me to jail for taking a few worthless rocks."

I stilled. For a moment I wondered if I was going to have to reevaluate my belief that scientists didn't carry valuable jewelry on research expeditions. "What rocks?"

Muttering, he turned and went to an old dresser that he kept downstairs for storage. "These." He ducked his head to hide his reddening face. "I *did* go through their pockets— like I said, I was just trying to find out who they were. But then I noticed that two of them had one of these weird rocks."

He handed one of the rocks to me. It wasn't a gemstone, as I'd expected, but a boring dark gray rock, each about half the size of an average brick.

Crinkles lifted on his toes to inspect it, too. "That's a rock, all right."

"Two of them?" I asked. "Which two?"

Boots frowned. "The woman and the man. The man that didn't have the antler in him."

Sam and Elaine.

"I thought the rocks had flakes of silver in them," Boots said. "But when I got them home and tried to polish one, it turned darker. Silver don't look like that. I'm pretty sure they're worthless."

"Then I wonder why they kept hold of them."

"Maybe they were fooled, too," Boots said.

Sam, maybe. But Eric and Elaine were mineralogists.

The fact that Sam and Elaine had been carrying the rocks but Eric hadn't puzzled me.

I didn't like this.

"When you took—some would stay stole—the rocks from

their pockets," I said to Boots, "you assumed they were valuable."

"I was just curious." He stubbed the toe of his elf bootie. "I wouldn't have killed for a few streaks of silver."

"You might have thought there was more, though," I said.

"If I was hoping they'd show me more where this came from, I sure wouldn't have stuck an antler in that man's back."

He had a point there.

"I save those people, and this is the thanks I get." He pushed the rocks back at me. "Take 'em back. I don't want them. What's more, I wish I'd never seen them, or those people."

Remarkable. He'd stolen from Sam and Elaine, but we left him pouting in his cabin as if *he* were the aggrieved party.

"Well, that's that," Constable Crinkles said over the whir of his snowmobile's engine as we drove back to Christmastown.

"What's what?" I asked, not getting his drift.

"Boots didn't do it."

"He might not have murdered anyone, but he stole those rocks."

"You heard him—they're worthless."

"But they rightfully belonged to the survivors."

"Unless *they* stole them."

That was something I hadn't considered. But now that I thought about it, why hadn't Sam and Elaine simply asked us about the missing rocks? Why the secrecy?

It was also peculiar that three people—two of them scientists—who were traveling through unfamiliar terrain under blizzard conditions and who were desperate not to carry excess weight kept, of all things, heavy rocks.

Crinkles indicated the burlap sack on the seat between us. "Are you going to return them to the visitors?"

"Of course." A moment later I added, "Eventually."

First I wanted to see if I could find out what those rocks were. Boots was no scientist, but he'd convinced me that they weren't silver. So what were they?

Crinkles and I parted ways at the constabulary. He made no effort to take the rocks from me, although he did load me down with red and green crepe paper to make pom-poms for the Twinklers' pep squad.

After I left him, I visited Doc Honeytree's house, hoping to find Algid. The doctor's house stood on the brow of a hill a short drive from the center of Christmastown. It was painted red and white, first aid colors, which made sense, since Doc sometimes saw patients here. Today I was more interested in the lab Algid had set up in the basement.

When Algid answered the doorbell, he looked even paler than usual. Almost as pale as Newton, the white rat who perched on his shoulder. Luckily, I was used to Newton now. The first time I'd been met at the door by those red beady eyes, I'd freaked out. Now I was more disturbed by Algid's appearance.

"What's the matter?" I asked him. "I hope you're not getting sick."

"Not sick," he corrected. "Just a little tired. I've been filling in today for both my uncle *and* Doc Snowball." He sighed. "This is the first quality time Newton and I have had in days."

"You've been filling in for the vet?" I asked.

"More reindeer have come down sick today." He shook his head. "It's hitting the Prancers hard."

"I wish we'd caught on to the reindeer flu before Nick's trip."

"It was unfortunate that we didn't. So is the fact that the Hop-n-Snort is scheduled for tonight."

I sucked in a breath. Cannonball was counting on attending. "It hasn't been canceled, has it?"

"No. But I'm going to be outside the Tinkertown arena checking reindeer for symptoms before they'll be allowed inside."

I was glad that at least some precaution would be taken to keep the Hop-n-Snort from becoming a super-spreader event.

"So you probably won't have time to take on an extra project," I guessed.

For the first time since I'd walked into the old house, he noticed the burlap bag in my hand. "What project?"

"It's a mystery I was hoping you'd solve."

I caught a glint in his eye. Maybe in Newton's, too. "Ooh, let's take a look."

He led me down over to the drop-leaf table that evidently served as a dining room table for him and his uncle. I placed the burlap bag on it and then extracted the three rocks.

"Igneous rock." Algid frowned, puzzled. "This really isn't my specialty."

"I know. But I need to identify what that shiny streak in the rocks is, and I thought you were the best person to figure it out. All I know about the rocks is what Boots told me—that the shiny stuff isn't silver."

Nose twitching, Newton crawled partway down Algid's arm to investigate. He sniffed, then ran back up Algid's arm and perched on his shoulders.

"Hm," Algid said. "Interesting."

I frowned. "What?"

"Newton doesn't like the smell of them. He says they smell like danger."

That tracked. "I think they might be the reason Eric Lynch was killed."

More curious now, Algid picked up one of the specimens and held it up to the light. "Come with me."

Newton stood on his haunches and squeaked.

"We'll have plenty of time to play Risk after the New Year," Algid promised him.

We descended to the basement.

For an elf who swore he didn't know much about rocks, Algid sure knew his way around classifying them. He set to scraping chips from the rock, weighing them, and then grinding the substance to a powder. Next he rifled through cabinets until he located a jar of clear fluid. The sizable skull-and-crossbones label on the bottle made me take two steps back.

Algid didn't seem to be concerned about safety, although he did put a pair of goggles over his eyes. "It's a very light mineral," he observed.

"Does that mean anything?"

He laughed. "Of course. Different minerals have different weights."

"I thought you didn't know anything about rocks."

"Well. I studied basic mineralogy, of course."

Of course. Who didn't?

"Luckily, what you brought me isn't hard to identify. A fool probably could have figured it out, given a little time and study."

By "a fool," I assumed he was talking about me. "I'm not sure how much time we have."

"I can understand, if you're trying to catch a murderer."

"Do you think there's anything in those rocks that someone would kill for?"

He lifted a beaker with the powder substance. "Oh yes." It almost seemed to glow in the liquid. "It's lithium."

I frowned. "You mean, like the stuff in batteries?"

"Exactly. The world is hungrier for lithium all the time, for just that reason."

I began to understand. And at the same time, I started to feel sick to my stomach. It all boiled down to money. Cold, hard greed.

"I should get going." I thanked Algid profusely for his help. "I'll let you and Newton get back to your quality time now."

He held out the burlap bag with the rocks. "Don't forget this."

How could I? They seemed to be linked to most of our troubles this week.

When I got back to the castle, the first person I ran into was Christopher, who held a box in his hands. "I found something to keep that guy Sam's mind off his missing camera."

He held out the box.

I gasped. "A Nintendo Game Boy!" Just the design of the dark blue lettering on the gray packaging stirred so many memories.

My ecstatic reaction caused a head shake. "I knew the minute I saw it that it would be one of those things old people loved."

I inspected the box. It looked in mint condition. "I haven't seen one of these in years—or even thought about it, frankly."

"I found some batteries for it and loaded it up. Maybe it'll keep him occupied."

"Thank you. I'll go upstairs and give it to Sam now." I had a few questions I wanted to ask him.

I was heading for the staircase but stopped and asked, "He *is* upstairs, isn't he?"

Christopher lifted his arms. "I don't know. I was looking for that thing."

Given how pleased I was with his find, I couldn't very well scold him for not keeping tabs on Sam.

Upstairs, Sam's door was slightly ajar. I nudged it open further to look inside. For an innkeeper to barge into a guest room was a no-no, but as a snoop I couldn't resist trying to catch Sam off guard.

But I didn't catch him. I caught Elaine, who slammed the

drawer of the bedside table so quickly that I knew she had been up to some snooping of her own.

I stepped inside. "Looking for something?"

"Uh, yes. I was searching for a notepad that the nurse at the hospital gave us. I'd jotted down some ideas for an article I might write, but I can't seem to find it. I thought Sam might have grabbed it by mistake."

It sounded like a reasonable explanation, but I didn't believe a word of it.

"Are you sure you weren't looking for a rock?"

Her eyes widened in shock. In the next moment, she crossed her arms. "So. They *were* stolen. Let me guess—the old man who found us?"

"He thought they contained silver."

"That would be peanuts next to what we found in the cave we were sheltering in."

"A mother lode of lithium." I understood now. "That's what Eric had meant when he woke up briefly and declared that he was a billionaire."

Her lips twisted. "Did he say anything else interesting?"

"No—although he mistook me for you. He said he thought I was Miss Mojito."

She laughed. "That's definitely not me. I'm not a mojito kind of gal. Madison might have been, I guess."

"Strange that Eric was already counting on the proceeds from the lithium. Boots said that he only found rocks in your pockets and Sam's."

Those sharp green eyes blinked in surprise. "That can't be. We all had them. We split them up on purpose."

"Maybe Eric dumped his for some reason."

"He wouldn't have done that."

"Sam mentioned something about Eric believing there was a North Pole Shangri-la?"

She shook her head. "Right. He was convinced that if we kept going we'd end up where Santa Claus lives."

I heard a cascade of nervous laughter and realized it came from me. "He seriously thought that?"

"You can laugh—but it got ugly. When we were in the cave and running out of food, our tempers were getting so crazy that Sam accused Eric of arranging the plane crash on purpose so that he would have an excuse to search for Santaland." She laughed. "You should have seen us. Rag-tag and starving, fighting like cats and dogs, and then suddenly we realized were staring at a seam of lithium that would make us rich."

"But it's not yours."

"Who does it belong to, then? Some indigenous people?" She waved a hand dismissively. "We can pay them off."

"That's not how things work here. The lithium will never be extracted."

She chuckled. "You're naïve. Every man on earth has a price—that's what Eric said."

"The way everyone talks about him makes Eric sound pretty ruthless."

"He is—was, I mean. But men like him have to be, don't they?"

I didn't understand. "Men like him?"

"Managers. He wasn't a top-tier scientist. His genius was vision, and selling projects. The trouble was getting him to stay focused on one. He'd get something together and convince people or institutions to invest in a project, but then the wind would shift and he'd go chasing some other butterfly. Same with relationships."

"Were other women why your marriage broke up?"

"That's a little bit nosy, isn't it?"

"He was murdered. I'm still trying to figure out why."

"Well, *I* didn't do it. Yes, our marriage broke up, but

mostly it was a problem of too many egomaniacs under one roof. Neither of us wanted to feed the other's vanity twenty-four seven. But we remained friends, and more importantly, coworkers."

She had the most bonkers worldview.

Her smiled died as she studied me. "Did you come up here to wrangle a murder confession out of me? If so, I'm sorry to disappoint you. I didn't kill Eric."

The rush I'd felt when I discovered that Eric had none of the lithium on him while Sam and Elaine did dissipated now. It didn't seem likely that they would have attacked him for two measly rocks. Of course, maybe they just didn't want a third partner in whatever they were planning for the lithium. But why would Elaine kill Eric? He knew about raising money for projects, and involved her even though their marriage had fallen apart. Whereas she didn't seem to have any respect for Sam at all.

I had to accept that the rocks weren't the smoking gun I was hoping for.

I extracted the Game Boy box from the paper bag and tossed it onto the bed. "Christopher asked me to give Sam this."

For a moment, Elaine froze in shock, her mouth agape. Then, with a gasp, she fell forward and grabbed the box. Tackled it, almost. This was the reaction I was expecting from her when I reunited her with her lithium rocks.

"Where did you find this?" Her gaze never left the box.

"My nephew dug it up."

"This was my favorite toy ever when I was a kid. *Tetris*!" Unable to resist, she opened the box and pulled out the gray-beige plastic console. It seemed laughably clunky and retro now. "It's in pristine condition!"

"Christopher put in batteries for you."

Sure enough, when Elaine pressed the power button, the little screen came to life.

"Oh wow. It's so chunky and cool—and these springy button controls. Don't you just love it?"

Within a split second, it was clear that she was lost. I could have spontaneously combusted and she never would have noticed.

Maybe she wouldn't notice a very blatant last question, either. "Tell me, do you think Sam was angry enough at Eric over Madison's death to have killed him?"

Still focused intently on the screen and her thumbs, Elaine shrugged. "Eric was maddening. I suppose he could have driven anyone to murder—even Sam."

I looked around the room. "Where is Sam now?"

"How should I know?" she said, concentrating on the tiny screen. "He went out."

That word, *out*, made my blood freeze. "Out where?"

"Exploring, he said. He's got his own wild ideas about this place." She raised a brow but still didn't take her eyes from her game. "If you ask me, that crash made Sam as deranged as Eric."

I was already backing out of the room. Sam was out just wandering loose in Santaland. Hopefully he hadn't gone far.

"Did he borrow some snowshoes from Leopold at the front desk?"

Her lips twisted in a smirk. "Last I heard, he mentioned finding a snowmobile in a garage. I think he intended to borrow it."

Chapter 19

"That fiend stole my Snow Devil 1100!"

Jingles stared at the empty spot where his souped-up snowmobile usually rested in covered splendor. Despair radiated from him.

"What am I going to do?" he moaned. "How will I ever get it back?"

"Don't worry. It's not like there's a huge highway network around here. I'll bet he just went into Christmastown. He shouldn't be too hard to track."

Famous last words. By the time I drove into Christmastown, I discovered Sam had been all over the place, flitting from one eatery and point of interest like a bumblebee in a field of flowers. He'd scarfed down polar bear claws at Puffy's All-Day Donuts and had a maple syrup latte at We Three Beans.

"How did he pay?" I asked Trumpet.

"He said to charge it to his room at Castle Kringle." He smiled at me. "I assumed you're good for it."

I dug money out of my purse. I also paid for a cranberry club sandwich and a stein of grog at the Midnight Clear Diner, plus three tankards of spiked mulled cider at the Mistletoe Tavern. The barman nodded in the direction of a clothes store across the street, the Tailored Tunic.

"Why would he have gone in there?"

"I doubt it was to buy a kazoo," the barman said.

Comedians.

The elf at the Tailored Tunic had artfully combed over his long hair to cover his ears and was wearing lifts in his shoes. It did my heart good to see how much care elves were taking to follow the directive—their track record was better than that of reindeer, snowmen, etc.

"An elf tunic?" I repeated when he told me what Sam had charged to the castle.

"A very nice one," the clerk explained. "I'm sorry—I've tried to keep our ostentatiously elfy stock out of the windows and front displays. The tunic he found was on our Boxing Day sale rack—size 8XL."

Elf sizes didn't always match up perfectly with human sizes.

"Oh, and a hat."

"An elf cap?"

"No ma'am. We've hidden those away. I sold him one of our snowman topper specials. And a scarf."

Okay. That made sense. The man needed clothes.

The clerk reached behind the counter. "If you see the man again, you might give him this." Pincering the garment with his fingertips, he held up the gray sweater Sam had been found wearing. "He said he didn't want to see it again."

I took the sweater.

"Not that I blame him. It's hard to believe people can put such boring clothes on their bodies. But the man was a little the worse for grog and might regret leaving his sweater behind."

Oh no. I knew Sam had been drinking, but . . . "How much worse?"

The elf's lips turned down. "I had to ask him three times to stop singing 'Frosty the Snowman' at the top of his lungs."

"Where did he go after he left here?"

"I'm not sure. But about five minutes after he walked out, I saw him speed off down the street on a snowmobile, heading east. But that was several hours ago."

This was not good.

Back outside, I stood on the sidewalk and looked down the city street. As if I could tell anything by staring off in the direction a man had headed hours ago. Fresh snow was coming down fairly heavily. For all I knew, Sam might have returned to Castle Kringle by now.

But no, Jingles would have called me if his snowmobile had been returned. I had promised him to look until I found it. So I continued to search, first on foot around town, and then getting on my sleigh and widening the circle. Where would Sam go?

For a moment I worried that he would try to hunt down Boots to get the rocks back—the rocks that he didn't know had already been returned. But there was no way a stranger would be able to find Boots's cabin all on his own.

Of course, since the discovery of those rocks and speaking to Elaine, Sam had been bumped higher on my suspect list in Eric's death. He clearly resented Eric for his treatment of Madison. He had something of a chip on his shoulder about not being as well off as the others, or as smart. Becoming a lithium tycoon had to be an appealing prospect. The chance to increase his share of the fortune with just a couple of syringes of frankincense might have been too tempting.

Of course, he and Elaine said they were playing chess when Eric died, so he had an alibi—albeit a flimsy one. What if they were both lying?

I was taking my second pass down Festival Boulevard when my phone vibrated. I pulled to the curb and ducked down to answer.

"Are you ready to go?" Juniper asked me.

I frowned. "Go where?"

"To the Hop-n-Snort."

I'd forgotten. I'd promised Cannonball he could drive my sleigh there, too. I sagged in my seat. "This has been a weird day in the weirdest Christmas week ever."

"All the more reason to go hop and snort!"

I was about to explain why I couldn't when I saw Cannonball coming down the street, the repaired girth guard in place again. He stopped when he saw me. "We'll pick you up in five," I told Juniper.

I flagged down Cannonball, then jumped out to retrieve the emergency harness from the back of my sleigh. I might have to disappoint Jingles when I didn't find his snowmobile, but at least I wouldn't disappoint Cannonball, too.

"I'm so nervous," the reindeer said as I harnessed him to the sleigh. "Be honest—does this girth guard make my rump look big?"

"You look fine. The important thing is how you feel."

"I FEEL NERVOUS!" He cringed in apology for his outburst. "I'm so sorry. It's just the first time I've ever worked up the courage to attend the Hop-n-Snort."

"Once you're there, you'll have a great time."

"Right. Thank you."

On our way over to Juniper's, I could swear I heard him repeating "great time" under his breath.

Juniper met us on the street outside her building, her pink coat standing out in the falling snow. "Hi Cannonball! Looking forward to the Hop-n-Snort?" Before he could answer, she remembered her mistake. "Oh! Never mind. I know you can't answer."

"Going to have a great time," he muttered anyway.

Juniper looked at me questioningly as she climbed onto the sleigh's bench seat. I shrugged and we set off for the Tinkertown Arena. Cannonball knew the way, so I only had to half pay attention to the road.

"Were you listening to the radio?" Juniper asked.

"No." Santaland had one radio station, which played Christmas music all year long. But everywhere played Christmas music all year long, so I never quite understood the appeal.

"Winkle Gladchime the weather elf is predicting snow."

Fat flakes were falling all around us. "It's already been snowing for an hour."

"I know—Winkle's amazing. He says it might get even heavier."

"I hope it doesn't get too heavy."

She smiled, shaking flakes off her wool cap. "I like a white Christmas."

"We're at the North Pole. *All* Christmases are white Christmases."

"Isn't that lucky? Maybe that's why I like Christmas so much." She tilted a curious glance at me. "Doesn't Oregon have snow at Christmas?"

"Not too often—except in the mountains."

"Oh." She frowned. "So when I go with you in the summer, it won't be snowy?"

"No, it's…" What was she talking about? "In the summer?"

"Yes, when we were talking at the Scoop, you said I could go with you next time. I can't wait—my first trip out of Santaland."

Had I invited her? I couldn't remember. Having Juniper down in Cloudberry Bay would be a hoot, but it would also pose certain . . . challenges. Like how to explain to the staff and my neighbors and everyone in town how I happened to have an elf staying at the Coast Inn. Cloudberry Bay was a small town, and with her red hair, large elf ears, and height topping off at four and a half feet, she wasn't exactly inconspicuous. If this week was any indication, Santalanders weren't the most adept at disguising their true identities.

"It's good I already have some human clothes to wear down there," she said, indicating her pink puffer coat and checked balloon pants that gathered at the ankles. "I'll fit right in."

"Uh-huh." I was glad the blowing snow across this flat stretch of snow path between the two towns allowed me to hide my skepticism behind a squint.

Also, Cannonball was slowing down. "What's wrong?" I called out to him.

He didn't say anything. Yet he stopped.

I hopped down and went around to talk to him. "Have you changed your mind about going?"

He shook his harness. "No ma'am. But that's Mr. Jingles's snowmobile."

I looked over. The vehicle was to the side of the snow path, half buried in new-fallen snow. I hurried over to inspect it. The other two joined me, Cannonball dragging our sleigh behind him as he pulled up alongside the snowmobile.

It was empty. No key in the ignition. Sam must have run into mechanical difficulty or run out of gas. Covering her eyes, Juniper surveyed the area around us. She pointed to depressions in the snow. "Looks like he headed toward Tinkertown, too."

Oh no. This was a disaster. The very thing we'd been trying to avoid. The elves of Christmastown knew to watch out for the strangers, and to try to mask their appearance. But Christmastown's sister city was far enough away that I'd thought it would be safe. If Sam wandered into Tinkertown, the place would be an open Santaland book: elves being elves, the Hop-n-Snort in full swing, snowmen . . .

Well, most of the snowmen seemed to be up on the mountain right now. I had that to be thankful for.

But not much else.

I took out my phone.

He answered on the first half ring. "Did you find it?"

"Yes," I said. "But I didn't find him. Sam is loose and headed to Tinkertown."

There was a hesitation over the line. "Then where is my Snow Devil?"

"On the Tinkertown snow path, about five miles outside Christmastown."

"He just left it there?" Jingles asked, aghast. "It's snowing!"

As if a snowmobile couldn't survive snow.

"Jingles, Sam is either lost in the snow or wandering around Tinkertown, soaking up Santaland unfiltered."

"Okay. I'll have Crinkles pick me up and take me to get the Snow Devil. Then we'll search the area for Sam."

"There's no key in the ignition," I warned him.

"That's okay. I keep the spare on a chain around my neck."

Juniper had overheard my end of the conversation, so when I ended the call we both headed to the sleigh. "Okay, we can go to Tinkertown Arena now."

Cannonball didn't budge.

Good grief, I thought. *Him, too?*

"On, Cannonball!" I urged.

Still no movement.

"Maybe we shouldn't go to the Hop," he said. "We should look for the missing man instead."

"Not on your life. You don't want to miss the big social event of the year."

He shifted legs. "That's just it—there will be another one next year. I can't selfishly let some poor man wander around in the snow because I wanted to have fun."

"Yes, you can," Juniper said. "Constable Crinkles and Jingles are going to look for Sam."

"Sure, but . . ."

This wasn't about Sam, or worrying about being selfish. I knew exactly what was going on in Cannonball's head. It was the same reason I had decided that it was essential to work on my *The Old Man and the Sea* book report the night of my sophomore homecoming dance. And the paper hadn't been due for another month.

Juniper jumped off the sleigh again. She understood, too. "Are you worried about the other reindeer?"

His head hung. "When I was young, all of the other reindeer used to laugh and call me names."

Where had I heard that before? I shook my head. Reindeer.

But come to think of it, that was pretty much why I'd dreaded that homecoming dance.

"Well, you know what, Cannonball?" Juniper planted her good hand on her right hip. "Just say Fudgsicles to those other reindeer bullies. You've got just as much right to be there and have fun as they do—maybe even more. What do those losers do all year? Compete in stupid games. And they obviously didn't even win them, or they'd be in Greenland right now. While you, you're a *working* reindeer, for Castle Kringle." She gave him a bracing nudge. "You are the crème de la crème."

"I don't feel like . . . whatever it is you said." He shook his harness again. "I can't breathe."

Butterflies, I thought. I still got them before walking into a party.

But Juniper was much more pragmatic. "That's because your corset is squeezing you half to death." She started yanking off the girth guard that Salty had taken such pains to fix. When the last hook was undone, Cannonball's flanks expanded like a memory foam pillow loosed from its shipping package. He even released an involuntary sigh.

"There, doesn't that feel better?"

"It sure does. But now I'm just Cannonball-shaped again."

"No, you're not. I can tell you've dropped at least ten pounds from last summer."

"Fourteen and a half," he said.

"Wow! That's amazing. You think the other reindeer aren't going to be in awe of that? You could probably become a YuleTube fitness star."

"It wasn't easy," he said.

"Right—so go reward yourself with an evening of fun. It's your night to sparkle and shine."

His withers twitched with excitement at her pep talk. "You'd better get on the sleigh then, because we've got to hurry before I miss most of the evening."

Juniper gave me a silent smile as she climbed onto the seat again. I was so impressed. Forget the library. She could have a second career as a reindeer whisperer.

By the time we reached the Tinkertown Arena, the place was jumping. Cannonball got as close as he could to the front. Juniper and I hopped down, unharnessed him, and walked him to the door. The Swingin' Santas' version of "Rockin' around the Christmas Tree" was thumping even in the parking lot, and all around the entrance, elves were dancing or singing along, or both.

Algid stood by the door with a pin light and a no-contact thermometer, checking animals for symptoms of reindeer flu as they went in. Luckily, Cannonball passed and was ushered right in. I peeked in the door at the crowd of reindeer in the stadium kicking up their hooves, playfully sparring, or hanging out by the refreshment troughs and tables. Cannonball looked back once, and Juniper and I gave him a thumbs-up sign.

"I hope he really does have a good time," I said, feeling like an anxious parent sending a teen off to the prom.

"How could he help it?" Juniper asked. "Just listening to the music is great!"

At that moment, Smudge appeared and the two of them started dancing. I was tapping my toes by the wall until a line of elves bounced past and urged me to join them. Even with the snow falling and the temperature dropping, a party atmosphere prevailed. I only wished Nick were with me. I hoped that Lucia had reached him by now, and that our supplies were bringing them some measure of comfort.

All the time I stayed at the party, I waited to hear word from Constable Crinkles or Jingles that Sam had been found. But no word came. While Juniper was occupied with dancing, I snuck off to my sleigh, flipped on the electric motor, and scooted off to see if there was any sign of him around town. At the moment, though, Tinkertown felt strangely deserted. Everyone seemed to be around the arena, so that the lighted and garland-draped streets felt almost like a ghost town.

Tinkertown is a factory town, and the factories mostly belong to Santa's workshops. These large buildings and warehouses are surrounded by workers' cottages, each with a small patch of yard usually containing a decorated tree. It had a rougher feel than Christmastown, but I found it charming, too. These were the elves that made children's dreams come true.

Every few blocks or so I'd see an elf out shoveling the walk, or come across kids out on the street having a snowball fight. I asked them if they'd seen a human man wandering around looking lost, but no one had. Of course, I didn't add that he was a possibly homicidal human. No need to cause a town panic.

I was considering where to go to next when the snowplow

driver came through. The single scraper blade had four reindeer pulling it. An elf in a heavy overcoat stood on the small shelf over the blade, which allowed him to steer the reindeer. I flagged him down, but he seemed eager enough to talk, especially when I mentioned the lost man.

"I saw a man like you're describing," he said, "but he didn't look lost."

My ears perked up. This was good news. "How did he look?"

"Drunk."

Okay, not such good news. "How could you tell?"

The elf laughed. "He was on the sidewalk arguing with a snowman."

"When was this?"

"About an hour and a half ago, outside the Tinkertown Tavern."

"Thank you!"

I sped to the Tinkertown Tavern, but the elves I spoke to there said that he was long gone.

"He left with Noggs," the proprietor said.

Noggs. I recognized that name. "The snowman?" *The derelict snowman*, I might have said. Sam had fallen in with unfortunate company. Noggs's weakness for drink was notorious in Tinkertown. "Were they arguing?"

"At first," the barman said. "But they sat outside talking forever and then that guy purchased a bottle of mulled wine and they headed out together."

"Where?"

"I think they were headed to the arena. You can hear the music from here."

I groaned. How had I missed them? After thanking the elves at the bar, I took off. When I pulled into the stadium parking lot, my heart sank. Sam and the snowman were near the entrance, leaning on each other. The new top hat Sam had bought at the shop in Christmastown was now on the snowman's head, while he was wearing a flat, battered porkpie hat that clearly belonged to Noggs.

Algid, small as he was, physically barred the door to the stadium. "All I Want for Christmas Is You" blared from within, but none of the elves outside were dancing anymore. All the focus was on Sam and Noggs.

"C'mon, Doctor," Sam said, "just let us in for one number. You think snowmen don't like to boogie?"

"We love it!" Noggs shouted. "Just as much as elves do!"

Oh no.

"And I love elves," Sam slurred. "All you wonderful little creatures who live in trees and make crackers and cookies."

One of the Tinkertown elves scowled. "We don't live in trees. This is Santaland!"

"Santaland!" Sam's bloodshot eyes widened in wonder. "Eric was right! Elves! Santa's helpers!" He practically fell forward to hug one of them. "Thank you for my LEGO sets. And Toby, my teddy bear. And all my Hot Wheels!"

I texted Constable Crinkles and Jingles that they could call off their search party. Then I hurried forward. "Hi Sam."

He whirled. He was wearing his new elf tunic, but it was covered in snow. If I didn't get him back to Castle Kringle soon, he'd freeze to death. "April!" He entreated me. "Please tell this doctor or elf or elf doctor to let me in. My buddy Noggs and I want to hear the music."

"You can hear it fine out here," I said. "But I should get you back to the ca—hotel."

He waved his index finger in my face. "No, no, no. I can't leave now that I've finally found the party. And all these wonderful little people! And my friend Noggs."

Noggs looked like he needed to go somewhere and sleep

it off, too. His long, tattered muffler had red stains all over it and reeked of mulled wine.

Sam took a long swig from his bottle, and Noggs let out a sympathetic hiccup. Sam thought this was hilarious. "I'm not going anywhere without Noggs."

"Come on, Sam," I said. "Look at this snow coming down. We need to go home."

"I'm not leaving without Noggs," he declared. "I told Elaine snowmen talked, but would she listen? No . . . She probably won't believe me about dwarves, either." He scanned the disapproving crowd. "Any of you dwarves want to come home with me?"

"Elves," Smudge said, seething. Juniper gave him a sharp poke with her elbow. Not that it mattered. The Santaland cat was clearly out of the bag.

It had been a long time since I'd tried to reason with a really inebriated person. It was exhausting. I finally had to lie to him that Noggs could come with us. Anything to get Sam on the sleigh.

He was back to thanking the elves again. "Thank you for my Android tablet, my train set, my Operation game, and all that chocolate you left in my stocking. I especially like those little peanut butter and chocolate Santas." He made a chef's kiss gesture.

I tugged on his arm. "Come on, Sam, let's go."

He grabbed Noggs's stick arm. "C'mon, Noggsy."

At that moment, the door banged open behind Algid and Cannonball came flying out. At first I thought he was being bounced out—the old heave-ho—but the expression on his face was one of pure jubilation. "Mrs. Claus!" he cried. "I'm in love!" He bounded like a deer and then flew over several parked snowmobiles and back again.

Cannonball, while fourteen and a half pounds lighter than

he was, still wasn't the most agile reindeer in Santaland. The result was, he undershot his mark and crash-landed on Noggs and Sam.

The crowd let out a collective groan as Noggs splattered to the pavement in an explosion of snow, sticks, coal, and carrot. Sam, while all in one piece, looked as if he'd hit his head on the packed snow on the ground when he went down. He was out cold.

Algid and I stood over Sam and Noggs while Juniper and Smudge helped a mortified Cannonball back to standing.

"I'm sooo sorry," he said.

Algid leaned down to take Sam's pulse and check his eye movement. "He'll be okay," he pronounced. "Probably have a whale of a headache when he wakes up." Then he looked over at the pile of snow and detritus that was Noggs. "Not sure about him, though."

"I was just dancing with a doe named Ripples and got so excited . . ." Cannonball hung his head in shame. "I'm no better than Adolph the Naughty."

At first it did seem like Noggs was a casualty of the reindeer's exuberance, but then, from somewhere inside the mess of snow, the snowman's inebriated voice started singing "Clouds."

"He's alive!" I found the largest snowball still left of Noggs and motioned for some of the elves to join me in reconstructing him. "Let's roll him back up."

A lot of the fresh fallen snow got incorporated into Noggs, which served as a kind of snowman blood transfusion. By the time he was standing and fully put together—he was sobered up and cheerful. Juniper even gave him her own knit muffler to replace his old one.

"What a great party!" the snowman said, hearing the sounds of the Swingin' Santas' rendition of "A Marshmallow World."

Then he noticed Sam being loaded onto the back of my sleigh, where a blanket had been laid out. "What happened to *him*?" he asked, with a look of disgust. He made a tsk-ing sound through his stick mouth. "I swear, some just don't know when to stop."

Chapter 20

Winkle Gladchime the weather elf hadn't been wrong. Snow continued to fall. And fall. For a while I worried we wouldn't make it home. It was slow going in near-whiteout visibility. Traveling up the mountain, in places the snow on the path was almost as deep as Cannonball's legs. It took motorized assist and some mini flights to get us to Castle Kringle.

At the castle, Jingles and Salty helped me haul Sam to bed—Elaine, evidently, was already asleep.

Overnight, the snow continued. By the next morning, it was still coming down even as we at the castle were trying to shovel out our doorways.

Santaland was accustomed to snow, but even we had our limits. This was nuts. For the first day, everyone at the castle padded restlessly from window to window, watching snow accumulate. The Christmas trees in the castle yard looked as though the snowy ground were swallowing them up. Salty and a shoestring crew of castle grounds elves aided the snowmen, making sure they weren't buried and smothered.

I tried not to worry about what this weather would mean for Nick's getting back—but of course I fretted nonstop. Tiffany, trapped now from going to Tea-piphany, kept busy baking in the castle kitchen. By noon we had enough scones to feed an army.

Christopher was particularly restless, especially after his mother wouldn't let him go into town on his snowmobile.

"If it starts blizzarding again," Tiffany said over lunch, "I don't want you to get stuck somewhere."

Remembering how difficult it was to get home last night, I could understand where she was coming from. Christopher, on the other hand, could not.

"The time after Christmas is always so draggy," he said as we all dawdled over the meal, which we were eating by ourselves in the servant dining room. It felt strange being in the castle elves' domain, but also rather cozy. The beam ceilings overhead, the old oak elf table that had seen a million meals, and the fire roaring in the open stone hearth made me feel snug and relaxed, if a little languid.

Because of the presence of Sam and Elaine, almost all the castle elves had been released for the holiday. That seemed like a futile gesture now, since Sam had gone walkabout last night and absorbed every fantastic detail about Santaland. The moment he woke up from his hangover, he would be able to reveal to Elaine that Centretown and the Castle Kringle Hotel and Resort were nothing but elaborate fictions. And that the truth was even stranger than fiction.

So far, though, Sam hadn't stirred from his room. The aftereffects of a binge like the one he'd been on last night were bound to be painful.

"More scones, anyone?" Jingles asked, holding up a platter. There would be scones for days.

"No," we all said in unison. Even Tiffany seemed tired of them.

"Most of the time after Christmas we've opened presents by now," Christopher complained. "Having new stuff at least gives you something to do."

"We're not opening gifts till Nick and Lucia come back," Pamela said. "Clauses are not early openers."

"Not even one?" Christopher had been lobbying for present opening all morning. "I mean . . . they're *right there* under the tree, practically begging us to unwrap them."

Tiffany shook her head. "No."

I laughed. "Christopher's got a point about the benefit of having toys. The only person who seems to be handling this blizzard day well is Elaine."

She hadn't stopped playing that Game Boy since it came out of the box.

Tiffany wasn't budging. "Your room is full of stuff for you to mess around with," she told Christopher. "Or you can read a book."

He moaned. "It's not natural." He appealed to me. "You've got a present that's almost the size of the Christmas tree. How can you stand it?"

I had purposefully avoided the living room since depositing my own gifts under the tree, so I hadn't seen this massive present he kept talking about. Surely he was exaggerating. Or maybe this was a ploy to win me over to the let's-open-presents team.

Pamela stood up and pushed in her elf-sized chair. "If you're all bored, why don't you all play a game?"

Tiffany, Christopher, and I looked at each other questioningly. "Monopoly?" Tiffany asked.

"No," Christopher and I said.

"Clue," I suggested.

"Ugh—that seems almost too realistic, given what's happened this week."

The game idea began to fizzle.

"They should be called *bored* games," Christopher said. "That's the only reason most people ever play them."

Pamela stood up on a sigh. "Well, if you'd rather curse

the darkness than light a candle, there's no hope. I'm going to my room to finish reading *A Christmas Carol*." She lifted an eyebrow. "Sometimes Scrooge seems like good company."

When she was gone, I laughed, relenting. "Okay—get out Catan."

We made it through one game before that stuck-at-home torpor took hold again. Christopher went out to sled on a hill close by, Tiffany got the sudden urge to bake ginger scones, and I wandered out to see what the guests were up to.

I ducked my head into the dining room. Elaine was sitting at the cleared table; I don't think she'd moved since lunch. The Game Boy was an extension of her hands now.

"Have you seen Sam today?" I asked.

"I heard moaning from his room sometime this morning." She shook her head even as her eyes never left the screen. "He must have gotten really hammered."

"Then you haven't spoken to him?"

"Please. He's hard enough to deal with when he's sober."

"I'm sorry we've left you on your own all day. Would you like to join us for dinner tonight, or play a board game with us?"

She shot me an *Are you kidding?* look.

"I just feel bad leaving you on your own like this," I said. "Especially during Christmas week."

She smiled and put down the Game Boy. "To be honest, I should really thank you."

The words sounded so sincere, I was taken aback. "What for?"

"For bringing me to this wonderful place. At Christmas. It's made me realize the reason I've always been so grinchy during the holidays."

"Wow—that's wonderful to hear."

"It's taken me all my life to understand how to do Christmas right," she said. "All those years when I was single, my folks would pressure me to come home because they didn't want me to be alone at Christmas. So I would, and I'd be miserable and cranky the whole time. And then I got married, and for several years I was never alone at Christmas, and oh boy, that felt lonelier than ever. And since the divorce, well-meaning friends have pressed invitations on me so I won't be alone at Christmas. But here I am"—she gestured around the cavernous, empty dining room—"alone at Christmas. And it's great! I'm finally spending the holidays with the person whose company I enjoy most in the world: me."

"Oh. That's"—not quite the holiday epiphany I was expecting—"good?"

"I'm just sorry I had to lose a toe to learn such a valuable lesson."

I started backing out of the room. "Okay, well . . . if you change your mind and want company—"

"I won't."

I bumbled out to the hallway, wishing someone were around to share *that* conversation with. I ended up in the family living room, where the tree was. Most years I loved to just sit with a hot beverage and bliss out in front of the decorated tree. There hadn't seemed to be time for zoning out this year. Until now.

I plopped down, expecting that the tree would work its magic and that I would fall into that dreamy Christmas mood. Instead, my gaze zeroed right in on a huge package behind all the others. Was that the present for me that Christopher had been talking about? It *was* the size of a refrigerator box. It was even wrapped in silver so that it almost resembled an appliance.

I went over and inspected the tag. *To: April From: Pamela*

What the heck was it? Not a sweater, Coco had said. That was obvious. What could Pamela have made me that would take up so much room? Even a comforter would squish down into a smaller box than this.

Overcome with curiosity, I pulled it out of its spot behind the tree. I was expecting that I would have to engage my long-neglected core muscles to heave the thing free of the other gifts, but the box was surprisingly light. Just unwieldy. I ended up stumbling backward and banging my leg on the coffee table. Hopping in pain, I let the box drop. Big mistake. The box fell against a crystal angel decoration, impaling itself on an angel wing tip.

I lunged for the angel—one of Pamela's favorite decorations. If I broke it I probably would be banished to the reindeer shed for the rest of my marriage. Quickly, I extracted the angel from where it had poked through the box, then took care in putting it back on the coffee table a safe distance away.

Now I would have to explain the damaged wrapping on the box. Unless I could disguise it . . .

I stuck my finger inside the rip in the wrapping paper and was shocked to feel something squishy inside. Was that wool? It felt more like foam.

Pamela had gotten me something taller than I was, made out of foam. What the heck was it?

I blame the blizzard. Even when I was a kid I had never tried to find where my Christmas presents were hidden. I certainly wouldn't have unwrapped one and peeked at it. But this day had dragged, and my mind had been preoccupied all week with murder and worry over Nick. Here was a pleasant mystery—and how easily solved! All I had to do was tear that box a little more . . .

Actually, I had to tear it quite a bit. And the more I saw of what was in the box, the more confused I became. It was something white. Large, foamy, and white. Although it *did* seem to have a tightly knit wool cover. I would almost have thought it was a mattress topper, but it was the wrong shape. This was bulbous. And big.

Before I could check myself, I was ripping the wrapping and the cardboard. Frustrated, I reached into the box and pulled whatever I could get my hands around out of the hole. To my horror, what popped out was a head.

"April! What are you doing?"

I cried in alarm—both at the unexpected voice behind me and the eyeballs protruding from the box. *Caught.* I turned around to see Audrey Claus in her maid's uniform, her face slack in bewilderment.

"Are you tearing into your presents by yourself?" she asked.

"It was an accident. The box hit the angel there and . . ." I gestured to the crystal angel, but even as I did I realized that it belied my claim of an innocent mistake. No way could that angel wing have torn open a two-foot gash. Not that it mattered. Audrey had already moved on to the more important question.

"What *is* this thing?" She gaped at the demented-looking head protruding from the box.

"I have no idea. It's my gift from Pamela."

"Wow." She circled the box as someone might a package that had *Danger: Radiation* written on it. "Do you have a mother-in-law problem?"

A half laugh escaped me. "I thought it was getting better, but now . . ." I stared at the squished-up snowman face. Where had I seen those eyes before?

Then it came to me. The night I'd run into Coco—after the caroling.

"Pamela made this—whatever it is—by hand." I tugged at it tentatively, extracting another few inches of white, knit-covered foam from the package. "Does she really think I want a stuffed snowman?" I wondered aloud.

Audrey tilted her head. "It's not just a stuffed decoration—it's a big-ass snuggy." At my confusion, she pulled even more of it out and showed me. "See? There's a zipper up the front, and beneath the eyeballs there's a hole cut out for your face."

Holy Moses. "So my face would be right below the snowman's face?"

Her lips twisted. "Yeah, it's kind of creepy."

"*Kind of?*" Did Pamela expect me to wear this thing? I yanked the rest of it out and held it up to me. In the bottom of the snowman there were two holes cut out for feet to stick through.

Audrey touched it. "This must have taken forever to make. Feel how they build the snowman segments over some kind of bendy plastic cage?"

I pushed a dent into the fake snowman body, and when I removed my hand, the indentation bounced back. "Ingenious. So in all the holiday pictures this year, I'm going to be dressed as a giant blobby snowman with two heads."

"*Hello? Anyone here?*"

At the sound of a voice coming down the hallway, Audrey and I locked gazes.

Was that Sam? I didn't want anyone walking in on this scene. I lowered my voice to an urgent whisper. "Help me hide this thing—and the box."

What if word got back to Pamela that I'd opened my gift? Or Christopher! We'd just been telling him he couldn't open his presents—Clauses weren't early openers!—and then I'd come in here and torn into one at the first twinge of temptation.

I had to give Audrey credit for snowman packing agility. She had that snuggy completely back in the box in seconds flat. Then she grabbed the box and looked around. "Where can I hide it?"

It was too big to stuff behind a chair. And left in the open, it looked just like what it was: a present that had been torn open by a very naughty person. Me.

Audrey stared at the small side door that led on to the servants' corridor. "I'll take it with me to my room and re-wrap it."

"You'd do that for me?" I asked.

"Of course—anything for Santa's wife!"

She scurried out, dragging the huge box with her. It was awkward getting it through the servants' door, but I helped shove it over the threshold and shut the door just as Sam weaved into the family room.

"Oh good—someone's here." He staggered to the couch and collapsed. After landing on his back, he winced and flung his forearm over his eyes.

"Headache?" I asked.

"Please don't shout." He sucked in a breath. "I was worried that I was the only one here."

"Didn't you see Elaine in the dining room?"

He swallowed. "No."

She must have heard him coming.

He shifted his arm enough to peek at me. "So tell me, what did I do last night?"

"You don't remember?"

"That's why I'm asking. I've had nightmares and visions, but I can't put it together so that it makes sense."

If he had no recollection of the night before, I certainly didn't want to remind him. At least of very much. "You stole Jingles's snowmobile—but he forgives you."

Sort of.

He grunted. "That's kind of him." His lips tightened. "Did I drive around much?"

"Mm . . . a little," I said noncommittally.

"I could swear something odd happened . . ." His face

tensed. "Like, maybe I met someone and we went to a concert, but we couldn't get in?"

I decided to change the subject. "Can I get you anything to eat?"

He paled. "That would be a really bad idea at the moment."

"Some ginger ale, maybe?" I sidestepped toward the door. "It won't take me a minute."

He peeked at me again. "Did you see me doing anything that would explain why I feel so uneasy?"

"No . . ."

"Weird." He sank further down on the couch. "Come to think of it, maybe that ginger ale isn't a bad idea."

"I'll be right back." I hurried out to the kitchen and poured a ginger ale into a glass. Tiffany was standing by the oven, arms folded as she watched the oven timer.

"How long can drunken amnesia last?" I asked her. "A day or two? Forever?"

She laughed. "Thinking of tying one on for New Year's Eve?"

I shook my head. "Sam's drawing a blank about last night."

"No memory of anything that you told me about?"

"He doesn't even remember Noggs, and last night it was like they were best buds."

She laughed. "Well, I'd say we've had a near miss."

"You're right. Let's just hope he'll stay clueless until Jake's witch gets here."

Maybe Imelda could hex these two out of our lives for good.

Chapter 21

The second day after the blizzard, restless people and elves began to dig out and take a look around. Midmorning, Juniper arrived at the castle for an impromptu visit. Tiffany and I were having coffee when she came in. Ever cautious, she was still wearing her Strawberry Shortcake coat and human shoes, which I supposed was a good thing, given that Sam still couldn't remember anything about his wild night in Tinkertown.

"I come bearing gifts," she said as she set down an assorted baker's dozen of Puffy's All-Day Donuts.

"Dibs on the polar bear claw!" Tiffany said.

I looked in the box and laughed. "Juniper knows us well. There are two bear claws."

Polar bear claws are paw-shaped éclairs with powdered sugar sprinkled on top instead of chocolate. Each one is an oversized pillow of custardy goodness.

"You're the best, Juniper," Tiffany said. "Even I was getting sick of scones."

"And you even carried the box with just one functioning wrist," I said. "How did you get here?"

"The sleigh buses are running today," Juniper told us. "Limited schedule, though. And since the library's closed until after the New Year, I thought I'd come to see how things are going up here. Has there been any word from Nick?"

"No."

"Oh." Juniper looked sorry that she'd asked. "But there's been no trouble with Sam and Elaine?"

"They haven't murdered us yet," Tiffany said. "Mostly the temptation has been the other way around."

I frowned. "I don't think either of them is a killer."

Tiffany shot me a look. "Come on, you don't think Elaine is cold-blooded enough to kill someone?"

She was joking, but I'd contemplated this. "I can't imagine her being able to hide it."

"The lithium, though," Juniper reminded me. "Money's a powerful motive. Who wanted money the most?"

That was a good point. "Sam's mentioned how poor he is a couple of times."

"So you think it was Sam," Juniper said.

"No . . ." I sank a little in my chair. "You've seen him. He's a goofball. He doesn't have a vicious bone in his body."

The door pushed open and Jingles came into the room in a flutter. Juniper hadn't seen him in his Leopold clothes before, and she couldn't help marveling. "Your outfit! It's very smart."

Jingles preened a little. "Thank you. And you look . . ." He frowned at the puffy pink coat. "Would you like me to take that for you?"

He helped her out of the offending garment. Her parachute pants and suspenders over a tight sweater with the word *FOXY* emblazoned on it didn't impress him favorably, either.

"Was there something you needed, Jingles?" I asked.

"Oh!" He stood at attention. "Yes, ma'am. There's a witch here to see you."

We all gasped. "Imelda?"

Jingles drew back. "You *know* her?"

"Aren't Jake and Claire with her?" I asked.

"Yes, I left them in the foyer, too."

I couldn't believe Claire had been stopped at my door. "You asked Claire to wait?"

"Excuse me," he said sharply. "She had a witch with her. I thought I should check with you about that. And there's another guest with them, too. I have no idea who *he* is."

"How did you know Imelda's a witch?" Tiffany asked.

He lifted his chin. "Oh, you can tell."

"Just show them all in," I said.

I crossed to the coffeemaker and started a new pot. If I knew Claire, she'd be ready for a cup after the trip she'd just made.

I'd only just set the brew cycle when our band of visitors entered, led by Claire. Behind her was a miniature elf woman: Imelda, I presumed. When I was growing up, my mother had collected figurines of people made with sticks with pecan heads, which had both fascinated and terrified me. Imelda was like a living, breathing pecan person. A dark wizened head with thin wiry gray hair sat atop a bony, hunchbacked body. She wore an eclectic assortment of clothes: garments that looked like burlap layered over chiffons and an apron made of fur from some mangy, long-dead creature.

"Is *this* Castle Kringle?" the old elf said in a voice that was a cross between a trumpet and a bullfrog. As she took in the dining table and the sideboard, her face collapsed in a few more wrinkles. "I was expecting something fancier."

Claire flashed me a long-suffering smile. "Imelda, let me introduce you to the current Santa's wife."

"That her?" Imelda poked a long-nailed finger at Juniper. More disappointment. "She looks like a regular elf to me."

"I'm not Mrs. Claus." Juniper stepped back. "My name is Juniper. I'm a librarian."

I extended my hand to clasp Imelda's wrinkly, long-nailed

claw. "I'm April Claus, and this is my sister-in-law, Tiffany Claus. We're very pleased that you could come."

Niceties didn't impress her. "Jake here says you have some folks who need hexing."

"Yes," I said.

Just then, her gaze alit on the table. "Polar bear claws!" Her hand snatched one of the prized donuts from the box and within the blink of an eye she was devouring it in a few gulps. It was like watching a lizard catch and consume a fly.

Jake ushered in the man they'd brought with them, who looked a stockier, shaggier version of himself. "This is my uncle Jasper."

"Pleased to meet you, ma'am," Jasper said. "I brought something for you." He presented me with what looked to be a large molar with the root sawed off. Tiffany bleated in alarm, but I reached forward and accepted it. I wasn't sure what Jasper was doing here, but my job was to make all Santaland guests welcome, even the ones who came bearing teeth.

"Thank you so much," I said. "I know your work, and this is"—I held up the tooth, which had stick figures dancing across the enamel—"amazing." It must have been extracted from a very large snow monster. It was at least six inches across.

"It's an ashtray." He shuffled modestly. "But you can always use it as a candy dish."

"What a thought," I said.

"I've got something of his, too." Not to be outdone, Imelda sidled up to me. She lifted a powdered sugar–covered hand and showed me a necklace biting into the folds of her neck. I recognized it—Claire's bracelet. I shot a glance at Claire, who smiled. "Imelda talked me out of it. It looks better on her anyway."

"You bet your sweet bazoo it does," Imelda said, cackling with delight. "She gave it as a down payment for my services."

"About this hex . . ." I wasn't quite sure how to go about this. "Is there any special equipment you need?"

"Just a potable beverage. Hot, preferably, but whatever you have on hand is fine. Not to brag, but my potions stand up even in ice water."

"I've made some coffee," I said.

Imelda looked back at Claire, wide-eyed. "Now? We're going to do this now?"

"You might want to wait," Claire explained to me. "It's a forgetting spell."

"Imelda says she doesn't do transportation," Jake added.

The witch wagged her finger. "Veeeeerrrrry risky, traveling spells. Now if you want a straight-up disappearance spell, *that* I can do."

The glint in her eye told me that the people she disappeared would never be seen again. Yes, I wanted to make Sam and Elaine go away, but I didn't want to obliterate them. "Forgetting would be sufficient. But I'm not yet sure when they should take it." Claire and Jake were right—it would be prudent to wait until they were about to be flown out.

Imelda looked exasperated. "I can't just give you a to-go bottle. That's what I was telling your friend Claire. A witch needs to deliver the dose."

"Okay . . ." The ins and outs of hexes was something I'd never contemplated before. "We probably shouldn't give them the dose until Nick and Lucia come back with the sleighs and are ready to take them back." Otherwise we'd have two amnesiacs on our hands. And they'd be soaking up new memories.

But what were we supposed to do in the meantime? Board this witch at the castle?

"I think I'll have another donut," Imelda said.

Tiffany and I watched in despair as the second prized polar bear claw disappeared.

I didn't see an alternative to offering her the hospitality of Castle Kringle until we could fly Sam and Elaine out of here.

The place really was turning into a hotel.

I smiled at Jasper and Imelda. "You're welcome to stay here at the castle as long as you'd like."

"That's very kind of you," Jasper said, though at the same time he was shooting a nervous glance at Jake. "But I'll need to get back to my cave. There's been some trouble recently . . ."

Jake stepped forward. "I brought Uncle Jasper here so that he could testify about what really happened to Eric Lynch."

His uncle took off his hat, revealing a thatch of salt-and-pepper hair. "There was a fight between that man and a neighbor of mine, Blurg."

"Blurg?" I asked.

"He's a snow monster. Usually he keeps to himself in his little cave, but a few weeks ago he went out with a few other abominables to hunt a snow leopard who'd been giving them some trouble. When he returned from the hunt, he discovered someone had been living in his cave, and left a mess."

Imelda gulped down an éclair. "Nothing worse than piggish guests."

"Worse yet," Jasper continued, "this uninvited guest had taken Blurg's ax and chipped at his walls, removing his favorite shiny rocks."

"The lithium," I said.

Jasper nodded. "Blurg wouldn't know lithium from a hole in his head. Neither would I. He just prized the shiny pattern on his walls. So he lost his temper, and—well, you know the rest."

"Those monsters have terrible tempers," Imelda said.

This seemed like extreme overreaction even for a snow monster. "Did he have to kill Eric?"

"Blurg swears it was self-defense. The man tried to shoot him with some strange weapon, but Blurg disarmed him and smashed it to bits. Then the man started to run away with the rock he'd stolen, and Blurg tackled him and hit him with the antler he'd found during his recent hunt."

"In the back," I said. "He stabbed him in the back."

"As to that, snow monsters have different ideas than us. Blurg was trying to get something that had been stolen from him. Now he's afraid there'll be trouble, and trouble between snow monsters and elves can escalate into disaster pretty quick. But Jake tells me that the man didn't die from the antler wound, so I'm hoping we can keep this from blowing up."

Nick would probably want that, too.

This new information cleared up a lot of questions, but left one big one. Who gave Eric that fatal dose of frankincense?

I was about to thank Jasper for making the trip to tell us all this when Sam burst in. He appeared to be in a fever about something. With his hair askew and a frenetic brightness in his eyes, he looked like a college kid who'd stayed up all night hopped up on Red Bull.

"Here you all are!" he said. "I've got it figured out. Mostly."

The rest of us exchanged confused glances.

"What figured out?" I asked.

"Everything! I've sent your man Mr. Salty to fetch the law."

Would Salty have gone to town to get Constable Crinkles? I doubted it. All he had to do was call the constabulary. In which case, Crinkles might be on his way soon. Given how crazy Sam looked, his arrival couldn't come soon enough.

In my calmest voice, I suggested, "Why don't we all take a seat?" and gestured to the oak table.

"No thanks—we're gathering in that room where I found you yesterday," he said. "The one with the big tree. Everybody else is waiting for us there." Sam sailed for the door, waving for us all to follow him. "Bring the donuts. They'll be Exhibit A."

"What's this about?" Tiffany asked.

I couldn't figure it out.

"It feels like we're being summoned for a big reveal," Juniper said. "Like Hercule Poirot gathering suspects together at the end of an Agatha Christie."

"The suspect rounding everyone up seems like a new twist, though," I observed.

Imelda eyed me curiously. "Was he the one I'm supposed to hex?"

"Eventually. First I want to hear what he has to say."

Everyone in the kitchen traipsed to the family living room, even Imelda and Uncle Jasper. I was curious to see who the others were that Sam had mentioned, but I wasn't prepared to see so many. Pamela was sitting in her favorite chair, knitting something in bright red yarn. She looked up at me briefly when I came into the room, and her gaze was not well pleased.

What had I done now? It wasn't my fault Sam had gone berserk.

Of course, the fact that I was leading a wizened old elf witch into the family parlor might have something to do with her displeasure. Imelda was agape at the size of the room. "Now, this is more like it!" she exclaimed. "Not shabby!"

Claire tugged her away to the other side of the room.

Audrey, in her maid's uniform, was stationed by a door, looking openly curious about what was going on. Jingles stood near her. Elaine slumped on the couch, game in hand. Strangest of all to me, seated in chairs near the coffee table, were Butterbean and Amory.

"What are you doing here?" I asked them.

"I came down to see how you were all doing here after the blizzard," Amory explained, "and to let you know that the lodge is still preparing for Grog Night, as usual."

"I'm helping," Butterbean said. "The zip lines were such a success at the send-off, we thought we'd put some up around the lodge. By New Year's we'll have zip lines running all the way from the lodge down to the castle."

Sam clapped his hands impatiently. "Can I have your attention, please?" He was distracted by Audrey sitting apart from us all. "You there—move in."

Audrey got up and crossed over to the main grouping, and Jingles followed suit. Those of us who'd just come in were still getting settled. Sam gave Imelda a pitying look as she crossed to the couch with the box of donuts.

"Here," he said. "Let me take those off your hands."

Imelda pulled the box out of his reach. "Not on your life, mister."

Juniper smiled at Audrey as she sat down next to her. She raised her forearm encased in its brace. "See, I didn't come out of the hospital unscathed that day, like you did."

Audrey's pinched brow telegraphed confusion, but she smiled reflexively. "I'm afraid I don't—"

A loud throat-clearing cut her off. Sam paced the rug between the coffee table and the Christmas tree. "I brought you all here because I've made some disturbing discoveries about this place."

Oh no. Did that mean he remembered his night out? Bracing myself for the worst, I checked the expressions around me. Elves and people alike looked alarmed. All except Pamela, who continued to calmly knit without any change in expression.

To my surprise, Sam's gaze homed in on me. "You *should* look anxious, April. It didn't take me long to figure out that you're at the crooked center of all this."

"All this what?" Juniper asked. "Are we here to talk about who killed Eric Lynch?"

"No." He looked confused. "Why would you think that?"

"You're doing the Poirot thing." She shrugged. "I just assumed. Never mind."

"Maybe Eric's another piece of the puzzle that I still haven't worked out," he said.

I also had no idea what he was talking about—he wasn't much more coherent now than when he was inebriated—but my brain was distracted by what Juniper had said earlier, to Audrey. How was it possible for Juniper to have seen Audrey leaving the Santaland Infirmary as she was going in to wait to get treated for her wrist? Clement and Carlotta told me that they were the ones who went to the infirmary that day, while Audrey was shopping.

"The day before yesterday," Sam announced, "I set out to do a tour of Centreville and its surroundings."

Jingles leapt to his feet. "You stole my snowmobile—and when the constable arrives, I intend to file a complaint."

Sam held up his hands. "You might change your mind when you've heard me out. I've spent the past day trying to remember the things I did and saw."

"We all know what you did, Sam," Elaine said in an exasperated voice. "You got drunk."

Sam nodded. "Yes—and do you know why?"

"Because you drank too much?" she guessed, deadpan.

"Because Centretown is chock-a-block with taverns, restaurants, and little stands selling stimulants. And sugar!" He pointed accusingly at the Puffy's All-Day Donuts box. "Every third business in Centretown sells something sweet. I can't count the number of chocolate stores, cake shops, and other bakeries I passed."

"Don't forget ice cream," Butterbean piped up. "The Santaland Scoop on Mistletoe Lane."

Sam gestured toward Butterbean. If the Puffy's box was Exhibit A, it appeared Butterbean would be Exhibit B. "And this is the sad result. Look at this unfortunate creature."

Butterbean's face froze in a bewildered smile. "*Me? Unfortunate?*"

"All over Centretown I found the same thing—chubby little people with manic smiles on their faces. And no wonder! The powers that be seem to have them geeked up on sugar and spirits twenty-four seven."

"Who are the powers that be?" Claire asked.

"I'm coming to that." Sam's expression grew grave. "Unfortunately, after a couple of hours I fell victim to my own research."

Elaine barked out a laugh. "Get real. You're hardly Madame Curie suffering the effects of radiation. You just got tanked."

"Not on purpose. You should have seen the proprietors of these taverns and shops—bending over backwards to ply me with free spirits. And always watching me." He looked around. "Just like we were always being watched here, Elaine."

"Leave me out of this," she retorted.

"But while I was in Centretown, I heard about this other place, and I set off for there. And . . ." Sam frowned as if in pain and held his hands to his temples. "I can't remember *all* of it, but I did see huge warehouses. I stopped at a couple of them and spoke to the little people guarding the entrances. One said that the warehouse was full of candy canes. Another said there were toys inside." He laughed. "Mind you, these places were huge enough to put Amazon to shame. And what would all this stuff be doing out in the middle of nowhere, in an area where we can't even access the internet?"

"The lines are down," I said.

He chortled derisively. "Oh right."

Pamela had heard enough. She put her knitting down. "Young man, you seem to be building to some sort of accusation, but for the life of me I don't understand what it could be."

"Only this." Sam paused for effect. "What's going on here is organized crime on a level that would put the Mafia to shame. And the bosses are the people in this house."

"Why on earth would you say that?" Amory piped up.

"You should have seen the faces on the people in town when I told them I was a guest here. They couldn't serve me fast enough."

"They were just being nice," I said.

He gestured toward Butterbean. "And what about all these little smiling automatons, with their sad potbellies. As far as I can tell, they're more like indentured servants than actual paid workers. They're just sent wherever the big people tell them to go." He glanced at Audrey. "One minute one's a nurse, the next she's a maid. That one"—Butterbean again—"purportedly works at an ice cream store, but he's all over the place. And I remember being at an auditorium where a rock band was playing, but all the peons weren't even allowed to go in. There's definitely second-class citizenship here."

"This is absurd," Jingles said.

"And don't even get me started on the reindeer," Sam added. "I saw a whole herd of them in a snowy field, looking like they were being forced to run some kind of obstacle course to get them into peak condition. I shudder to think what their fates will be."

I glanced across the living room. Pamela was sending me a significant look, as if this were my fault. Which it kind of was. I was the one who relented and invited Sam and Elaine to come here. Of course, he might just as easily have jumped to these wild conclusions if he'd stayed at the hospital.

"So why did you send for our constable?" I asked.

"Because I'm giving you fair warning that I'm going to tell the world the story of the crazy regime here. And once I've got it down on paper and maybe have a lucrative magazine deal, I'm going to inform the FBI or Interpol, or whoever will listen."

This was not good. He sounded like a crackpot, but crackpots got media attention all the time. What could we do to stop him?

Elaine stood up. "You know, Sam, I think I liked Eric's idea better. You should have stuck with the belief that this place is Santaland." She pointed at Amory and said, tongue firmly in cheek, "Look how much that man resembles Santa Claus. And the housekeeper here could be the spitting image of Mrs. Claus."

All the Santalanders seated in the living room laughed, nervously at first but then a little more robustly when Elaine joined in.

"Just wait till he finds out reindeer can fly," Claire said in a stage whisper.

"This is no joke," Sam said.

He looked so anguished, I almost felt sorry for him.

Elaine, though, was merciless. "But keep going, Sam. I haven't been this entertained since the bellboy juggled oranges from the breakfast room fruit basket this morning."

"I know what I saw," Sam insisted.

Just then, Constable Crinkles walked in, followed by Ollie. "What did you see?"

Before Sam could reply, a brainwave washed over me and everything—or almost everything—clicked into place. Unwittingly, Sam had revealed Eric's murderer after all, albeit in an indirect way. I shot to my feet. "The fruit basket!"

"Why did you do it?" I asked Audrey.

She grabbed the sides of her chair as if to brace herself.

"Do what?"

"Kill Eric," I said.

"I didn't!"

"I suspected you days ago, but Carlotta and Clement lied to me. They told me *they* had delivered the fruit basket to the hospital."

Her face flushed. "They did."

"No, Audrey. You were there. Juniper saw you."

"I did," Juniper confirmed. Then she frowned. "But she didn't have a fruit basket."

"Because you saw her as she was leaving the infirmary and you were going in. When you two passed on the sidewalk, Eric was inside either dying or already dead."

"You're crazy," Audrey said. "Clement and Carlotta left the fruit basket. Why would they lie?"

"To cover for you. Did you confess to them?"

"Of course not—why would I confess to something I didn't do? If they told you they took the fruit basket, you should believe them."

"That's what I thought, but something's been bugging me about that fruit basket all along. It wasn't there when I left to meet Plummy Greenbuckle at Tea-piphany. Tiffany said it wasn't there when she was at the infirmary, just after the egg-nog spill happened, and while Fuzzy from the eggnog factory was being treated. But when I returned to the infirmary, the fruit basket was there."

"Yes, because Clement and Carlotta took it in," Audrey insisted. "Will you listen to yourself? You sound nuts."

I shook my head. "Clement and Carlotta were never at the infirmary that day. They told me they took the basket in through the front entrance where Mildred was. But the entrance was covered with frozen eggnog and blocked off. If they'd gone by the infirmary when they said they did, they would have seen the eggnog and the sign telling them to use the ER entrance."

Audrey stood, fists at her side. "Forget the stupid fruit basket. Why would I have murdered Eric Lynch? He was just a patient. I was barely in his room for five seconds."

"Just long enough for him to recognize you and for you to panic and run," I said.

"That's absurd."

"I saw you that morning as you were fleeing the infirmary, Audrey. You'd told Nurse Cinnamon said you couldn't stand the sight of blood. But I looked in on Eric shortly afterward. His dressings were perfectly clean. No blood at all. You were just using your squeamishness as an excuse because seeing him flustered you."

She looked flustered again now. Flustered and increasingly frantic.

"When Eric saw me that morning, he mumbled that he thought Miss Mojito had come back." I crossed my arms. "I assumed Miss Mojito was Elaine, even though she told me I was wrong. But now I guess you and Eric shared a few mojitos on a Florida beach sometime recently. And that after a few of them you told him about a magical place between two mountains at the North Pole."

Audrey's mouth opened and closed, but no words came out.

"*Murderer!*"

The word was shouted from the other side of the room, where Elaine, her face a mask of fury, was reaching for the nearest thing to hurl at Audrey. The nearest thing at hand, as it turned out, was the crystal angel. The prospect of a Claus family heirloom being thrown across the room brought everyone surging toward her.

"Stop!" Pamela said.

Crinkles nearly knocked over a side table in his rush to disarm her. Jingles hurdled over an ottoman.

"Seriously?" Elaine said to everyone converging on her. "You care more about this stupid angel than catching a killer?"

"No—"

But when I turned back to see if Audrey could be subdued by some other means, she was gone.

Chapter 22

"She's disappeared," Juniper said.

"How?" Elaine asked. "People can't just disappear."

No they couldn't, unless . . .

I crossed to Imelda, who'd been so quiet. "What did you do with her?"

She blinked at me, all innocence. "Nothing. I've barely been listening, to tell you the truth. I've been keeping my eye on the donuts."

And devouring the donuts, by the looks of that empty box.

Ollie pointed to an elf-sized door built into the room's paneling, which led to the servants' corridor. "She went through there."

"Why didn't you try to stop her?" I asked.

"I thought we were trying to stop the crazy lady with the angel."

I couldn't help releasing a sigh of exasperation. "We've got to find her."

That, it turned out, was easier said than done.

The corridor provided no clues, nor did a search of the kitchen and the servants' dining room. The most likely explanation was that Audrey had ducked outside, but several of us ran outdoors and couldn't see anything in the yard. Just trees and snowmen. Footprints led away from the house, but everyone had been going in and out all morning—tracks radiated from the portico in all directions, some made by small elf feet, larger human feet, reindeer hooves, and snowmen trails.

"We'll keep looking," Salty assured me. "She just didn't vanish."

I was just turning to go back inside to tear the house upside down when two familiar figures came cross-country skiing up the drive: Clement and Carlotta, in matching snowsuits and reflective goggles that made them look like a pair of puffy insects. They waved and smiled, oblivious to what had happened this morning. But they knew a good part of the story of Audrey's actions, I was sure of that.

The siblings had glided up to the portico before they noticed anything amiss. Carlotta pulled off her goggles. "What's wrong, April?"

"You'd better come inside."

They stepped out of their skis and followed me into the castle. "What's happened?" Clement said when we arrived in the family parlor.

"You lied to me about dropping off the fruit basket at the Santaland Infirmary."

The two of them exchanged guilty glances. "Yes, we did."

"Why?" I asked. "You must have known what Audrey did that day. A man had died."

"She swore it was an accident," Carlotta said.

Clement nodded. "Just a matter of the dosage being stronger than she expected. She was trying to help him—but she just didn't know anything about nursing."

Carlotta added, her voice heavy with disapproval, "Nurse Cinnamon never should have left a novice in charge of such a serious case."

I didn't know which to feel more, disgust or pity. They

were either willfully blind or they had been totally bamboo-
zled by their prodigal sister. "Audrey wasn't even supposed to
be at the infirmary that afternoon," I explained, "and she certainly wasn't supposed to be administering medication. The
first thing Nurse Cinnamon told me, and I'm sure Audrey
too, was that we shouldn't do anything more therapeutic than
plumping pillows. Never would she have directed Audrey to
administer frankincense."

"Oh." Carlotta's lips turned down.

"But why would Audrey have murdered that man inten-
tionally?" Clement wondered aloud.

"She's been trying so hard to be a model Santaland
citizen," Carlotta added.

Bingo. "I assume she crossed paths with Eric Lynch somewhere in Florida recently," I said. "The reason he ended up
here was because someone told him about Santaland, and
even tried to explain how to get here."

Their faces paled. "She knew she couldn't divulge the secret of Santaland to anyone," Carlotta said.

"My guess is that she had one mojito too many and wanted
to impress a great-looking, intelligent guy she ran across at a
bar. When she heard that he was bound for the Arctic, the
temptation to do some bragging about her native country
must have been too strong for her."

"Oh." Carlotta's face collapsed.

"She is fond of a mojito," Clement admitted.

"But it still could have been a mistake," Carlotta added,
more feebly. "Just a terrible mistake."

"If it was, she should have fessed up right away. But she
didn't. She lied, and finagled you into lying, and now she's
fled."

The siblings' eyes went saucer wide. "Where?"

"We don't know. Salty, Jingles, and some others are out
hunting for her now." My gaze narrowed on them. "If you

know where she is, you should tell us now. Let her throw herself on the mercy of Santaland justice."

"What good will that do?" Carlotta said mournfully. "The best she can hope for is exile."

"Whether she escapes and hides," Clement said, "or is caught and banished, we've lost her again."

"This time forever."

I couldn't contradict them.

"We'll let you know if she turns up at the chateau," Clement promised, putting an arm around his sister.

Somehow, I disliked Audrey even more for having let Carlotta and Clement down.

After they were gone, I felt drained. I collapsed on the sofa, eyeing the Puffy's box that had been left there. All the donuts were gone.

Pamela breezed into the room and saw me staring at the empty box. From her clucking at me, I guessed she thought I'd polished off the entire baker's dozen on my own.

I sat up straighter. "Why do you seem so put out with me today?"

She crossed her arms. "You can sit there, in *this* room, and ask me that question?"

I looked around the room, trying to figure out what especially about this room indicated that I had committed some unknown offense against her. I drew a blank. "I don't know what you mean."

The reason finally exploded from her. "My gift! I've been knitting my fingers to the bone to make a special holiday surprise for everyone for when Nick and Lucia return, and you just took it. You're worse than Christopher—he hasn't sneaked a peak at his gifts in years."

A flush of shame rushed into my face. I *had* opened the gift, but how did Pamela know that? One glance at the tree gave me my answer: The present was gone.

I hopped to my feet. "It was only opened accidentally," I said. "Well, sort of accidentally. The package ripped and then"—a realization struck me—"Audrey was supposed to re-wrap it and bring it back."

But she hadn't.

"So you're telling me you didn't peek?" Pamela asked.

"No, I did." I gasped. "Oh my gosh! *That's* how Audrey got away—she's wearing the snowman snuggy." I gave Pamela a bracing hug. "You're a genius!"

Immediately, I alerted Salty and Jingles. "We're not look-ing for someone who looks like Audrey, we're looking for Audrey in a snowman suit."

Soon after we realized what we should be on the lookout for, Salty reported finding a large box and wrapping outside a cliff-facing window.

"She probably hopped into that suit and hid in plain sight in the yard when we first started looking for her," I said. "Then she crept away."

"It's been over an hour now," Salty said. "She's got a big head start."

I began pulling on outdoor wear—coat, scarf, hat, and two pair of gloves. "But I'm willing to bet there are witnesses who can tell us which way she went. Witnesses who wouldn't be fooled by a snowman snuggy."

"Who?"

"The snowmen."

Unfortunately, I didn't hear the approaching footsteps be-hind me until it was too late.

"You're going to interview snowmen?" Sam asked. "They *do* talk?"

I was too wound up to care if this noodle-brain learned snowmen could talk or not. "Of course they can talk. What do you think their mouths are for?"

He didn't appear inclined to argue with that reasoning, and when I went out to get my sleigh from the sleigh barn, he was right on my heels.

I stopped at the first snowman I came to. Jaggers, a large old snowman in a bowler hat, stood alone in the yard between the side portico and the reindeer barn.

"Hello, Mrs. Claus!" he said cheerily in answer to my greeting, before noting that I had one of Santaland's guests with me. Panic seized him. "I mean . . . never mind. I'm not talking."

"It's okay," I assured him. "I need you to tell me if you've seen any strange snowmen lurking about this morning."

"Lurking about, no." He thought for a moment. "But I saw an odd-looking snowman practically running for the snow path about an hour ago."

"Did you see her get on the snow path?" I asked. "Which way did she go?"

"Where all the snowmen have been going—toward Kringle Lodge."

"Perfect!"

Juniper and Jingles ran out of the castle. "Did you find out anything?" Juniper asked.

"Audrey was sighted headed up the mountain toward Kringle Lodge."

"I'll take my Snow Devil up there," Jingles said. He darted a resentful glance at Sam. "Juniper, you can come with me."

The four of us set out, Sam and I in my hybrid sleigh, Jingles and Juniper behind us in his Snow Devil.

Another northbound snowman confirmed that a rather rude snowman had scooted right past him without even saying hello. "Don't know what the world's coming to, Mrs. Claus, when you can't even trust the snowmen to be friendly. Or even to be a real snowman."

"If you spot her again, give someone a shout."

"We can shout now, can we?" he asked, brightened. "And sing again?"

"Sure." What was the point in silencing them now? The Santaland cat was clearly out of the bag. "Belt your heart out."

Sam shook his head when we left the snowman warbling out a stanza of "Jingle Bells." "They talk. I knew it." He frowned. "And did he call you . . . Mrs. *Claus*?"

"It's a common name around here."

We followed the path up to Kringle Lodge, slowing down to inspect each snowman we saw. If I saw Audrey in the snuggy head-on, she would be easy to spot. But all snowmen, even fake ones, looked alike from the back.

At the timberline, the trees thinned out and snowmen became more numerous. They were migrating from the castle in preparation for Grog Night. Also thick on the ground were elves involved in multiple construction projects: erecting a stage for the elf cloggers, putting up canopies for seating in case of snow, and elves climbing trees—I wasn't sure what they were doing. Overseeing the work was Butterbean in his reflector jacket and hard hat. Seeing me, he rushed over.

"See?" He gestured to the elves in the Christmas tree we were standing next to. "Zip lines."

I couldn't work up much enthusiasm for those now. "We're still looking for Audrey," I told him. "She got hold of a snowman suit and might be lurking around here."

Butterbean scanned the many snowmen who now dotted Amory's yard just as they had populated the castle grounds a few days ago. They all looked genuine, but it was surprisingly hard to distinguish between yarn and snow at a distance, especially since a fine powder had begun to fall.

All at once, Sam's arm shot out. "Look—by the road."

Jingles and Juniper had rounded the approach to Kringle Lodge's drive a little too quickly, nearly colliding with a snowman. Instead of taking the hit, though, as a real snowman would, this snowman dove out of the way.

"That's Audrey!" I called out, waving for Jingles to stop.

Sam and I ran toward Audrey, but she was agile even in her snowman snuggy. Her feet moved fast, barely protruding through the bottom of the costume, and she evaded all pursuers by assuming the serpentine pattern. She looked back and saw us gaining on her. She unzipped the front of her snuggy and shed her snowman skin. And then she started climbing the tall Christmas tree in the middle of the yard.

"What is she doing?" I asked, astonished that she would trap herself at the top of a tree.

Butterbean shaded his eyes with his hand. "She's going for the zip line!"

One day soon, the zip line would run all the way down to the castle, Butterbean had said earlier. And his elf workers had obviously made great progress. If we didn't grab Audrey now, she might zip over our heads and out of our grasp.

Juniper, who was coming up behind Jingles, sized up the situation immediately. She lifted her good hand to her mouth and let out a piercing whistle. "Elf pyramid!"

A swarm of hard hat elves converged where she stood. Several beefy ones dropped to their hands and knees, and just that quickly, the pyramid building started. Unlike the night of the send-off, this time the elves were sober, and their pile grew swiftly.

"Get out of my way!" Audrey warned them from inside the tree.

But the pyramid kept building. Audrey emerged from the cover of the evergreen branches, gripping the pulley at the top of the wire.

"She doesn't have a harness," I said.

Amory had joined me. "Then she doesn't have a chance."

The elves didn't have a chance, either, once Audrey took

off. I winced as Juniper scrambled to the top of the pyramid even with her sore wrist—right in Audrey's path. What happened next was a sight I'll never forget. Juniper and Audrey collided so hard that Audrey lost her grip. The two dropped to the ground, and the entire pyramid came crashing down after them. Audrey was buried.

I knew what that felt like.

Belatedly, Constable Crinkles drove up with Ollie, followed by more people from the castle. Seeing the mountain of elves, Crinkles jumped out, arms akimbo on his Canadian Mounties jacket. "What's going on here?"

"At the bottom of that pile you'll find Audrey Claus," I said.

The elves began hopping up. Juniper rose and limped a few steps. I ran over to her. "You were magnificent. Are you okay?"

She grinned. "Fine—just a twisted ankle. Not a big deal."

"Audrey wasn't so lucky," Amory said.

When all the elves were on their feet, only Audrey was lying in the snow, her leg jutting out at an unnatural angle.

Painful as it looked, I couldn't muster up much sympathy for her. She had killed a man. I moved to stand over her. "Why did you do it?"

She began to speak, then winced as if just taking a breath were painful. "Why didn't I let the man ruin my life, you mean?" She bit her lip and swallowed. "He would have told everyone that I was the reason that he'd found Santaland."

"So rather than have him ruin your life, you ruined it yourself," I pointed out.

Her eyes closed. "It's so unfair. I never meant to tell him, I swear."

"Blaming it on the mojitos?"

Her face tensed as a wave of pain hit her. I wasn't sure if it was her leg causing it or the memory of Eric Lynch.

"Partly, yes. You didn't know him. He was like a snake charmer. It all just spilled out of me. One minute we were at a bar together and the next I was wittering on about this place. I knew he was interested in the Arctic. I thought maybe if I told him something he didn't know, he might change his mind about failing me."

"You were his student?" Juniper asked.

"Just for a half a semester—he was part of the reason I had to drop out. Who knew geology could be so hard?"

I couldn't hold back my disgust. "You divulged Santaland's secrets for a grade?"

Her eyes flashed at me. "Easy for *you* to be judgy—you in your fancy-pantsy castle. You've got it made. But what did *I* ever have that was my own? I've even felt like the odd person out in my own family. My whole life, I've been trying to fit in somewhere, but everything and everyone's always against me. First Eric, then yoga, and now you. Why did you have to go poking into Eric's death? Why couldn't you have just left it alone?"

How many times had I asked myself that question? "Because you killed someone."

"He was a selfish jerk—and *not* a good teacher, either. He hit on students. If I hadn't given him that frankincense, I bet he would've blackmailed me to keep him quiet about what I'd done."

From what I'd heard about Eric, that wouldn't have surprised me.

What did surprise me was the fierce growl from behind me as Elaine hopped off Salty's utility sleigh. Hobbling on her boot, she hurled herself toward the woman on the ground until she loomed over her. "That jerk was a human being! One of the few I was ever close to."

"His ex-wife?" the younger woman sneered. "You should have heard what he said about *you*, you old toad."

"Loser!" Elaine raised her crutch.

"Don't," Juniper pleaded. "Leave her to Constable Crinkles. Her leg's broken."

"I'll break the other one for her." What she had done to an MP3 player she clearly wanted to do to Audrey's right knee. Sam and I lunged to disarm her, but we were both stopped short by a shout from behind us.

"Everyone! Look!"

We all turned toward Butterbean. He tipped his hard hat further back on his head and pointed down to the mountain to the top of the Old Keep, where the lantern was lit. "It's the sign—Santa's coming back."

Elaine froze, her crutch in midair over a terrified-looking Audrey. "*Santa?*"

Sam turned to her in a state of feverish excitement. "It's true, Elaine. We're in Santaland. I talked to a snowman."

She laughed. "Oh god. This again?"

"This one was real. You can talk to one, too." He looked over at the nearest snowman. "You—Mr. Snowman. Say hello to Elaine."

"Hi, Elaine," the snowman said, though half-heartedly. We were all distracted in that moment.

Sam followed all our gazes, which were now trained on the sky. "Look!"

My heart bounded in my chest. Off in the distance was that familiar silhouette I'd been longing to see—a sleigh and nine reindeer. In the waning afternoon light, I could just make out the lead reindeer's glowing nose. And of course, I recognized Nick's outline, too.

All at once, the dozens of elves around us were hopping and waving—even though there was little hope of Nick's seeing them. Or me. I couldn't stand still. I needed to get to my sleigh and get down to the landing strip. But Amory squeezed my arm, stopping me. He pointed at Butterbean, who had scrambled to the lodge's roof and was holding glowing orange sticks aloft to guide the craft in.

The sleigh banked then and followed the beacon up the mountain. Elves scurried out of the way to clear a path in front of the lodge. And with a swiftness that never failed to rattle me, the sleigh came down in a thunder of hooves, jingling harness bells, and ancient creaking wood. Nick called out a final "Whoa!" and pulled the reins taut to bring the sleigh to a stop.

Elves surged toward the sleigh. I was still in shock, until Juniper hopped toward me and gave me a nudge. "See? He always comes back."

Nick leapt down from the sleigh just as I managed to find my feet and rushed forward. I practically tackled him, gripping him as if afraid he might fly away again. "Thank heavens you're here, safe!" I said.

Earthbound for another year, I could only hope.

He leaned down and kissed me. The feel of those whiskers made me so happy I didn't care how many elves were watching and cheering.

"Merry Christmas," he whispered to me. Then, remembering himself, he added another "Merry Christmas!" to the rest of the crowd as well.

I glanced over at the sleigh. The team was the one Nick had left with. "Where's Lucia?" Although I have to admit I was mostly concerned about Wobbler.

"She'll be along. We had all the reindeer feeling stronger and there seemed to be a break in the weather, so we decided to go for it."

I looked out at the crowd, some of which had already started to dance.

"I'm sorry we don't have fruitcake for you, Santa," Salty called out.

"Seeing April here is all the treat I need," Nick replied, bending down to kiss me again.

I flushed happily as a chorus of snowmen broke into "A Holly Jolly Christmas," and elves began to jig through the snow. Even Juniper joined in, although she was doing more hopping than dancing. We might end up visiting Nurse Cinnamon this night.

Two nearby faces in the crowd stood out. Sam looked positively rapturous, while Elaine gaped at Nick as if he were a Martian instead of flesh-and-blood Santa.

"Holy moly, Eric was right. This *is* Santaland." She turned to Sam. "Forget lithium—we're gonna make a bundle from this place. Think of it, Sam—North Pole Adventures!"

"That's what I've been trying to tell you," he said.

"We need to draw up plans."

Imelda sidled up to them. "Sounds like you should drink to your new partnership. Don't tell the others, but I have some delicious spiced cider. It's got the perfect amount of kick."

Elaine looked doubtful at first, but then laughed almost giddily. "Oh, why not?"

Claire appeared with two tankards, which Imelda filled from her flask. "To North Pole Adventures!"

The two visitors took the offered drinks, clinked their tankards in silent celebration, and drained the contents.

I sank into Nick in relief. "That's that, then."

He frowned. "Were those two making plans to commercialize Santaland?" he asked, unable to keep the outrage out of his voice.

I hugged him again reassuringly. "Yes, but don't worry. In five minutes they'll have forgotten all about it."

Epilogue

Nick looked extra Santa-like in the Santa snuggy Pamela had knitted for him. Alas, my snowman snuggy had been retired after Audrey's commandeering it as a getaway disguise. Instead, I was luxuriating in the gown and raw silk robe Nick had had designed and made especially for me by Madame Neige. I was also luxuriating in Nick's exclusive company.

We'd ducked out of Grog Night a little early. The revelry was especially wild on the top of the mountain this year, so I doubt many noticed that Santa and Mrs. Claus had snuck out to ring in the New Year in the privacy of our suite at Castle Kringle. After the week we'd all had, everyone deserved to celebrate as they saw fit.

I retrieved my bottle of champagne and handed it to Nick to do the honors.

"I put another bottle on Lucia's sleigh for her and Amory to celebrate with," I told him.

In spite of Amory's protests a few days ago, he and Lucia had gone together to deliver the amnesiac Americans to a hospital in Alaska. What stories Sam and Elaine would tell, or what they would make of the missing month of their lives, it was hard to say. Before she returned to her cave on Mount Myrrh, Imelda promised that the forgetting spell would only encompass the month of December. So Sam would hopefully still know his way around a camera, and Elaine, minus one toe, could go back to analyzing sea ice. Still, I wondered if vestiges of what they'd experienced here might pop up in their unconscious brains from time to time. Maybe Sam would dream occasionally of a strange night out with a sozzled snowman.

The champagne cork popped, and Nick poured out two glasses of champagne, not spilling a single drop.

"You did that so carefully," I said. "But of course you do everything carefully."

"You—and this past week—made me realize that I can do better." He smiled ruefully. "I'm going to see about putting seat belts on the sleighs. And for the next few months, I'm going to work on some emergency plans, too."

"I'm glad to hear it, but I'm not sure Christopher will be. He admires the old-school, dangerous ways."

"Good thing he's got eight years of growing up to do before he takes the reins of the great sleigh, then."

I laughed. "Says the man who was arguing against seat belts just a week ago."

"Says the man who learned the hard way instead of listening to his better, wiser half."

He pulled me in for a kiss, and how could I resist?

I didn't want us to get carried away, though. Not yet. "I think we're supposed to wait for the stroke of midnight." I looked around for my cell phone, but I didn't have it on me. Now that Nick was back, I wasn't frantically checking messages all the time.

"I don't have a watch, but here's one way to tell time tonight." He leaned over an unlatched window. Cold air gushed in, and so did a din of cheering, noisemakers, and a thump of music coming from the top of the mountain. The Grog Night revelers obviously thought it was midnight already.

"That's the sound of happy elves," he said.

"And New Year's optimism." I wound my hands around his nape, wondering what would be ahead for us during this next trip around the sun. With Nick at my side, and all the wonderful friends and family in my life, I felt confident that it would all be good.

Acknowledgments

My thanks go out to my agent, Annelise Robey, as well as to all the people at Kensington who are a writer's dream team, including my editor, John Scognamiglio, Carly Sommerstein, and Larissa Ackerman.

If you were strolling through a bookstore and picked up this book by chance, what drew your attention was probably the fabulous and fun artwork and cover design by Olivia Holmes and Kristine Mills. Many thanks to them for the eye-catching covers that have been a hallmark of the Mrs. Claus series from the beginning.

As always, I'm also so grateful to my husband, Joe, and to my family for their encouragement. And to all the readers who have picked up the Mrs. Claus series and have reached out to me to let me know that you've enjoyed reading about April, Juniper, Jingles, and all the Santaland gang, I'm lifting a tankard of grog to you in thanks!

Visit our website at
KensingtonBooks.com
to sign up for our newsletters, read
more from your favorite authors, see
books by series, view reading group
guides, and more!

Become a Part of Our
Between the Chapters Book Club
Community and Join the Conversation

Betweenthechapters.net

Submit your book review for a chance to win exclusive
Between the Chapters swag you can't get anywhere else!
https://www.kensingtonbooks.com/pages/review/